# WARRIOR'S INSTINCT

CERBERUS TACTICAL K9 TEAM BRAVO

CERBERUS TACTICAL K9

FIONA QUINN

# WARRIOR'S INSTINCT

### TEAM BRAVO

FIONA QUINN

## CERBERUS TACTICAL K9 TEAM BRAVO

- Juan Ortega, Chief of Tactical Operations Center
- Ares (Heath Sterling) and Judge (M. Malinois) – nose and a bite/ war veteran/urban SAR
- Mace and Diesel – (M. German Shepherd) – nose and a bite/ war veteran/ urban SAR
- Ash and Hoover – (M. German Shepherd) – nose and a bite/ war veteran/urban SAR.
- Bear and Truffles (F. blonde British Lab) Urban SAR
- Knox and Zydeco or cocoa (F. Coonhound) Urban SAR
- Red and Whiskey – (F. bloodhound) SAR/tracker
- Mongoose – the vet and TOC liaison

## INIQUUS TACTICAL LOGISTICS

- Kiyana Swabi
- Jerry
- Ben

**WORLDCARES NGO**

- Hailey Stapleton
- Jay'la Packson, translator
- Kibbi
- Dr. Orni

**WASHINGTON NEWS-HERALD**

- Remi Taleb – war reporter
- Cindy Au – videographer/photojournalist

Readers, as I know many of you like to do further research after reading my novels, please note: In this work, I have compressed geopolitical information from several locations and therefore have created my own fictitious names for these areas. Unlike my other novels, these places will not show up in a search.

HATARI, EAST AFRICA

BRATE DESCHISE, ROMANIA

NEZDOLANNYY, RUSSIAN DISPUTED LANDS (NEHZ-DOH-LAWN-KNEE)

*This novel is my love letter to all of those who leave the comfort of their homes to go out and relieve the suffering of others. I am so appreciative that there are people like you in this world.*

*I also dedicate this book to those who are facing the destruction of war. I am so deeply sorry this has happened to you.*

# PROLOGUE

**Hailey**

THREE YEARS AGO, HATARI, EAST AFRICA

HAILEY WASN'T SLEEPING. There wasn't enough time for that. But it felt good to close her eyes and rest there in Ares's arms.

Her cheek was pillowed on his expansive chest; her naked thigh tossed casually over his hips.

Ares combed lazy fingers through Hailey's long blonde hair, catching on a tangle and slowly working it free.

Tipping her head to plant a kiss, Hailey breathed in the scent of Ares's post-coital sweat and the fresh herbal scent of his soap.

"I love you." She tucked back in. "With you in my life, I have a new lens to focus through," she whispered.

"Rose-colored glasses?"

"Rose? Mmmm, no. Does peace have a color? Does happiness? 'Butterflies dancing on a sun-brightened flower' colored lenses. How's that?"

"Nice." He reached for her hand and pressed it to his heart.

"Happiness? Yes." His other hand painted along her back and cupped the swell of her bottom. "Very happy." His sleepy voice wrapped her in a moment of contentment.

The sheets tangled around their feet.

A warm breeze lifted the white gossamer curtains that tented over the queen-sized bed, keeping the deadly mosquitos at bay.

Ares twisted and lifted his head from the pillow.

She knew he was checking the clock readout on the side table there in her little hut on the outskirts of Hatari, a remote village in Eastern Africa.

He dropped his head back down. "Five minutes." There was so much disappointment packed into those three syllables that Hailey smiled and answered with another kiss pressed into his warm skin.

Straightening her leg, Hailey pulled her hand free and walked her fingers down his goody trail. "Five minutes?" she asked flirtatiously. "Five minutes could still be fun."

He pressed her shoulder, so she'd roll onto her back, her hair fanning over the pillow.

She could just make out Ares's expression in the first light of a new day. His face wasn't soft with sleep anymore.

There was an edge to it.

"Five minutes. That's not enough time for this. But I wanted to talk to you about us." His gaze searched over her face. Ares's voice had an uncharacteristic stickiness to it. A growling kind of intensity that she'd never heard before. The timbre of his voice alarmed her.

She tensed.

"I'm happy that you've been part of my life," he said.

*Shit* was the word that bubbled up for Hailey and was left unspoken. She waited for a "but." She'd heard this conversation with past boyfriends. "You make me happy when you're here, *but* your job—your always being gone is too hard." Or "You make me happy, *but* my career takes precedence. You understand, don't you?"

Hailey tried to imagine what Ares's "but" would be. She landed on: *But my Green Beret unit has been deployed here for fourteen months, training our counterparts. We're about to be sent home. Nice knowing you. See you around.*

"Shhh shhh shhh." He brushed his finger over her temple and down her jawline. "Don't look so stricken. It's nothing bad." He dropped a quick kiss onto her lips that she didn't return. "I don't think so anyway." When Hailey shifted her gaze up to catch his, Ares said, "I want to get your take on things, is all. If you think this happiness might be something that—" He stopped to clear his throat.

Judge—Ares's three-year-old military K9, an amazing Malinois—stuck his nose over the mattress and fixed his gaze on her. He must have sensed her stress.

Judge was hyper-protective of Hailey.

"Lay down, Judge, Hailey's okay."

Ares waited until Judge plunked back down on the cool cement floor.

"You were asking if there might be something?" Hailey reminded him.

"If you thought you'd be happy with me in the long term."

"Long…" She let the word draw out, hoping he'd give her some context.

"I didn't plan this for today. I've been thinking about it for— almost since the moment I laid eyes on you, sprawled out there in the earthquake rubble, your arms in the hole being someone's lifeline." He swallowed loudly. "Okay, here it is. Hailey, I love you. You bring color and good things to my life—that butterfly on a flower thing. I'm a selfish enough man—especially given the limits to what I can offer you—"

She shook her head. What he offered her was *amazing*. They were *amazing* together.

"I'm selfish enough to want you in my life always. I want to marry you. Would you consider that? Being my wife?"

Hailey's eyes flashed wide.

"It's sudden. I get that." He paused.

Hailey should say something, but this was such a one-eighty from where she thought this conversation was going that she was scrambling to get her thoughts and emotions lined up.

"Hailey, you're *everything* to me. Marriage would be challenging given our jobs, but you are the queen of organization. And I'm willing to go to *any* lengths."

With the first threat of heartbreak, Hailey had shut down. She hated the process of ending a relationship whether it was she who made the decision or her past boyfriends. She'd learned to throw a kind of blackout curtain over her emotions until she could get herself to a private space.

Now she was trying to claw that curtain down, trying to focus on what Ares had said. "Marry?"

"My heart is yours if you'll have me."

And she laughed. The laughter bubbled up from the tips of her toes, up the length of her legs, into her hips, and belly, then burst, all glittery and shiny, from her system, to fill the room.

Ares pulled a hand down his face. Then rested back on his elbows. "You're killing me here."

Just as suddenly as the effervescent bubbles tickled through her, they stopped, and she sobered. "No! No. This is joy. I'm not laughing *at* you. I'm just filled with unexpected...I had no idea it would feel this way. Yes. *Absolutely*. Without reservations. I will marry you."

His kiss, warm and soft, brushed her mouth. "Yes?"

"Yes," she said with her lips still pressed to Ares's.

Warrior's Instinct | 17

"Yes?" he asked again as he reached under her, pulling her even tighter against him, claiming Hailey as his.

"Yes!" She grinned.

Judge put his head back over the bed and gave a high-pitched bark.

"She said yes to us," Ares told him as Hailey lifted her head for another kiss.

With that kiss, Hailey gave Ares a piece of her heart and filled that now empty space with the commitment he was offering in return.

That kiss was a bond, and she sank into the intensity of it.

When her old-timey windup clock jangled its brassy intrusion, Hailey moaned, "I will always hate that sound, now," she whispered as Ares reached out to tap it quiet. "Killjoy," she grumped.

"I'll ask you, again," Ares promised. "I plan to do it right. The ring. A romantic setting."

"This was romantic! Surprising! Wonderful. You don't have to do it again." She laced her fingers together and stuck her hands under her chin as if she would burst apart with happiness if she didn't hold herself tight.

"Okay. 'Officially' then." He sat with his back against the headboard. "When I put the ring on your finger, I want to make that special."

"If you want to. But for me? I don't need anything. I am," she closed her eyes and inhaled as her lips bowed up in contentment, "bliss."

"You are indeed," he said with a chuckle. "Miss Bliss. You're also about to be late for work. Me, too."

She swung her leg over the bed and pushed herself to standing. "Mr. and Mrs. Heath Sterling. Heath and Hailey Sterling. Hailey Sterling. Whew! It's not far off from Stapleton, but it will take some getting used to."

"Only if you want to. Your name is your decision."

"Oh, I want to take your name." She stretched and let him take in the length of her naked form. "I don't want to confuse our children."

"Children, huh?" He put his hands behind his head, elbows wide, muscles bulging, watching her with a smile curling his lips. So *damned* sexy. "How many?"

"Ten?" She shrugged. "Fifteen?"

He threw himself toward her, grabbing her up and kissing Hailey in what he called her 'sweet spot', just behind her ear. It always made her giggle and squirm.

The alarm sounded again. He must have hit the snooze.

"Work." She stuck out her lower lip in a pout.

"I know. I feel the same. Go on and get in the shower first. Should I get breakfast?"

"Uhm, no." She lifted the mosquito netting and ducked under, turning to slide her feet into her shower flip-flops. After tugging on her robe, Hailey reached for the towel hanging from a hook by the door. "I'm eating with Kibbi this morning, staff meeting. We have a new doctor coming in to run the clinic. She'll be here this afternoon, and we want to go over some reports before she gets in." Hailey moved toward the hall door.

Judge padded after her.

"Judge, stay with me." Ares reached for the pair of tactical pants that were in a pile by the bed, tugging them on, commando. Slung low on his hips, showing off the drool-worthy V, Ares was looking painfully yummy.

She sighed; her libido would have to be patient for tonight.

Judge stomped the ground.

"Sorry, you can't go in the shower with Hailey." Ares looked up to find Hailey's gaze fixed on him.

"They call you Ares, and I think they did you a disservice with that name." She turned and swayed her hips as she pulled the door open.

"Yeah?"

She flung, "Adonis is probably a better fit," over her shoulder and caught the grin on his face as she headed through the door.

HAILEY DANCED her way through her morning routine. She floated over to her all-terrain vehicle, climbed in, and buckled up. The next twenty minutes of her teeth-rattling drive over the rutted dirt roads to the WorldCares NGO station where she worked as a humanitarian aid manager were punctuated by her singing good morning songs to the fields, and clouds, and any birds she happened to see.

This was an astonishing day. Hailey was about to embark on a new trajectory.

Arriving at the station, she parked under the shade of a neem tree. As she dragged the stick shift into neutral and tugged the emergency brake into place, Hailey stopped to inhale the earthy splendor.

This morning was glorious.

Hailey couldn't wait to tell Kibbi her news.

Pulling a box filled with treats that Ares had brought in from his post along with her as she jumped down from the cab, she spotted a new face.

"Doctor Oni?" Hailey raised her voice over the children's call and response game. Hailey hadn't thought that the new doctor was arriving until late afternoon.

Tall, with a brightly colored headscarf wrapping her hair and bright blue scrubs draping her wiry body, the woman turned.

Hailey tucked the box under one arm with her other hand lifted in a greeting and made her way over to the older woman.

"Miss Stapleton?" Tattoos made lacey designs on the doctor's face. She stepped forward with a wide grin that flashed gleaming white.

"Hailey, please." They shook hands. "I'm sorry we haven't prepared our welcome yet. We anticipated your arriving—" Hailey adjusted the box on her hip and pointed toward the community center. "Has someone greeted you?"

The heat of the day was just starting to shimmer on the horizon.

Hailey always tried to get her high exertion chores done in the mornings when the atmosphere was less dense with heat and dust. She hoped Dr. Orni would understand. Hailey decided to orient the new doctor, then let her explore on her own.

"Yes. Kibbi showed me to my room last night." Dr. Orni fell in step with Hailey.

"I came in last evening as I had an opportunity to travel with some friends."

"That's nicer, isn't it? Have you had a tour?" Hailey looked around. "Do you know where Kibbi is?"

"Of the tour, no, it was dark when I arrived. Of Kibbi, she went to check on a new mother."

"Okay, good." Hailey would have to hold off sharing her exciting news until later. "I'll walk you around. I need to set this box down first. It's art supplies for the children."

They moved toward the front door of the main building. "Let me start here. This is our community center. It's an all-purpose building. We eat and meet here. We have computers available for the village. We have battery charging stations over on that wall."

"What is this?" Dr. Orni stepped toward the neat shelves filled with black boxes plugged into the line of wall sockets.

"WorldCares NGO provided each family in the area with a UPS—uninterrupted power supply unit." She pointed to the ceiling. "We have solar panels on the roof. It works out pretty well. The women bring the UPS units here in the morning to charge. If they have school-aged children, they leave the kids to play in the yard until the school bell rings." Hailey pointed toward the window. "The women fill their buckets with water from our well. It saves them the two-mile walk to the river and back. It's safer."

"It's heavy to carry water that far each day."

"I don't know how they do it." Hailey shook her head. "I couldn't. So, in the evening, the women come pick up the batteries." She pointed back to the wall of black boxes. "That way they can get more water, pick up their children and have lights after dark, charge their cell phones, what have you. It still amazes me that there's better cell reception out here in the wilds than we had back in rural Kansas." She focused on Dr. Orni. "Kansas is the state I come from in America. It's not quite in the middle of our country, but close."

Dr. Orni gave a polite nod.

Hailey gestured toward the door and started out. "The women will have come and gone already today. I'll come earlier tomorrow and introduce you if you'd like."

"Yes, please."

They rounded out of the building. "Behind this is the clinic and your apartment where you must have stayed last night?"

"Yes. I walked through the facility this morning. Impressive. I can do a lot of good in that clinic."

Hailey gestured toward the structure to the right. "That's the schoolhouse. We educate local children and children sent to live in the orphanage. The dorms are behind the school." Hailey turned and nodded to the left. "There, we have food storage along with building and farming equipment that we lend out to the villagers."

Dr. Orni fell in step beside Hailey as they walked toward the children. "Have you been here long?" she asked.

"A year." Hailey smiled. "A lot has happened in that time. I feel we've made good progress. WorldCares NGO originally came in to support the people following an earthquake that wiped out their village. We hoped to support area families who survived." Hailey stopped, focusing on the children at play. "Many of our students were orphaned in the event," she said quietly so only Dr. Orni would hear. "We supplied medical care and food. As we got to know the area and figured out the long-term needs, we began to set up this social net. Now, their local council is strong. Kibbi and I will only be here for another month. Then, the council will take over."

"Is the village stable enough for your organization to pull out? The military is in the area. I drove past them last night. There was a checkpoint."

"There have been warring factions forever, people vying for power. And violence always seems to be just over the horizon. I haven't experienced any. The government requested that America send in a Green Beret group to teach and advise. The checkpoint you encountered was probably set up as a training evolution. I know a few of the men on that team, my fiancé is with them." That was the first time she'd publicly called Ares that. It felt good. "They seem pleased with how well their counterparts are performing. It's not a perfectly stable situation, mind you. There's a lot of unrest as I'm sure you were warned about before you took this position." Hailey thrust her hands into the pockets of her khaki shorts. "Outside of an occasional patient that comes to the clinic for treatment from the bush, I haven't seen anything that looks violent."

"That's good to hear. I'm leaving an area that isn't so blessed."

Hailey caught her eye. "I'm so sorry. Well, I hope that this is a good assignment for you." She stepped forward. "Shall I show you the school before classes start?"

The women strolled toward the building.

The sun, though still low on the horizon, glared at them with intensity. Hailey was glad that most of her to-do list that day was comprised of reports that she could compile under the relief of her office ceiling fan.

Just outside the schoolhouse door, the children's singing came to an abrupt stop.

Hailey swung her attention to the group.

They stood there, hands on their heads, bodies rigid, and absolutely silent.

Hailey turned to the west, to see what they were seeing. Sometimes there were issues with the wild animals scrounging for food.

Kibbi, with her traditionally patterned skirt hiked up to her hips, ran full tilt toward them. Her eyes were held wide and white. Her mouth hung open. Her lips peeled back showing her teeth. Her face was a mask of sheer terror.

Over the horizon thundered a militia on horseback.

The leader with his tan turban and olive fatigues, stained with sweat, and draped in weaponry, pointed at Hailey. He yelled out. The others whipped their horses to make them fly over the slim space, overtaking Kibbi who disappeared behind the cloud of dirt churned up by the hooves.

And what happened next, Hailey couldn't understand as anything other than flailing limbs and desperate screams.

The men smelled of rot, like corpses left bloated in the sun.

Hailey vaguely understood someone was tearing at her clothing.

She was fighting.

Running.

Falling and being dragged by her ankles.

She thought maybe she tried to protect. To escape. But she couldn't be sure.

The slaughter went on and on.

A face, glistening sweat with flaring nostrils, pressed closer.

His broad tongue licked over her lips. A machete blade flattened under her nose, dripping with blood. Her blood?

Violently, there was fur, black and tan.

Judge's white fangs chomped into the man's arm that held Hailey down.

Shrieks rose from the man as Judge's jaw clamped down tighter.

The machete's edge slit across Judge's side instead of Hailey's.

The crack of gunfire made her ears echo and ring.

Death rattled the man's chest as his shirt bloomed red.

Blood.

So much blood all around her. Everywhere, red.

Screams.

Hailey was forced to lie down in a basket. She was lifted through the sky, as the helicopter downwash spun her wildly.

The next thing she knew, Hailey was pushing through the grogginess, coming to after surgery. Ares was holding her hand. Judge had survived surgery, he said.

But the others did not.

She alone left WorldCares NGO Station #642.

And she *only* survived because Judge and Ares were hard focused on saving her.

She got airlifted to an American military hospital because of her passport.

Ares and his brother Green Berets along with the group they'd been training saw the militia riders heading toward the village from a drone image and had raced to the fight, destroying every last member of the attacking militia.

But not fast enough.

Kibbi died.

The children died.

Dr. Orni on her very first day at the clinic died.

WorldCares NGO didn't need to close up shop. It had all burned to the ground.

And Hailey? She was simply flown home to her family in Kansas to recover.

As if that could *ever* happen.

# 1

---

Ares

THE SHOCKS on the Iniquus Security SUV struggled to keep up with the challenge of the unpaved road. With every bump, drop, and hill, the vehicle bucked and shimmied beneath Ares.

Mid-forties in January, the ground was saturated with the melt off from the recent snowstorm that had dumped eight inches in the D.C. area over the last few days. It left the backroads oozing slime, making today's task that much more challenging.

Briefly, Ares's gaze caught Judge's in his rearview mirror. Tongue out, panting in anticipation, the Malinois braced on the back seat in his safety harness, not bothering to lie down, where the violent jolts wouldn't tax his energy as much.

Judge was primed for the adventure.

Judge's job was to be a nose and a bite. That meant he was trained to find specific scents and if there was a bad guy around, he'd gladly do the chomp down.

He could go from kitten-loving, belly-rolled-toward-the-sun manic goofball to fur missile in the blink of an eye.

His go-switch was greased and ready.

Working with Judge, Ares had learned that his K9 was intelligent enough to understand the situation, sometimes better than Ares did himself.

Ares always trusted his dog.

That Judge kept swinging his attention between Ares and the back window told Ares that he needed to power forward to stay ahead of the team that was chasing them down.

Already, Ares's boot pressed the gas pedal nearly flat to the floorboard, sending a muddy spray in their wake.

It was hardly a clandestine way to make it up the hill.

The back tires fishtailed through the slippery red clay of rural Virginia as Ares powered up the steep incline. He figured, there was no way to get through the mud and not leave a trail, might as well chomp up the terrain in the off chance it slowed the vehicle that Judge was telling Ares was closer than comfortable.

The SUV tipped hard as Ares plowed through a deeper than expected puddle. His windows were suddenly opaque from the shower of mud he'd sent flying.

Without a second thought or stall in forward momentum, Ares toggled on the washer fluid. The wipers scratched a hole for him to peer through.

There to his left, almost with his sixth sense, Ares found the trailhead.

Dragging the steering wheel around, they came to an aggressive stop under the pines. After throwing the gear into park, one hand rounded over the seat to press the quick release clasp on Judge's harness.

Without taking the time to turn off the engine, Ares released his own belt, wrapped a hand into his pack, and threw the door wide.

"Let's go," he called to Judge.

Behind him, Judge leaped to the front seat and scrambled out of the open door. Within seconds, he was beside Ares as they sprinted alongside the trail. Ares hoped to mask their footprints by staying off the path proper and leaping from rock to fallen trunk.

This was a scent training, not a visual tracking evolution.

Footprints would wipe away any challenge, making this exercise both a gritty mess and irrelevant.

The croon of the bloodhound pair, Whiskey and Chaser, rode the wind from the trailhead.

Reaper would be at Ares's SUV letting his trackers sniff the driver's seat to capture Ares's scent. Reaper, the new Cerberus trainer, had signed an Iniquus Security contract about a year ago. After finishing up his observational stint with Strike Force, he was now training K9s full time with Cerberus, Iniquus's tactical and rescue K9 unit. Reaper was definitely proving his capacity in honing working dog skills.

While Whiskey was a permanent member of the Iniquus kennel, her littermate, Chaser, was being trained for Virginia State Police to track the bad guys when they abandoned their vehicles and plowed into the night.

With their prized hotdogs zipped into a plastic bag in Reaper's pocket, Ares knew the two bloodhounds were motivated for the find and the ensuing reward.

Ares pushed hard, keeping an eye on Judge. Where Judge covered the terrain with graceful ease, Ares—though, he hated to admit it—felt like he was slogging through quicksand as he sprinted through the leaves. Yeah, there was the hazard that his foot would slide into a covered hole, and he could jack his whole body up, but when the enemy was tracking you, it wasn't time for a leisurely stroll. Even if the word "enemy" was in quotation marks.

In real-world scenarios, a person performs the way they train. Train hard was the only way Ares knew to do it.

And Judge? That was a no-brainer, Judge thrived on this stuff.

"I wish you could talk," Ares told Judge. "I'd like to know how hard to push, how far back they are. The wind is whipping their noise back down the mountain." He grinned at Judge. "They've got those little legs, though. I think we can make it to our designated hiding spot before they get to us."

Ares's radio crackled. "TOC to Arz." Someone from the Tactical Control Center. Ares didn't recognize the guy's voice.

"TOC to Arz."

"Reaper to TOC what's an Arz?"

"TOC. Alpha Romeo Echo Sierra," he spelled out.

"Reaper. TOC that's pronounced Air-ease. God of war. We don't have any pirates on our team. Man, who's training you?"

"TOC," the guy stammered. "Sorry. I…I'm…eh-eh-hem. TOC for Ares."

"Ares," he said, laughing. "New guy, you owe me a case. None of that microbrew crap. I want it cold, and I want it by my locker when I get back from mud mountain."

"TOC. Yes, sir, excuse me, sir. I was…I'm not old enough to buy beer, sir." His voice cracked.

"All right. TOC go for Ares."

"Yes, sir. Uhm, Mr. Ortega is conferencing with Iniquus Command and asked me to tell you to have your uhm training team to uhm stand down."

Juan Ortega was chief of Cerberus Team Bravo's tactical command center.

New guy cleared his throat. "My apologies, sir. Mr. Ortega says he needs you for a briefing. I'm quoting, 'Here. Now, if not sooner.' Sorry again, sir."

"Wilco. Standing down. Returning to base. And tone down the apologies, they take up too much airtime. Reaper?"

"Reaper. What's the plan?"

"There's a rock outcropping just ahead of me. I'm going to crouch behind it to give Whiskey and Chaser the win, then I'll head back."

"In cuffs."

"That's going to be a no-go." Ares rounded the boulder and gave a soft whistle for Judge to come hide with him. "My orders are 'now.' I'm not running down mud-splash mountain with my hands behind my back. Over."

"Reaper. I just pulled your red dot up on my GPS, Ares. We're about five minutes south-southwest. We'll let Whiskey and Chaser do a sniff and howl. I'll give them their hot dogs, and you can head down to see what's cooking."

## 2

**Hailey**

HAILEY DROPPED her phone onto her lap and leaned her forehead onto her desk.

With closed eyes, she exhaled, letting the news wash over her.

The route she'd so carefully developed to get her supplies into Nezdolannyy in disputed Russian territory wasn't going to work.

This was her fourth attempt.

Contracts signed. Everything was a go—then the trucks were diverted.

Priorities. Hailey got that.

Every situation had a hierarchy of needs. She had hers, NATO's military arm had theirs.

Which would save more lives?

A crystal ball and some psychic skills might help.

No one was sure that a crisis ensued.

In her job with the humanitarian organization, WorldCares

NGO, pre-positioning was one of their fortes. If they could see a disaster on the horizon—a hurricane, for example, or an encroaching forest fire —they could get out ahead of the crisis. WorldCares would position survival supplies outside of the danger zone, wait for the event to pass, and move in.

When the events had to do with social upheaval, be they natural or manmade—post-war unrest, famine, floods, and volcanoes—her NGO found that people did best when they weren't evacuated to a different space but supported amongst the familiar. It kept families and communities together where traditions and norms could help ease the psychological effects of the disaster.

When they could, WorldCares' policy was to support folks where they lived. And having spent the last decade managing catastrophes worldwide, Hailey was good at doing just that.

Now, Eastern Europe was staring down the barrel of a gun.

Russia needed a distraction. Their president had cancer, their economy flailed from the most recent pandemic, and the government was desperate for a win, something that would bolster national cohesion and pride. Instead of putting effort into improving their citizens' lives, the government, instead, turned to their military and the idea of "denazification" of their neighbors, where Nazism wasn't an issue.

"Bring us glory! Move us back to the time when we were the USSR, strong and vast."

For the sake of an individual's greed, humanity would suffer.

While Hailey was given the task of supporting one tiny city. Other coordinators would do the same. In this way, they hoped to shore up the citizens with what they needed to weather the assault.

Like the populations that Hailey's NGO mobilized to support post-hurricane, sometimes they prepared, and the storm would break up with no catastrophe. Sometimes, they thought the storm would have little impact, and it blew in with destructive ferocity.

Plan. Prepare. Get on-site.

Then thank the fates if it all blew by.

In this case, though, 'better safe than sorry' wasn't a useful idiom. Hailey felt it in her bones. The war was coming.

She had this window to help the most vulnerable.

The rich and connected would get out. It was the poor, the sick and disabled, and their caregivers who would pay the biggest price.

It always was.

If Hailey failed, the result wouldn't just be a disappointment. The lack of supplies could cause intense suffering. Even death.

Hailey wasn't giving up. She'd keep trying until there was no more hope.

And she knew that last thread of hope would be severed by the first bomb dropping.

She just wasn't sure what to do next.

Pulling the map back over, Hailey stared down, hoping for inspiration.

WorldCares hired retired American military strategists as part of their humanitarian efforts. It seemed an odd marriage. Warriors and caregivers were often on opposite sides of the spectrum. Since many of the people in dire straits found themselves caught up in geopolitical issues, WorldCares needed the military's input.

The strategists had looked at the satellite images, the lists of amassing war machinery— including several mobile cremation units—and pinpointed the places where they thought the populations would be most impacted.

For each circle that the strategists put on the map, WorldCares put together a two-person team—an organizer and a translator—and sent them off to do their thing, making sure that basic survival supplies were in place.

Larger teams only went in when they were going to sustain a presence. That would not be the case in a possible war zone.

Hailey was assigned to Nezdolannyy in the south-east. According to her WorldCares report, Nezdolannyy was at high risk of a siege in the first days if not the first hours of an incursion.

When she did her research, Hailey thought it looked like an odd place to attack.

But incursion planning wasn't her skillset. She'd just follow through with needs.

Her time frame when she was handed the task? With fingers crossed for bad weather and good diplomacy, she had had three weeks.

At the outset, it was a herculean effort. But Hailey was determined.

To Hailey's relief, Nezdolannyy, like many cities in this part of the world, had learned the benefits of being underground from back in WWII.

The subway systems served a dual purpose of transportation and bomb shelter.

Using evacuation tents in January, when the climate traditionally had fifteen days of snow, and the rest of the days were hail and fog, was a terrible idea.

It was a relief that Hailey could simply check the shelter box, and call it done.

Hailey discovered that the modern buildings included underground parking decks that increased the shelter capacity. There, she could construct an underground clinic.

The Nezdolannyy city planners provided Hailey with schematics to help her. And looking them over, she thought that the city had done a pretty remarkable job designing their infrastructure to help their people survive a catastrophe. Tunnels ran from building to building.

Should a building collapse, there would still be a way to get those seeking shelter out.

Hailey had worked with the mayor on what was most needed —diapers, formula, MREs, sanitation stations, batteries, and medicines. But these supplies couldn't help the Nezdolannyy people sitting in a warehouse on the Poland-Slovakian border.

Her latest attempt at transport had been planned.

Hailey was supposed to be at the warehouse at five in the morning to watch the truckers load and go.

And then came word, the trucks were diverted.

Hailey pressed the maps away from her, letting the disappointment settle so she could think of another way in. Daunted, but undeterred, Hailey had learned long ago to expect roadblocks and hurdles.

Hailey pulled up her messaging app: **Hey, Wombats. Is anyone working in Eastern Europe right now? I'm staging supplies in Poland and can't get them from Point A to Point B in advance of the war. I'm looking for inspiration.**

The Wombats were a closely-knit group of women who worked in conflict areas. Among their ranks were other NGO staffers, medical types, war correspondents, and photojournalists.

The name for their group came about when they were on base with the French troops. Hailey had been there with the original Wombat women drinking away their angst as the enemy sent RPGs into the camp. Someone there started talking about how she wished she were a wombat with an armor-plated ass.

That's when Hailey learned that wombats were the kind of animals that in the devastation of the Australian fires, allowed fleeing animals down into their burrows to shield them from the heat and smoke. But if a predator tried to get in, the wombats would wedge into the opening of their homes. The threat couldn't pass through. Wombats have buns of steel.

Hailey's friend Remi said that they, as a group, were like the wombats. Willing to help, willing to protect. And with lifted glasses clinking together, they christened themselves "The Wombats."

Later, they discovered that a group of wombats was called a "wisdom."

Their group depended on the wisdom each had developed as they worked in the most dangerous places in the world. They leaned on each other both for survival techniques and when they used each other's networks to get a job done.

Hailey's cell phone pinged.

Remi — **Did a quick search. It looks like AgilitiCorp is in that city. They're American.**

Hailey — **Do they have semis that can transport containers?**

Remi — **I don't think so. They're about computer stuff, software engineering. But they'll be obliged to safeguard their workers. The American ones at least. This might be a good story to follow. I'm going to reach out to them and see with whom they've signed security contracts. How much stuff are we talking here? What kind of supplies do you need to move?**

Hailey — **8 intermodal containers. 2 = mobile medical clinic. 6 = humanitarian supplies.**

Remi — **I'll get back to you.**

Hailey wasn't sure how the information about AgilitiCorp would help, but Remi obviously had an idea working in that brilliant brain of hers.

*Rely on the wisdom of the wombats.*

Dressed in a pair of black yoga shorts, Hailey's tank top hung loosely from her frame.

As usual, the external pressures from her job seemed to tighten down around her, making even this much clothing feel suffocating. She reached under her shirt to unhook her bra. Tugging the straps down to her elbows, Hailey wiggled her arms free, tossing the bra onto her low boy, then flopped back on her bed, peeking at the clock. She hadn't realized how late it was.

Another day. Another world crisis.

Such was her job.

Not really a job, more of a lifestyle.

A life of purpose.

A life that had meaning.

Hailey had been a child when she'd chosen this path. At six years old, Hailey was supposed to have been in bed sleeping, but she'd had a nightmare and had gone off in search of her babysitter.

Hailey couldn't remember the teen's name, or much else about her other than that the girl was wearing jeans and sitting cross-legged on Hailey's family room couch, crying into the tissues until they were damp wads. She'd toss them like a ping-pong ball into the trash and pluck a fresh tissue from the box, resting on the sofa's arm.

Not ever having seen empathy displayed before, Hailey gripped the handrail on the stairs and slid down to sit in the shadow of the balusters so she wouldn't be noticed, observing this strange spectacle and trying to decipher it.

Hailey's nightmare still felt fresh and raw. Her anxiety still prickled. But finding solace from the babysitter might not be the safe thing to do.

The television was playing an interview of a family talking about their experience surviving a tsunami. Hailey mouthed the word "tsunami", thinking that whatever a tsunami was it was a monstrous and dangerous entity, willing and capable of killing children.

Well-loved children.

Ripping a baby from her mother's arms never to be seen again.

This lined up with Hailey's nightmare.

The tsunami monster sounded more dangerous than the lava floor that sprang into her imagination when she flipped off the light switch and leaped from one tossed article of clothing to the other across the room and safely onto her bed. It was worse than the monster that could extend his furry claws and grab at her if her leg slipped from under her covers. The tsunami monster, it seemed from the stories playing out on the television, came when you were awake and didn't disappear when the lights flashed on, pressing the darkness away.

And the adults seemed incapable of saving the children. They were snatched from their parents' arms and dragged away never to be seen again.

No hope of them surviving.

Hailey watched the reporter talking to family after stricken family. She remembered clinging to the balusters, forcing her face through the opening so she could see the TV screen better. The prickle of the carpet fibers worked their way through her thin nighty, and she could feel them on her rump and thighs.

Soon, she was crying as hard as the babysitter.

And the babysitter heard her. "Oh, Hailey, baby." She clicked the TV off.

Hailey liked that babysitter; she was soft. Soft voice, soft touch, soft body for snuggling up to when she read books.

"Hailey, I thought you were asleep." And even though she'd newly turned six and wasn't a baby to be carried around anymore, Hailey was swept up into the babysitter's arms and carried back to bed.

She was offered a sip of water, a kiss, a backrub…

But Hailey couldn't let go of the mother's crying about dead children.

Hailey had just learned about that—about death. Her grandpa had died when his heart got tired. They put him in a box lined with slippery cloth, the lid was shut, and they put him in a hole.

With the family crowding around, Hailey's dad had picked up a shovel and threw some dirt over her grandpa's box.

It was terrifying.

Hailey wondered why they needed the hole to be so deep. She wondered if her grandpa was scared down there under all that dirt. It seemed a bad thing to do to someone you loved. They should have waited until he woke up. Then, Hailey could at least have given her grandpa another hug. The best she could do was slip her favorite stuffed rabbit under his arm—the one she'd had since she was a newborn baby that she dragged around by its ears as her constant companion.

Hailey had had nightmares every night since she did that.

But she wouldn't ask anyone to get her rabbit back.

It was a little friend for her grandpa so he wouldn't be scared.

She could do that for him because she still got to see the sunshine, and he didn't.

Hailey thought about the woman on the TV who sat with her shoulders up to her ears, clutching a rabbit very similar to the one that Hailey had just given to her gramps. The mom talked about the tsunami dragging her baby boy from her arms and out to sea.

That seemed worse than under the dirt.

As Kerry—Kerry! Her name was Kerry—as Kerry tucked the sheets up to Hailey's chin, she sat down on the floor, risking both lava and under-bed monster arms. "I'm going to tell you something," she'd said. "And I want you to remember this. It's important. Bad things happen in this world. The world will never be perfectly safe or perfectly peaceful. So it's important to know that we can't fix everything, but sometimes we can fix *some thing*s."

Hailey had stopped sobbing but had to talk through the hiccoughs that always followed her crying jags. "That mommy is sad."

"Yes. There are lots of very sad mommies and daddies in the world."

"Can we fix her?"

"No. She is going to have to be sad for a long while."

"Did the police catch the tsunami?"

"No, baby, a tsunami is what we call a big wave in the ocean. It only happens after an earthquake. Do you know what that is?"

"No."

"Well, it almost never happens, and you shouldn't be afraid of a tsunami. Now when this wave came, it didn't just take the people out to sea, it also took the food and the clothes and the furniture. It washed everything away. But people helped. They brought in fresh food and cooked it. The doctors and nurses showed up to put on bandages and give medicine. All over the world, people tried to help. My mom and dad are there. They're photographers, and they're taking pictures to try to help families find each other."

With a hitched breath, Hailey said, "That's nice of them."

"I think so."

The seed planted; a path was determined. "That's what I want to do. Go help people who are crying."

"If you do that," Kerry said, "you'll make the world that much better of a place. Now, I want you to scoot down and get your head on the pillow. Where's bun-bun?"

"I gave him to Grandpa so he wouldn't be scared in his box."

"Oh, well, see? You already know how to help and be kind. Roll on over, and I'll sing you a song until you fall asleep."

Kerry was the reason Hailey was ultimately here in Poland.

A tsunami was about to hit. And most of the people had no high ground.

# 3

---

Ares

ARES ROUNDED into the parking lot at Cerberus. The Iniquus vehicle was red with a thick coating of clay, only at the roofline was the underlying charcoal gray exterior visible.

Fun times! Some days on the job were a blast.

One of the support staff stood patiently. It was the vehicle pool's task to keep the Iniquus fleet pristine and in top working condition.

"Not gonna lie, man, glad this isn't on me." Ares shot him a grin and tossed the keys into the guy's cupped hands. "I tried my best to keep the goop out of the cab."

"Appreciated." The guy pulled off his ball cap as his gaze slid over the length of the SUV. "I've got it handled."

Yeah, Ares was off the hook for the SUV, but he had Judge to deal with. Instead of going in the front door of Cerberus Tactical Headquarters, Ares jogged around back. They had a shower room with an outside door where both the operators and their K9 could get spiffed up.

Judge jumped into the tub, he loved to get cleaned, especially when Ares took extra time massaging the suds into his coat. Today's clay adventure required a lot of massaging, and Judge was blissed out. He'd stand under the blow-dryer hood while Ares did his own scrub.

After shucking his clothes and dumping them in the hamper, Ares sprayed off his boots and placed them on the drying jack. Everything was set up for efficiency and military-level cleanliness and order.

Showered, a towel wrapping his waist, Ares rounded into the locker room for a fresh uniform with a pristine Judge prancing at his heels.

"Yo, got a clue what's spinning up?" he asked Bear who was lacing up his boots.

"Nada."

Ares reached in his locker for his boxer briefs, pulling them on, then chucking the towel into the hamper. "A new voice came over the comms. I wasn't sure how serious the call-in was."

"Serious. The whole team is pulling in. The guy on the radio was our new kennel apprentice. First day, he's learning how to clean the water bowls. Juan was having his fun. Best bet, when you show up, Juan's going to be stomping around like a wooden-legged pirate yelling, 'Arrrrz there, matie,' giving the kid a hard time. Teaching him to be humble."

"Wish my hazing was a tickle like that," Mace said, dragging the Iniquus gray uniform compression shirt over his head. "I swear, if I opened my mouth, it was 'Case of beer!' and if I didn't open my mouth, it was 'Case of beer!' I ended up having to have my girlfriend loan me money to make my car payment that month. Talk about humble. Shit."

"How'd he get here, the apprentice?" Ares asked.

"His mom works at Headquarters in IT. The kid thinks he wants to join the military to handle K9. He figures Cerberus on his resume will get him the plum position he wants to negotiate with the recruiter. He asked for the opportunity to volunteer to work with Reaper."

Reaper was Cerberus's master training advisor.

Cerberus Tactical K9, while on the Iniquus Security's campus, had its own headquarter building, along with a kennel, and training yard. Cerberus looked to the main Headquarters for support with everything from the vehicle pool, to communications, to larger logistics pictures. This was true when they went out to provide search and rescue assistance in mass disasters, and when a K9 team joined with one of the tactical operations forces. On mercenary-styled missions, be they hostage rescue or a tactical stand-in for a governmental alphabet—CIA, FBI—that didn't want to get their boots dirty, the tactical K9s were a force multiplier.

Ares and Judge were often sent downrange with one of the Iniquus tactical forces because of their skill sets, both finding explosives and taking down bad guys.

"Smart kid," Ares said of the new intern. "Strategic. Yep, I like him already." Ares dragged on his uniform gray camo tactical pants. "He needs to work on his comm skills, though."

The men, now presentably dressed, strode to the conference room.

Ares looked around. "Reaper's not down from the mountain, yet," he called over to Juan. Typically, when they got their assignments, the trainer was there to listen to the details. They would be part of the decision-making when it came to which K9's name went on the roster.

While each Cerberus operator had their own K9, Iniquus maintained a kennel of dogs that teams rotated through training. Bear's dog Truffles was trained for urban search. She didn't like searching rural areas, so Bear would handle a field dog in that instance.

Outcomes depended on training and reliability.

Judge wasn't a people tracker; his nose was all about explosives.

On search and rescue assignments in natural disaster areas, Ares and Judge would search for anything that might go BOOM. Gas leaks, munitions, bad guys with guns, it was Ares and Judge's job to make sure the area was secure.

"Reaper didn't follow me in," Ares told Juan as he found a seat.

"Reaper's on his way home. We've discovered a breach," Juan said, reaching out to a brown cardboard box and sliding it closer. "Everyone will be going through a digital pat down to make sure that all systems are secure. Phones go in this box. Computers get stacked on the trolley." He tipped his ear toward a gal in a gray suit with her back pressed against the wall. "Charlotte from IT. She's going to make sure your equipment hasn't been compromised. She should be back with them—" Juan turned to catch her gaze.

"Oh, yes." She pushed off the wall to stand straight, shoulders thrown back. "We know what we're looking for so I should have everything back in say two to three hours. Since you're deploying, you've been prioritized."

"Within three hours," Juan repeated, placing his phone in the empty box, then passing it to Mace.

One after the other, the men placed their phones in the container and handed it along. They pulled their computers from their backpacks and put them in place.

Silence filled the room until Charlotte left.

"You need to be vigilant with anything that communicates through the airwaves," Juan caught each of his operator's gazes, then shifted to the next, making the point that this was imperative.

"Do *not* become complacent when it comes to what you say and where you say it." Juan pressed his fingertips onto the surface of the conference table, leaning forward. "Back story: Reaper was traveling with his service dog last week to Boston. Houston found a thumb drive attached to a seat at the airport."

The men sent up a cheer.

Reaper had been working on training K9s for the FBI that could detect hidden thumb drives as the special agents raided homes of child pornographers. There was a little controversy around it. Like any scent trained K9, there was the question of what the K9 was picking up on. Was it the scent or was it the subtle body language of the handler? Reaper had worked with Houston as a test case. That Houston had functioned in the field, when there was no way that Reaper could know there was a stash, proved the point. It was doable.

"Unfortunately, that drive was being monitored. The individual figured out who Reaper was and was looking for retribution."

Reaper had a new baby in his house and a wife who had already gone through hell and back. What did retribution look like?

"This individual set up surveillance systems in both his neighborhood and in his home."

Bear leaned forward. "How were they found? Houston?"

"Houston is trained to find flash drives and SD cards. She wasn't trained—and I'm not sure how you'd go about training a dog—to find surveillance electronics since they're typically hidden in places that already have those components. How would you weed a legitimate circuit board that's always been there from an illegal circuit board that was layered in? Cameras that are supposed to monitor the contents of your refrigerator versus cameras that are now monitoring a kitchen?"

Yeah, the K9 nose was an amazing organ. But this wasn't

finding an apple amongst the oranges, this was finding a specific Fuji apple in a bin of Fuji apples. Okay, there were exceptions. Reaper had trained a K9 named Digger to find anything electronic —but that was for a specific job of finding electronics hidden in the woods for the Asymmetric Warfare Group. Not electronics hidden within other electronics.

"Stepping back," Juan continued. "Last night, the individual that targeted Reaper was shot and killed by a sniper. That's under FBI investigation."

The men leaned in.

"Reaper wasn't doing the shooting. He was standing next to the woman when she went down. She was already in cuffs. Someone didn't want her talking."

The room shifted its energy. These men were now on a war footing. That wasn't a deranged person, that was a professional with ties to something larger.

"As usual, when we find out we've had a brush with that level of expertise, our tech team did a sweep of their area. They started immediately after the arrest and subsequent death. Reaper's home and neighborhood were *loaded* with equipment. If any of you have a smart fridge, it needs to be gone. If your security systems need an update, you need to signal tech, and they'll take care of it while you're gone."

"They got into Reaper's house and messed with his smart fridge?" Ash asked.

"The babysitter let someone in. Cameras were found in his electronics among other very high-tech equipment. The exterior sniffing technology that we pulled out of Reaper's neighborhood was significant. This included parabolic listening devices. Strike Force's puzzler, Lynx Sobado, and Reaper Hamilton live side by side in the same duplex. Anything said in either of their homes could be picked up. Anything they said on their phones, despite end-to-end encryption could be heard—at least one side of the conversation."

"That's messed up man," Mace said.

"Since we've all been in contact with Reaper and his surveillance kooties if you have a residence off-campus—" Juan's gaze swept around the table. "Right now, that's Ares, Ash, and Mace. You'll be getting a knock on your door. The tech team will do a sweep. Expect that in the next five hours. Also in the next five hours, you will be gearing up for deployment."

Cerberus Tactical K9 was divided into two teams, Alpha and Bravo.

Based on the training of Delta Force operators, Iniquus deployed in rotation.

The three months when they weren't on call, the teams rested and trained.

Alpha had just completed its three months on.

Now, it was Bravo's turn to step up to bat.

# 4

Hailey

"Hey." Hailey grabbed up her phone on the first ring. She was wrapped in a bath towel following her shower, lying back on her bed staring at the streetlight outside her window in an otherwise pitch-black room. It wasn't late but stress and an early setting sun left Hailey exhausted. Hailey hadn't been sleeping well. Anxiety. Trepidation.

"Bingo." It was Remi's familiar voice.

"Yeah?" Hailey sat up, eyes wide, holding her breath.

"You're in Poland, you said?"

"Yes, that's right. In Krosno. That's about a thirty-minute drive heading south to get to the Slovakian border."

"And the problem moving your humanitarian supplies into place is an issue with the trucks crossing the border?"

"No." Hailey swung off the bed to pace, sliding her feet into her flipflops. "The problem is finding drayage. I need a convoy of eight trucks."

"Dray-age?" Remi pronounced carefully. "I don't know what that is."

"Uhm, drayage is a logistics term for moving containerized cargo, like what I have ready. We use a crane to put the containers on a skeleton trailer. It's the kind of truck where the driver can secure the intermodal container, loading it in one place and moving it to another without needing to unload."

"Drayage. That's a good word to know."

"I can't find any providers in my price range. Or double my price range. There's high demand as people are getting geared up for the possibility of a war. Especially up in the north."

"You aren't positioning in the north, though. Can you tell me why?"

"We have teams that are working with individual cities. I was given Nezdolannyy. Our military experts think it's going to be a two-pronged assault. The capital and the southeast on day one. Though, in talking to my cohorts, that's not the conventional wisdom on the ground. On the ground their saying the focus is going to be on the capital."

"What do you think?"

"Not my bailiwick. I don't do war." Hailey paused, then said quietly. "I try very hard not to do war. I was promised that this was setting up humanitarian aid and out."

"Mmmm."

"That didn't sound encouraging."

"I have good news and—I don't want to say bad news. Let's say more concerning news."

"Okay." Hailey put her palm to her forehead and continued to pace. Was she too late to help?

"Which do you want first?"

"Since I've spent the last week fielding bad news, let's switch things up. What do you know that's good?"

"I spoke with Iniquus—Auralia put me in touch with them. Her brother—"

"Gator Rochambeau?" Hailey asked. Gator was an operator in Iniquus's Strike Force. Hailey had met him when he'd brought a group of traumatized kids to one of her stations in Dominica after the last earthquake. He didn't hand them over and call it done. He'd stayed, lending a hand to Hailey's overwhelmed staff. He made sure the kids were fed, played with them, got them settled in their tents for the night then asked for chores. "Chores? Can you fix a truck?" Good guy. Golden-hearted. That was also where Hailey met Auralia who was there providing network coverage of the rescue efforts. Hailey and Auralia had immediately hit it off. "I've brushed past Gator in the field. Auralia and I—"

"Are friends, yup. I remember that now. We need to all get on the same continent at the same time and meet up for some girl-time."

"That would be amazing. Let's make it happen. Hey, is Auralia heading to Europe?"

"Mmm, no. She's working a story in Israel. An American reporter was shot and killed. The government is lying about the circumstances."

"I've been following that in the papers. Does Auralia have new information?"

"She got a video in her inbox from someone who happened to be filming at the time of the murder. It didn't capture the crime, but it did show the scene. There were no bursts of gunfire, the way the authorities claimed. No unrest. No cross firing. Just a single, precise shot."

"Sniper?"

"I can't speak to that. Auralia's going to see what she can figure out. Her news station authenticated the video, so that should help. Yeah, just tragic. Folks were walking around calmly, there was the sound of a gun being fired. The reporter, in full attire, mind you, with big PRESS badges across her chest, was dead before she hit the ground."

"I'm so sorry." Hailey paused as the sheer vulnerability of moment-to-moment life settled into her gut. It could be a normal day, with a normal to-do list; then suddenly, hell. "Did you know her well?" Hailey whispered, her hand wrapping her throat.

"I didn't know her personally. But war reporters are all family. To your question, you won't see Auralia on the ground. You'll be in and out of the country before she gets her Israeli assignment handed in. You're not staying in place, right? Just unloading and hightailing over the border?"

"That's the assignment."

"First, let me say—and all of this is on the down-low—that before reaching out to Gator and then Iniquus Command, I talked to my contacts at the Pentagon. I'd hoped they were going to say that you shouldn't feel like you were in a pressure cooker, that there was time. Or better, that they thought this was smoke and mirrors, some kind of distraction for the Russian people's benefit. Instead, they told me that if I wanted to be inside the borders when things got rocking, I should get in place now."

"Oh." *Crap!*

"After that, I checked in with Auralia. She gave me Gator's number. By the way, Gator's off the market. He just got married."

"And hearts are breaking all over the world." Hailey chuckled. "A gladiator with a heart of gold, his wife must be a special woman, if for no other reason, hearts are breaking all over the world. Jealousy can be a thing."

"Yup. She's a Night Stalker, though. She can hold her own."

"I don't know what—"

"She flies military special operators to their missions. They're the ones that flew SEAL Team Six in to assassinate Osama Bin Laden."

"Oh, wow. Okay. She can definitely hold her own then. Okay, you talked to Gator?"

"Yup. He went up the food chain and asked Command to speak with me."

"Good guy. Why all this about Iniquus, though?"

"Skipped that part, didn't I? The American company I mentioned to you—"

"AgilitiCorp?"

"Right. AgilitiCorp contracts for disaster security with Iniquus."

Hailey's brows pulled together. "That's your good news?"

"Yeah. Yeah, it is. It means things are going to run smoothly. Their logistics team has been on the ground staging in Romania for about a month now."

"Interesting choice, Romania." Hailey pulled the curtain to the side and rested her head on the cold pane.

"I'm sure they have their reasons. I figured I'd ask at the source when I get there."

"You're coming?"

"Sort of. You always get out ahead of the story. Let me lead you through this for a second."

"Okay, but you spoke with Iniquus Command? What do they think, timing wise?"

"Same as the Pentagon. They're speeding up their date for extraction to this Thursday, so the day after tomorrow."

"How many people are they pulling out?"

"They didn't go into that with me. I'm not sure they know yet. People have to make their decisions. It's a big upheaval. Iniquus Command was speaking in terms of thousands. Some will want to stay. I do know that if they leave, it's going to be light. They'll be able to take one personal bag and a roller bag that fits in the overhead bin per person and a rolling suitcase per pet."

Hailey smiled. "I have two pieces of luggage, but one of them is for my pet goldfish in this sandwich bag."

"Ha! That would be one way to thwart the system."

"Overhead bin?" Hailey asked. "Are they flying them out? Thousands…you'd need a dedicated airport and fleet for something like that. Buses? At around fifty seats per bus, it's twenty buses per thousand people. That could take weeks."

"It's trains. When you're talking thousands, you need trains."

"Yeah, not a lot of trains where I've worked. It didn't immediately come to mind in this case. I did rule it out though for moving my goods. A bunch of reasons that I couldn't work my way through in terms of cost mostly."

"Noted. So listen, after talking with Iniquus, I called AgilitiCorp back."

"Back and forth gathering nuggets with each conversation, I'm getting a picture of how you fenagle information out of people."

"I do my best. So I spoke to one of the AgilitiCorps executives in Nezdolannyy. And as an aside, I did ask him about planes, at least for the executives or those with special needs, medical or whatever. The company's not gung-ho about putting people in the sky after that jet fighter killed almost three hundred people on that Korean passenger flight shot down in Russian Airspace."

"They wouldn't be flying over Russian airspace. They'd head…I guess south or west, right?"

"Russia believes that it owns all the airspaces over former USSR countries. If the war starts, they'll be in the sky looking for targets."

"I can see their concern *after* the war breaks out…"

"You never know when that might be. Iniquus Command said that regardless of the concerns for getting shot out of the sky, there are simply too many employees and their families to move with planes. This works in your favor."

"How's that?" Hailey exhaled to make a fog patch on the windowpane. With her index finger, she drew a frowny face, then wiped it away.

"I mentioned your issue to Iniquus. I can't confirm this is a go—"

Hailey held her breath.

"I'm going to text you a contact name. Iniquus is all about adding to humanitarian aid when they're in a region that's facing a disaster. You know that. You've seen them operating on your various assignments."

"Yes. Well, not so much in terms of logistics as their search team. I don't know any of their logistics folks."

"Hopefully, that's about to change. The thought that their logistics commander batted around—her name is Kiyana Swabi, she's been boots on the ground in Romania this whole time—was that the trains are going in to Nezdolannyy empty. There wouldn't be any excess weight on the trip from Romania into the city. You said you needed flatbeds for containers. Maybe they could add flatbeds to the train configuration—I told them eight, right?"

"Yes, two for my rapid set up clinic and six for other humanitarian supplies."

"If we can get those containers on the train in Romania, then the engineer could decouple that section when they got to the city. The city will have the resources to unload the cars, I'd imagine."

"How… let me pull up a map."

"I pulled up a directions app while we've been speaking. It looks like a full day, and I mean thirty hours, by train to get you into place, Poland to Romania," Remi said. "I checked to see if there were rail lines that connected the two countries in a straight-ish line. A truck with a direct link would be faster. But, you said there aren't any trucks. You could make it there in time if all the pieces fell into place quickly. Iniquus might have the resources to help you with that since they're already contracting with a rail line."

"Thank you," Hailey said with as much warmth and conviction as she could express with her words. "You're right, once the containers are in Nezdolannyy, it would be pretty simple. A crane moves the container onto a local truck and then to the designated site, I've already cleared with the mayor. He has a team of volunteers for unloading and setup. I already have a shipping company who said they could do local runs on my timeline. Though, when I was having that conversation, I thought that was unhelpful."

"You have a translator traveling with you?"

"Yes, Jay'la Pakston," Hailey said. "She's got all of the major Slavic language family under her belt."

"That should help. I'll admit, getting your containers loaded onto a train and down to Romania in the next forty-eight hours? That's going to be a logistics Hail Mary."

Hailey laughed. Nerves. "It's worth a try if Iniquus lets me glom on. No wiggle room, huh? Forty-eight hours?"

# 5

Ares

"Gentlemen." Juan stood at the front of the conference room. "The situation is coming to a head with Russia. The intelligence community believes that a Russian column will cross their western border into the disputed territory and attack in the next four to five days."

The men sat a little straighter in their seats.

"Iniquus has security contracts in country. Logistics, headed by Kiyana Swabi—"

The men responded to her name with nods and smiles. She'd have the mission whipped into shape, everything humming along.

"—has been on the ground staging in Romania, developing plans to remove all of the individuals who wish to leave and are under the umbrella of Iniquus protection. This includes university students and faculty with American passports as well as company personnel for different American organizations who have a footprint in the area. As far as Cerberus Bravo is involved, our focus will be narrow. There is an American company called AgilitiCorp in Nezdolannyy. We're looking at thousands of people who need to be brought out."

"Are they being cooperative?" Ash asked. "Do they see the risk of staying? After all, threat is different than decided risk."

Juan said, "To your point, few have taken us up on the offer for immediate extraction. Those who have, were flown out already. There is no more seating available on international flights. That window is now closed for the foreseeable future. Granted, flying into the country is much easier. Far fewer people are heading in country. Mostly tacticians and press is my take." He leaned over and tapped his computer to bring up a map. "To the north," he circled the capital with his laser pointer, "the numbers were small enough that we've been using regular flights. Tickets were already purchased. Also buses and trains. The extraction push in the north is to be completed in the next twelve hours. With the capital nearby, they're feeling the heat of the Russian bear's breath on their necks. For some reason, those in the south seem to think they're not in a potential conflict zone."

If Juan was talking in terms of hours, and the IT woman was putting their electronics at the front of the queue for Bravo's imminent deployment, that meant things were coming to a head quickly.

"Those in the north who did not accept our help have signed waivers removing Iniquus from culpability. We're a land of free will. This is completely their choice. However, once Russian aggression is in play, there will be consequences for those decisions."

Judge was getting restless under the table, responding to the tension that was filling the room. Ares reached down, putting a calming hand on his K9's head.

"Here in the south," Juan made a loop with his laser pointer, "we have a bigger problem. AgilitiCorp is American owned. They have about four thousand under an Iniquus security contract. That number includes all members of the employees' households. About a third hold American passports or green cards, some have EU documentation, some from other nations, a lot are local citizenry. Of those who are from Nezdolannyy, many never obtained travel documents. There's a sudden flood of requests. It's going to take a while for the local government to move through the backlog. Point blank, they'll have to cross the border with whatever they have in hand, birth certificates, driver's licenses…"

Ares wasn't sure what this could do with Cerberus K9. Extraction wasn't normally part of their job description.

Juan tapped the computer. "Ares is wondering what the heck this has to do with a dog team." Juan caught Ares gaze and grinned. "I'll get there, brother. Let's look at the most recent satellite image from the southern border."

Bear crossed his arms over his chest, pushing back in his seat. "Those three sentences put together? It's not sounding good."

"Exactly," Juan said. "The Pentagon is saying five or six days until the breach. Iniquus Command thinks we cut this too close. Not we, Logistics has been ready for the green light. The contracting company didn't want to interrupt their workflow if it's Russian saber rattling, and posturing. Company upheaval and all that goes with it. Our command believes the five-day window, that the Pentagon projected, is optimistic."

Ares leaned forward, reading the images with a practiced eye.

That had been one of his jobs with the Green Berets, to train American allies how to interpret and prepare.

Of course, with standing national armies it was one thing…

On Ares's last mission, three years ago, in Hatari with the Green Berets, yeah, they had no window of opportunity to extract the vulnerable.

With militias—agile and small, that hide in the bush to appear on the horizon—it was a rare catch.

And they'd certainly missed the guerrillas hiding in the forest mists in Hatari.

His team in Africa hadn't had anything like the clarity of this image or time to prepare.

If only they had known, they could have thwarted the station's massacre.

The people alive and living their lives, Kibbi and the children…

Hailey would be his wife. And they'd be living their happily ever after.

Judge…

Three years ago, and like yesterday in Ares's mind, when his team saw the drone images, they'd raced onto the scene.

The carnage and tumult were like nothing Ares had ever experienced before. The gratuitous destruction and brutal murders taking place, there was so much turbulence of action that Ares wouldn't have seen Hailey in time.

Judge found Hailey immediately.

He'd leaped from the still moving vehicle and raced to Hailey's aid.

Ares owed Judge *everything* for his bravery, saving Hailey.

Out of her own physical recovery, Hailey associated Ares and Judge with that terrible day.

Ares understood why Hailey distanced herself while she worked on her mental health. For Ares, that Hailey was alive, healthy, and doing the thing she loved to do—serve those in desperate circumstances—meant he could maintain his own sanity.

That slaughter was both life destroying and life changing.

After the bloodbath at Hailey's station, Judge was given emergency transport and care at the hospital. Ares was told that

Judge's injuries would necessitate the K9's being retired from service and put up for adoption.

With Ares's contract coming up for renewal, he decided he was done with that chapter of his life.

Retiring military K9s are first offered to their handlers, if they were in a position to care for the dogs. Ares made darned sure he was in that position.

Judge was Ares's hero.

And no, there was nothing Ares wouldn't do for this dog, including upend his life and take a new job.

Signing on with Iniquus was the very best decision Ares could have made for Judge.

Mongoose, the Cerberus Team Bravo vet, guided Ares in helping Judge to rehab. Ares poured all of his soul into making it work. It kept him sane as he adjusted to life without Hailey.

And now, Ares and Judge went out with the Cerberus teams to serve humanity. To lift up those who were in desperate need.

That, very soon, would be those in Nezdolannyy on the edge of Russian disputed territory.

Seeing the image projected onto the screen, Ares knew exactly what *should* happen. Everyone who wasn't serving a role as a fighter or support staff needed to get the hell out. *Now.*

The placement of the troops. The number of tanks. The roads that encircled the city…

Citizens that were consuming the supplies, would drain them from the fighters. Civilians who needed protection would be a distraction. All eyes, all bodies, all minds, and every ounce of conviction would need to press back, or the city would fall.

It was absolutely, unequivocally, the most important thing to do—evacuate anyone that wasn't part of the security structure.

The finger crossing, head in the sand, maybe we'll be okay executive decisions on the ground with AgilitiCorp, meant that, instead of smooth and easy, this was heading to a crisis.

And what did Cerberus Tactical K9 do? Urban search and rescue. That wasn't the team walking down the road, calling out someone's name. It was crawling in the rubble, looking for survivors.

Yup, Ares got the mission, now. The team was being staged for impending disaster.

In a natural disaster, it was tough, but there were rarely monsters breathing down their necks, complicating their efforts.

Looking closer at the image, Ares thought that the Russians were staging for a siege. And if Cerberus couldn't get the players out in time, the team might well be caught in the lasso, as the enemy pulled the loop tight.

Ares thought he'd left the wars behind.

The one thing he could be grateful for was that Hailey only did humanitarian interventions. She'd be somewhere preparing shelter for flood victims or setting up mobile clinics at a forest fire. Possibly, her NGO was looking at similar satellite images, and they were setting up to receive the flood of humanity that would heave away from the war zone.

Ares needed Hailey safe.

"Let's talk about why we're along for this ride," Mace, Ares's number two, said. "I get it that Command thinks the Russians will go kinetic sooner rather than later. We're going in in case the sooner happens before the extraction?"

Juan put his knuckles onto the table and leaned in. "Exactly. If the Russians decide to drop bombs, we still need to protect our contracted individuals in the area. Everyone who put their name on the list to evacuate if Russia advanced will come out. That's our contract. What's not part of our contract is changing minds. If this goes down, and our last train has rolled out, Iniquus isn't going behind enemy lines to perform a rescue. Free choice, yes. But also, now or never."

"Trains?" Ash asked.

"Let's go over that," Ares said.

Juan put up a different graphic. **Approx. 4,000 people under contract.**

"That number isn't workforce. It's their workforce's household numbers?" Mace repeated for clarity.

"Exactly. About a thousand workers hold American passports. Those who are nationals may wish to stay and fight, and possibly some US citizens will choose to stay to fight as well. Logistics has clarified that there is a window of opportunity when fighting aged men will be allowed to leave the country. We are butting up against that time frame. As soon as there is cross-border aggression that window will slam shut."

He flipped the slide.

"The company wants to evacuate all of those people who live with the employee so spouses, children, parents, what have you and their pets."

"Pets?" Knox asked.

"As you know from our disaster interventions, many people refuse to move to safety themselves when it means abandoning their pets. This is particularly true in this area of the world. Cats are the biggest animal population in our group."

Knox looked under the table. "Hear that, Zydeco? Cats. You *will* behave."

Juan nodded. "We don't want anyone to die because we refused to transport their kitty. It complicates evacuation to the United States, but the government in Romania has signed off on the pets coming through. Romania is our hub."

He flipped to the next slide.

"The evacuation is performed as a triage. The first train will carry the most vulnerable—those with disabilities, the elderly, pregnant women, women with infants and toddlers up to school age. This train will have the fewest people being transported out as the train will contain sleeping cars and medical staff. There are a few people presently hospitalized, and they're being evacuated on the company's jet as we speak. That plane will land here in D.C. this evening. It will refuel, and that's our transport to Nezdolannyy."

"Sir," the men said as a unit.

"The others are stable enough for the train ride. Train one arrives in Romania and our evacuees are transported to temporary hotels. The train is cleaned. The sleeping cars will be replaced with seating cars. It will then head back into Nezdolannyy. Families with children school aged to eighteen will be loaded. This will be our most crowded night."

Ares thought this was the right tactic. He wondered about contingency plans. If he were Russia, the first thing he'd do was disable the rail lines.

"The third night will be singles, younger employees, those who are the healthiest and most fit. In preparation, all of the employees were asked to fill out questionnaires and the AI systems determined their placement on the train."

"Our role?" Ares asked.

"You will be there from first train to last. We will have a car on that third train for your exfil. You'll fly home from Romania. The AgilitiCorp jet will bring you out. This is scheduled as a six-day deployment, plan accordingly. While you're there you will be assisting as you can. The K9s are to monitor the tracks, the train, and the passengers. The last thing we need is some nut with an unknown zest for Mother Russia to be blowing themselves to smithereens or disable our trains."

Mace leaned forward. "How possible is that scenario?"

"We don't have a good read on the political bent of the employees. Don't get complacent. It only takes one."

"Sir," the men said.

"Obviously, those who don't wish to leave have the right to stay in place," Ares said. "What's our responsibility for their safety after the last train leaves out? You said that in the north they were signing waivers."

"There's nothing different in this contract as with our clients in the north. If the individuals aren't on that train, they forfeit our assistance. Their personal decisions will have personal ramifications. Though, I want to be clear, if a worker is staying, we are extracting everyone within their home that wishes to go. If a Nezdolannyy mother is staying, we'll take out her parents, husband, kid, and kitty."

"If the adults want to stay and want their kids out of the area? How are we handling that?" Ash asked.

"Since my time here at Iniquus, this hasn't been a mission that I've come across. Having been in war zones, though, human trafficking is a real danger. Young women in particular going missing…" Ares added.

"Right, the logistics team is drilling down on that. We need to make sure that any minor children are connected to friends or family that the parents agree are safe. The adult women—anyone over eighteen is free to make personal decisions, but we are there to safeguard their wellbeing from the point when our first train arrives up until they've reached their destination home. That means Romania and on. Logistics has that. That's not part of the Cerberus mission. I'm answering for clarity."

Ares shook his head. "This is why I'm glad not to be an operations guy. I prefer the simplicity of a leash and a nose to work with."

The team chuckled in agreement.

Juan waited for silence. "*If* this does go kinetic, Europe is going to have an enormous evacuation flow. We'd like to get as many as we can to the U.S. to free up space for other vulnerable people." He flipped through a file laying beside his laptop, stopping on a page and tapping it with his finger. "Iniquus has rented out long term hotel rooms near corporate headquarters in

Colorado," he read. "Those who don't have the documentation to get to the US will be housed in Europe." He looked up. "Other questions?"

"As we choose our K9 partners," Ares asked, "what are the priorities?" All the men on Cerberus Team Bravo handled K9s while in the military. And like in the military, sometimes the handlers would choose from the tactical kennel rather than take their usual K9 partner. The tactician chose the K9 for the job and the dog's expertise.

"I need a good mix." Juan responded. "Your team will be thirteen members strong. Six K9 and six handlers with Mongoose going in with you."

Ares nodded. Mongoose was the vet that deployed with their team when they did off-site training missions as well as regular mission work. His job was to assess and care for the dogs, to make sure that under high-stress high-danger work conditions that the K9s were well cared for.

Besides being tightly bonded with their handlers, and the emotional cost of a dog being injured, there was also the financial cost. Each K9 after purchase and training was worth about a hundred thousand dollars.

"Ares, I'll let you work the details out with your team. Train station security is what we're hoping. That's best case. But there's a significant chance that we'll need urban search and rescue in there. Logistics wouldn't request our team if they weren't seeing signs that we were cutting this exfil close." Juan pointed at Bear. "Truffles is a must." Truffles was aces with urban search and rescue. She had a special knack for tunneling through debris to make live finds.

"We find people," Bear said. "We're not equipped to extricate the victims or provide medical care."

Cerberus could handle light extraction tasks. But crush injuries and major infrastructure took a different kind of expertise.

Iniquus was successful, in part, because everyone trained to be the best of the best in their own lanes and knew when to step out of the way and let another team with the right skillset step in. There was no room for ego or territoriality when it came to lives on the line.

"We'll be depending on your years of experience to get everyone to where they need to be." Juan's gaze caught on the wall clock. "I'm heading over to Headquarters to get an update from Command. I'll let you get to planning." He turned. "Ares, I'll reach out to you when I'm back, and we can fine-tooth comb the specifics." He rapped his knuckles on the conference table. "You have all worked in disaster situations, this is a bit different. Normally, you are battling Mother Nature and natural conditions. In this case, you're battling the clock to get people out."

This last bit confirmed what Ares had been speculating. Command expected bombs to drop.

Otherwise, Cerberus deploying made little sense.

With languages and efficacy in tactical operations, Panther Force was a better match.

True, Ares was comfortable speaking the Russian language, and many people in that area were Russian speakers, he was rusty though. It had been years since he'd crouched in front of the evening fire and spoke with the tribal councils.

"We need plates and helmets?" Bear asked.

"The intelligence community believes that this city will be among the first hit. The capital in the north of the country, and Nezdolannyy in the south. Gear up accordingly."

"Is there something there they want from Nezdolannyy?" Mace asked.

"Several somethings," Juan said, gently shutting his laptop. "They want the citizens to feel physical and emotional pain to force compliance. They need to grab a foothold while the grounds are frozen to be in place for the mud season when their tanks will be useless. Now, having said that, our intelligence community believes Russian leaders are blowing sunshine up the president's skirts. Overly optimistic. They believe that our area of operation will happily turn to Mother Russia, grateful that the citizens can, like a prodigal son, return into the fold." He scratched at his jaw. "Indications from our resources on the ground indicate that is far from the truth. 88% of the people say fight. 11% say do whatever it takes for peace and 1% don't know what to do. With a super majority willing to fight, our military officials have gamed this out. When Nezdolannyy citizens don't stand in the roads, cheering and waving their flags, handing out welcome flowers to the Russian tank parade, this city will be besieged. Now is the time for the vulnerable to get out."

*Now is when, exactly.*

Juan looked from man to man. "This looks like it's going to be a protracted war. You've been through this, every one of you. If things go down while you're boots on the ground, remember, as hard as it is, you can't fix everything. You can't save everyone. Stay focused on the tasks before you and let's bring this mission safely to a close. After this briefing, you'll have eight hours to gather you kit, kiss your loved ones, and get on the tarmac."

Ares was acutely aware that their team was unattached. Team Alpha made a big deal of last year's string of engagements and marriages. It made the bachelors on Bravo the butt of Alpha's manhood jokes.

Ares was agnostic about relationships. He enjoyed parts, disliked others.

Since Hailey, Ares dated for comfort. He liked the dichotomy in his life. He lived in a hard world and soft appealed to him.

But then, he'd found that soft could also be needy.

And honestly, after Hailey, Ares didn't have a ton to give.

# 6

Hailey

WHEN HER PHONE'S tone jangled through the car's speaker, Hailey tapped the button shaped like a telephone receiver on her steering wheel and called out hopefully, "Hello?"

"Hey. It's Remi."

"Oh good!" The background was filled with the sound of crowds and a PA announcement. "Where are you?"

"Türkiye, still. I'm boarding a plane here in a couple minutes."

"Heading where?"

"Nezdolannyy. I was wondering if you want me to get you a room next to mine at the hotel."

"Maybe. I wanted to stay near where the Iniquus folks are staging. I'd like to solidify those connections because, I'm telling you, I've never seen anything like what they can do and how quickly they can do it. I'm seriously blown away. Thank you so much for helping me make the connections."

"I'll always be there for my Wombats."

"Same." Hailey inhaled deeply, feeling gratitude. If Remi hadn't connected the dots and made opening phone calls for her, Hailey would still be pulling out her hair in Poland with no good ideas.

"About the hotel," Remi said. "That works then. I know for a fact that I'm staying where at least some of their team is. Same reasons, I want to develop those connections since I seem to be crossing paths with them more and more. Bonus, the hotel is across the street from the train station's main entrance."

"As long as that doesn't make your husband jealous," Hailey sing-songed. She still couldn't believe Remi was married. And that Hailey had never even met the man. It had been a whirlwind romance.

Remi said that when you knew, you knew.

Hailey had felt the same. Almost from the moment that Ares had quite literally moved into her path and cast a long and much appreciated shadow over her. Hailey had looked up at his kind face and thought, "Yup. I think it's him." She'd been right, until she was very wrong.

Not his fault.

Ares was a good guy.

*The best.*

But life had decided that their paths would go in different directions.

"T-Rex?" Remi's laughter brought Hailey back to the present and away from nostalgia lane. "He has nothing to worry about. Where are you?"

"I'm on my way toward Romania. Right now, I'm crossing through Slovakia, heading to Hungary. I was able to book a flight from there. I just made it over the mountains. Those roads! Whew, that was pretty hair raising."

"Alone? Is your translator with you?"

"Jay'la? No, she had a personal thing she had to attend to. She's meeting up with me later at the train. She's got her own way there."

"So it worked out with Iniquus? You said Romania."

"Are you asking as a friend or a reporter?"

"Bit of both. I'm working a couple of story angles. I thought I'd reach out to you and see what was going on in the minds of some of the relief and humanitarian aid NGOs." She used the initials for non-governmental organization. "You're top of my list."

"I'd be hurt if I wasn't." Hailey smiled. "I'm allowed to talk to reporters on background. I can't give you permission to mention me or WorldCares by name. I'm just a cog in the machinery. If you want something that's a quote, I can give you our PR guy's number."

"I might get that from you later."

"Hey, did I say yes to the hotel room? That's a yes from me. I was going to ask Kiyana when I got to Romania, then call ahead for reservations. But you already know where some are staying."

"Yes, it's not their logistics folks, though. It's the Cerberus Tactical K9 team. They're flying in as we speak. They're on an AgilitiCorp private jet. They'll be in Nezdolannyy tomorrow probably about the time the first evacuation train is pulling in."

"And you know them?"

"I'm alive because of them."

"Wait. What?" Hailey slowed to a crawl as she passed a horse cart, then had to dodge a pig walking down the highway.

"Yeah, they were training over in Israel last year at the time of the Beirut explosion. You know I was trapped."

"For days with your hunky husband."

"I was lying there, contemplating what it would be like to die of dehydration."

"No!" Hailey gasped. "What? But you're always so prepared."

"We had enough for a few days. We were there a lot longer than the supplies I had with me. We weren't going to make it much longer when I met Truffles."

"Truffles! A doggo? What a great name."

"Beautiful dog. My hero. She found us and got us comms. They sent in Rory, that's a Delta Force team dog. Anyway, it all worked out. But I'm hoping Truffles is going to be here. I promised her a steak, and I never got to give it to her because they flew us out. We were with the senator."

"Right. I remember that. Oh, man, Remi. That's terrifying."

"You know, there might just be a handsome dog handler for you in this Cerberus mix."

"No, thanks." Hailey frowned. "I was in a relationship with a dog handler once. I'm good."

"I've interviewed enough working dog handlers that I know you really can't be a bad guy—the dogs seem to smell that on a person's skin. I mean, I know there are bad people who handle K9s, but the doggos disrespect their handler and that creates chaos in difficult situations."

"Like?" Hailey was so grateful for this conversation. It was helping time pass. This was going to be one heck of a long drive. She had to get into Hungary to catch a flight to Romania. It was a stupid schedule, but everything and everybody seemed to be in an upheaval. It was this or drive the eighteen hours straight through. Hailey didn't think she could do that without Jay'la to trade off with and cat naps on the back seat.

"A police officer sends in the K9," Remi was saying. "The K9 gets the wrong person in the bite. Or the right person, he's been subdued but the K9 won't release."

"Because the dog didn't know the commands? Wasn't trained?"

"Maybe? Sometimes? I've seen it happen. I've been there when the handler couldn't get the K9 to release. You can usually spot the dogs that are in a bad circumstance—be it the wrong job, poor training, bad-guy handler—because they have shock collars on. The handler is shocking the shit out of the dog to get them to comply with the command."

"Cerberus K9? That doesn't jive with what I know of them. Which is very little. I've seen them working at different disaster scenes. I haven't talked to them at all. You know, they had their dogs in the rubble piles, and I didn't want to distract their work. These are their urban disaster rescue K9s they're bringing in?"

"Yup."

Hailey had to listen hard to hear Remi respond past the noise of what Hailey assumed was a passing group of very enthusiastic people. "They're night and day with that police bite scenario."

"And why are they sending in a K9 team?" Hailey asked. "Does that make sense to you?"

"I have an explanation in my imagination," Remi said. "But I'd rather not talk about it until I can confirm it. Taking off my Wombat badge and replacing it with my press pass, I'm going to ask you a few questions, so I have a jumping off place when I land in the city. I need to focus us on that for a minute. They started loading my plane. I'm taping you now."

"K." Hailey took a breath. "What angle are you taking with this assignment?"

"AgilitiCorp gave me permission to gather information from Iniquus. Still, Iniquus was tight-lipped about the details. I know a bit about the trains, though. They will have three trains on three consecutive nights, moving *some* of their employees. I'm most interested in meeting those who are planning to stay. The reluctant who didn't take their places on the first two, and what nationals

Iniquus can get out of the potential conflict zone. Iniquus believes that the government might step in to stop fighting aged males from leaving."

"Those men wouldn't want to leave anyway. I've been talking to the mayor and the city planners. They will fight to their last breath. No fear. Steadfast. It's… I can't find a word with the emotion I want. Heart-pounding and impressive." Hailey pressed down on the gas as she powered up the hill.

"I agree. What's going on with your containers?" Remi was the queen of not getting derailed by side conversations and deflection.

"To make the deadline, I was able to find two trucks that were going down to Bulgaria to pick up a load from the Black Sea port. As a humanitarian gesture, they let me load two of my containers on, and they're dropping them in Romania with Iniquus."

"Free? You weren't worried they'd just disappear?"

"I made sure Iniquus thought it was a good idea. I had already placed trackers in the different modules and boxes. But yes, their logistics commander, Kiyana, has the trackers on her computer, and she's following them in. If there are any issues, she said she has a team that would follow up."

"That's sounds like a bad outcome for any would-be robbers."

"My thoughts. They should get the containers about two hours before I get there. Iniquus will load them from the truck to the train."

"Two containers out of eight. Which did you choose?" Remi asked.

"Mobile clinic and medical supplies. That's going to take the most time to set up. And I want to be there for that."

"And the other six?"

"They're loaded onto the train cars back in Poland. They should have left out of there already," Hailey looked down at the clock read out, "about an hour or so ago. The train will decouple them in Romania. Iniquus will just add them to their train config-uration on their second run. The train itself won't be empty. They won't tell me what they're bringing in. It's not people. It's secret. I'm thinking from the kinds of things that have been said to me along the line, both from those in Nezdolannyy and from Iniquus, that they won't bring in guns and ammunition. They're not inter-ested in overstepping American diplomacy or doing anything that might trigger Russia."

"Right. Stab in the dark, what is it?"

"My guess is practical stuff that would be helpful to their citizen soldiers. I bet the young adults who are signing on to fight are shopping for sturdy boots."

"That could be right. I'll snoop."

"Hey, Remi, they're doing me a ginormous favor…"

"I would ask those questions if you'd said something or said nothing. Your name will not come into play. Remember, I'm a nosy war correspondent. And I have a personal relationship with some of the K9 team from Beirut."

"Okay."

"Where are you putting the clinic?"

"Is this going in your article?"

"I wouldn't put a map with a red pin. Iniquus is saying siege. I'm wondering where you think it's safe to set up."

"Siege is what my people think, too. And from your reporting, I'd think that Russia being Russia, and what happened in Syria, that they'll target the hospitals. I've found an office building with four levels of underground garage. On the lowest level, I will have places for the elder and disability care. The second I'll have maternity and pediatric space."

"God."

"I know. I *hate* that. And the third level, hmm, they call it 'blue level', imagine you're standing on ground level, and you go to your car, and it's parked two floors down, that's where I'm putting the war wounded. There will be an operating theater with four operating stations."

"What's on the highest level of the garage?"

"Buffer. Our engineers looked at the schematics. They think that might have some collapse if the office building takes a direct strike. The lower floors were built to withstand that, and there are tunnels to nearby buildings in several directions. It's pretty safe. I hope."

"That's train one. And you'll be coming in on that train. It'll be here tomorrow evening?"

"Right, Thursday. The containers will be there, and Iniquus said they had it handled getting them onto the trucks the mayor is providing."

"What comes next?"

"The subsequent trains are shelf-stable precooked meals, baby supplies."

"For whom?"

"General population. We're staging those along with first aid, sanitation, and water stations."

"Huge job."

Hailey looked over her shoulder, touched her blinker and changed lanes. "Thankfully, things have been ticking right along, now. It seems that when one miracle appears on the horizon, that the universe conspires to continue apace."

"So where are you putting the stuff?"

"You *can't* print this." Hailey reached up and clawed at the turtleneck that now felt overly warm.

"On background. You're sketching a general picture."

"There are a network of underground areas where the population can retreat, including the subway system. The city government wants to get the food into the underground areas to prevent mass dehydration and starvation. You know what, Remi? I'm caught on Iniquus bringing in urban search and rescue dogs. And they're flying them in? That's…surprising. I don't have anything from my NGO about an uptick in Russian activity." Hailey adjusted the car's temperature ten degrees lower. "They haven't moved up my 'get everything in place' date."

"Which is when?" Remi asked.

"Next week. Not because of their assessments of an impending assault, but I'm needed to get nutrition stations set up in Haiti."

"Huh," Remi said. "Word in my circles is that Haiti lost international support and relief work when those missionaries were held for ransom."

"That's true. A few people thought of themselves and scared away assistance programs. I'm going in with security. I'm not staying. I'm just supervising a supply shipment."

"Who's providing it? The security not the supplies."

"My boss didn't say. Before I head in, I'll get the name, check them out, pass the name by the Wombats to see if anyone has the scuttlebutt. It would make the most sense if WorldCares hired locally because they'd know the language best, the terrain, the no-go areas. My concern is that if my company were to hire locally, that that could be a set up. As sad as it is, corruption is an issue. They could fake an ambush. The gang issues are problematic right now."

"Is that where your head is?"

"Ever since the massacre at my station in Hatari, yeah, that's where my head is. I love the feeling I get when I help, seeing faces shift from anguish to smiles. But I'm also always looking over my shoulder to see who's casting a shadow. My sense of safety is non-existent. I mean, there I was finishing up my Hatari project, so pleased with what we'd accomplished. The new clinician had arrived. Hours later all that was left was pain and destruction. We were out in the middle of absolutely nowhere. We shouldn't have been on anyone's radar. Someone had to have led those guerrillas to us. And they must have been attacking to make some terrible statement that they knew would get to the right person."

"And you never found out those reasons?"

"No, well there was no one to interrogate after the military moved in."

"I know this in my soul, people can be evil incarnate, and there are saints walking amongst us. My hope is that the good at least balances out the bad. Though, honestly, I'm always hopeful that the good will do more than that balancing act, that they will conquer. It's hard in our line of work not to burn out and not to grow cynical. What are you doing for self-care? Are you taking regular times off? Taking care of your mental health?"

"Regular times off? Yes, I try to go to beautiful places and bask."

"And dating? You never bring up anyone—though, amongst the Wombats that's kind of a thing. Everyone has their head down, pushing through whatever adventure or misadventure that our jobs have laid before us."

"True. I thought you were recording me for an article?"

"Nosey is all. The recorder is off."

"As for me? Mmm, not so much with the dating scene."

"Interesting." Remi muttered something under her breath, then Hailey could hear rolling wheels. "I get that it's hard with all the traveling. I mean, I met my husband on an assignment and got to know him pretty darned well while we were stuck under the rubble in Beirut day after excruciatingly long day. He kept me sane. I figured I could use that in my life."

"That and he's darned cute with an action-hero's body."

"Were you checking out my husband?"

"Auralia showed me pictures. I was just making sure he was good enough for you."

"You're deflecting."

"Yeah. Well, I met a guy on assignment, too. We were engaged. Things kind of fell apart."

"Loading now! You never told me you'd been engaged. I want to know that story."

"Safe trip." Hailey wished that piece of her personal story hadn't popped out. "I guess I'll see you tomorrow. And you've got the hotel arrangements for me starting tomorrow night, right?"

"Yup. I've got you covered," Remi said.

"Hey," Hailey called out before Remi hung up, "if this doesn't work out for some reason, and I miss seeing you, stay safe, promise?"

## 7

**Ares**

DEPLANING WAS A SLOG.

Twenty hours flight time was long. And though Ares and his teammates were used to traveling globe-circling distances in miserable conditions, it always took some time to shake it off.

A long run with Judge, an intense workout in the gym, a solid eight hours of sleep would help get his body comfortable and reset his system as he adjusted to the new time zone. Get his mind and body ready for whatever came their way.

Mongoose had managed the dogs with medication. These were high-drive K9s that never wanted to stop. Twenty hours in a crate would drive them bonkers. They'd found that on long flights, the dogs could bounce back best when they weren't stressed from the trip.

Mongoose gave each doggo a wellness check as the handlers coaxed their woozy partners from their blanket nests out into the frigid air on the tarmac. The dogs stretched and dopily took in their new surroundings.

Judge pushed his nose under Ares's arm and breathed humidly into the fabric. Ares spoke soft encouraging words as he rubbed over Judge's body, loosening up the dog's muscles. At six-years-old, Ares could see the effect. He hated the idea that a time would come when Judge would be retired. After years of constantly being side by side, that transition would be hard on both of them. Though, Iniquus cared for the dogs for their full life. Judge would want for nothing from warm therapy pools to Mongoose's vet skills. It would be a good life for Judge. Ares would make sure of it. But it would still be a dark day.

Judge looked up, catching Ares's gaze.

"Good? Do you want to walk it off a bit? Go potty while Goosey checks on your friends?"

As the team focused on their dogs' care, Mongoose, who was in the dual role of vet support and team logistics manager, monitored the airport workers as they unloaded the plane, folded the crates, and placed their gear onto the waiting bus that Kiyana had arranged.

Everything flowed smoothly and they were on the bus headed for their next destination.

Ares hoped this was the tenor of their whole mission.

Getting to the hotel added another forty minutes to their trip. It gave the men an opportunity to see the city and get a feel for the mood.

Nobody in the streets seemed anxious. It all seemed very calm. Normal.

It was hard to fathom that very soon bombs could be dropping from overhead, tanks rumbling through the streets.

Was this bravery? Steadfastness as was the translation of their city's name?

Or was he being naïve?

They passed by the hospital, and a school, that Ares thought, strategically, weren't great to have in proximity. They were the kinds of soft marks that Russian generals loved to hit.

Violence of action against the most vulnerable was supposed to bring people to their knees.

It either worked or it had the opposite effect, enraging the population to fight harder, longer, more ferociously.

Ares had spent hours poring over intelligence reports on the plane ride over. If Russia used its normal tactics, they would awaken the warrior's blood that flowed through the citizens' veins. Far from making the people of Nezdolannyy cower and grovel, Ares was convinced that they'd awaken a beast.

Yes, the chances of a World War III were high. No lie. A madman with his finger on the nuclear buttons was an existential threat. The only thing, in this moment, that gave Ares a sense that that wouldn't happen was that the winds blew from west to east. The Russian government would have to decide that irradiating their own people was a fine tradeoff. And for a crazy person, it might well be. But the people who actually placed their hands on the switches and decided to let the warheads fly, they had families, too. They were the ones that Aries hoped were sane.

The bus slowed as it approached their hotel.

It was located across the street from train station. Honestly, as long as the conductors weren't blowing warning horns through the night, the rattle of a train might be sleep inducing.

As the bus came to a stop, Mongoose went in to register and get the key cards for their team.

Ares stood at the front. "Listen up. I want you to exercise and feed your dogs and get them settled. Order room service. Get a good night's rest. Get on the Nezdolannyy clock. Our schedule for tomorrow: After you've run your dog and had breakfast, we have a video meeting with Juan. That's at zero six hundred local time. No one is late. Once we have our updates, we'll spend the day getting to know our area of operation. We need to scope everything that might have an impact on our assignment. Find out where the shelters are. Where the fire department and police station are. The hospitals and clinics. Everything in a five-mile radius. I'll develop a grid assignment for each of you. Tomorrow noon, we'll share our observations."

"Sir."

"Now, the first extraction train is coming in from Romania tomorrow at sixteen hundred. We'll learn more about that from Juan in the morning. Before it gets here, Mace, Ash, and I will walk the train station and tracks, sniffing for anything that might go BOOM."

"Sir," Mace and Ash said.

"The nose and bite K9s will help maintain security. The rest of the team will do whatever it is that Logistics needs us to do to make it a smooth transition for our clients as they get safely onto that train and leave. After the train departs, we'll head back to the hotel. I'll get Mongoose to secure a meeting space for us if Kiyana hasn't done so already. You can present your reports at that time. We'll assess how the day went and how we can smooth the wrinkles. Yes?"

"Yes, sir."

Ares looked over his shoulder as Mongoose arrived back at the bus.

"Dismissed."

Ares looked down at a woozy Judge. "Yo, man, you're getting to be a light-weight in your old age." Ares scrubbed his hands into Judge's fur. "Come on, you'll feel better after you run a bit."

Knowing that Mongoose would handle the baggage and crates, Ares pocketed his key card, checked Judge's collar and lead connection and started off at a slow jog.

~

## Thursday, Nezdolannyy

It was zero six hundred on the dot. The team had assembled.

The dogs sprawled, panting at their feet, relaxed from their runs.

The men were fresh from their showers dressed in the Iniquus uniform of gunmetal gray long sleeved compression shirts under fleece jackets specially treated to perform under extreme conditions. For this assignment, their digital-camouflage tactical pants were the winter wear choice—fleece lined with Lycra and modern fibers that made the clothing both wind and moisture resistant. They kept the team as comfortable and flexible as possible as Bravo performed their duties, moving from indoors to out. Each team member had a black MOLLE backpack with emergency equipment and encrypted comms sitting by their chairs, ready to grab and go.

Juan was on the big screen leading their brief.

After his greeting and check in about their accommodations, Juan said, "You'll be happy to learn that our friend and war reporter extraordinaire Remi Taleb is registered at your hotel."

"Crap," Bear said under his breath. Then louder, "If Remi's here, you know this is going to turn into a shitstorm."

"I hope that's not the case. We think she's here reporting on advanced humanitarian efforts."

"Ours?" Mace asked.

"Not necessarily. Logistics is allowing an NGO to use the train to bring in supplies to support the citizens should things turn kinetic."

Ash leaned forward. "How did Remi find out about that?"

"That's pretty easy," Juan said. "Remi is the connector of the dots. She's following a story out of Poland where the charity ran into a logistics headwind. Remi figured out that Iniquus held security contacts in the area and put the two efforts together. Since Beirut, Remi's added Iniquus to her network. Iniquus's stance is that we're glad to partner with her to share info, but we also appreciate advanced intelligence from her reporting, the background material that's not working its way into her articles or compromises her objectivity and ethics." Juan panned his gaze toward Ares. "To that end, Remi said she'd meet with you tonight, Ares, to share anything tactical that she learns that might impact our mission. Forewarned is forearmed." Juan paused as he shifted to the next topic. "Speaking of arms, until the first bullets or bombs fly from Russia, you will not have weaponry on you outside of a multitool and your K9. If aggression comes to pass while you're still boots on the ground, Command will make decisions. Russia cannot think that America is fighting, that could be the start of World War III. Because of our military backgrounds, that is a fine line. And we're walking that tightrope. The train coming in is not empty. Along with the flatbed cars with humanitarian assistance from WorldCares NGO, it contains gifts from Iniquus."

Ares system tingled with adrenaline when he heard the name WorldCares. The last thing he thought would happen on this mission was that he'd hear Hailey's NGO named in a briefing.

He focused back on Mace who was saying, "…tactical?"

Yeah, he'd missed something important while he was distracted by Hailey thoughts. He couldn't allow that. Ares scooted his chair closer to the table, propped his elbows, and focused in, trying to catch up.

"We're working with US officials on best practices here. There's a lot of concern. If America, or any of its entities, seem like they are preparing to fight alongside the nationals, well, this could put an exponent next to the risk factors. Like I said before, we aren't interested in becoming a player that catalyzed a world war. We're quietly going in, getting our people, leaving some support products, and getting out. My understanding is that our supplies include helmets, ballistic vests, night vision, boots, tactical gloves, pants, MOLLE systems, tactical first aid kits, and the like. We won't be unloading. That will be handled discretely by one of their military units dressed in railroad uniforms. This is just a heads up, so you know what's going on."

"Let's say things go sideways while we're here—" Mace started. "Logistics personnel traveling on that train aren't military tacticians. Are we supposed to provide security? At that point, would we have access to weapons? Do we have a plan if we end up fighting our way out of here?"

"Chances are not zero that things will ramp up during your mission window. Otherwise, Command wouldn't have sent your team in. You've got that figured out. Right?"

"Yes, sir," Mace responded.

"Your job is to get the people on our list out safely. That's why Command decided to put urban search and rescue in place. Command is concerned that we're butting up against a time crunch. We may have arrived on the knife's edge of disaster. If the bombs drop before we can get our precious cargo out, Bravo will be tasked with finding the employees and pulling them, whole or not, from the debris. Logistics is monitoring all of their locations via GPS. Tags were mailed out as necklaces two weeks ago. Everyone is supposed to have them on as part of their identification."

"Cell towers are likely to fall first," Ares pointed out.

"Possibly by friendlies," Knox said. "I mean, it can make things a nightmare for those trying to maintain contact, but can you imagine? Throw off the GPS for the incoming foreign fighters, they'll be driving in circles."

"Positives and negatives to that scenario, brother," Juan said. "We'll all have our satellite phones and backup ham transceivers with us. I don't need to hand hold and slow walk you through this.

You've seen what can happen. Think through the scenarios in advance. Be strategic. Protect those tracks and protect that train. All right men?"

"Sir."

"Okay good." Juan looked down at the sheet of paper in front of him. "Next, as I mentioned Remi Taleb is in the area and that she was going to share some observations with Ares this evening. She'll probably also want to interview our team to see what's going on. If you see her in the field, everyone is to point her back to Ares."

"Sir."

"And if you can be of any help to the WorldCares, as long as it doesn't detract from our mission, I am authorizing that."

"Sir."

Juan gave a nod. "Good luck, gentlemen. Dismissed."

The screen went blank.

Ares wondered who WorldCares was sending in. It was a huge international organization. It had thousands of employees.

But Ares knew in his gut, it was Hailey.

Man, he hoped he was wrong.

For her sake.

…and for his.

The idea of seeing her and having his heart ripped back open.

Three years became yesterday. The attack. The helicopter. And the life he'd envisioned—as challenging as it was going to be—flew away.

After Hailey was back at home, Ares tried to stay connected.

He'd sent her videos, so she knew that Judge was recovering. He let her know that his contract was up with the Green Berets and that he was adopting Judge and helping him convalesce.

When he mentioned Judge's recovery, that seemed to lift a bit of the weight that she took on. She was survivor's guilt personified. She said she'd started therapy. And Ares had a glimmer of hope which dimmed with time.

It wasn't a sudden crack that severed their relationship.

Texts were left without response. Phone calls left unanswered. Video visits without joy.

Ares had talked about his situation with his sister Leslie; she was a student guidance counselor.

Leslie had listened with an empathetic ear, then said. "You know that crap phrase 'what doesn't kill us makes us stronger.' It's a terrible burden to put on people. Some people thrive in adversity but that isn't typical. What's typical is that people bow under the weight of the baggage they carry. It's exhausting."

True, when Ares and she had spoken, Hailey sounded exhausted.

And the last thing Hailey needed, Leslie told Ares, was someone who wanted her to be the person she was before. Someone who was waiting for her to snap back. That wasn't going to happen.

"What do I do, Les? How do I let Hailey know that I'm here for her?"

Leslie had looked at him with troubled eyes. "Waiting for the old Hailey back? Personally, if I were Hailey, I'd break up with you."

It was a punch in the gut that winded him for long minutes. Finally, he stammered, "What? Why?"

"Because you knew her *before*. Personally, I'd surround myself with new people."

"Why? The people who love her want to—"

"Make her snap back to who she was. Will keep looking for signs that she's emerging from the fog."

Ares stilled. She was right.

Leslie picked up her kid's stuffed bear and wiggled it at him before tossing it into the toy bin. "It's rare to find a Pooh."

"Lost me," Ares said with a shake of the head.

"Eeyore was depressed."

"Okay."

"And no one tried to fix him. He'd be invited. He'd mope along. And he was accepted for what he was, depressed. That's what I'd look for. New people who knew 'traumatized me'. They'd either accept and invite, like Pooh, or they'd not be in my circle."

Ares felt his heart crushing in his chest.

"By letting you fade out of her life, that's one less person who would be watching from the corner of their eye to see if she was blooming again. And why would this happen specifically to you and not everyone?"

"Because I was there and didn't stop it in time. Because when she sees me, she sees the scenes from the attack."

"Maybe. I can't speak to that. But perhaps, it's because you knew her in a unique way. Unlike her parents or childhood friends that she might speak with once a week, once a month, once in a blue moon, you had decided to spend your life with a certain person. And she isn't that person anymore. You made a commitment to the previous-Hailey. She *isn't* that person."

"Those aren't the vows. The vows are through everything we will walk together."

"Ah, but you hadn't made those vows yet. Not officially. I bet in Hailey's mind—having met her and knowing what a generous, kind person she is—she's answering fewer and fewer calls because she thinks it's best for everyone that your feelings slowly ebb."

After that conversation, Ares had paid close attention to his thoughts. Leslie was right. He kept hoping for *his* Hailey back.

It didn't stop him.

He'd called on a specific schedule, right down to the minute of the day of the week, so she wouldn't be surprised.

He sent a text every morning.

The texts that she answered were short and unencouraging.

He kept trying until it felt like stalking. He was obviously not welcome in her life.

The last text he sent read: **I'm always here for you. If you change your mind about us, reach out. And if you don't change your mind, just know someone out there loves you. Always.**

He'd seen her at a distance at disasters when he was out doing his job for Iniquus.

It had been a trick to keep Judge busy on task, and then headed in the opposite direction.

It was something surreal to land in a foreign country under the devastation of a natural disaster. Things weren't all kumbaya. Disease was rampant in the aftermath of the event, cholera, respiratory illnesses... The darkest souls found ways to exploit the situation—rape, theft, murder. To see Hailey was to worry for her safety.

Hailey was usually there in her khaki pants and bright-colored t-shirt, clipboard in hand, someone's baby bouncing on her comfortably round hip, phone calls coming rapid fire over her earphones as she scooted from tent to tent making things hum with efficiency and compassion.

Hailey was *kindness* personified. Soft features, soft voice, warm heart. A genuine smile. Her long blonde hair made her easy to spot in most parts of the world. The freckles that splashed across her nose felt sunny and warm. She was good stuff. When she walked into a tent, smiles lit otherwise ashen faces.

Hailey knew he was with Iniquus.

She saw the Search and Rescue teams working their K9s.

If she wanted to talk to him, she could have found him pretty easily.

In that she didn't reach out to him or mention him to his teammates, it told Ares to stay away.

"Please, don't be associated with this crap," Ares whispered under his breath.

He pushed to dismiss the weird feeling of doom.

Hailey didn't do war zones.

Heck even Cerberus didn't do war zones.

WorldCares NGO was sending supplies. There was no disaster to manage. No fleeing refugees to feed and house. If Hailey was involved in this at all, it would be over a border. Poland where Juan had said things were being organized. Poland was the perfect place to stage.

In Poland, Hailey would be safer.

Those thoughts did little to calm Ares's pounding heart.

**8**

---

Ares

Ares paced the length of the footbridge. Below him, a busy thoroughfare ran on his right, the train tracks ran on the left. He'd talk to Kiyana about using her area contacts to sign up local vets with experience from the Middle East fights. Ares wanted experienced eyes on that road a couple of kilometers in either direction to watch the vehicles for anything that might look questionable. He'd put Bravo on it, but that would put them two men down and their team was already small to police the tracks and assist the travelers.

Today, the most vulnerable were going out. Invalids, infants, pregnant women. Six hundred of them. This would be a good stress test for Kiyana's systems. They'd find the holes and fill them for tomorrow when the evacuation numbers would double.

Ares focused on the team of local soldiers unloading boxes from the cars like ants transporting food back to their nests.

Iniquus was doing right by their allies. The number of boxes being unloaded were substantial.

If there was a war, this country would be the barricade that stopped encroachment into NATO territories, and that would be a world disaster.

Ares was on his satellite phone that was encrypted end to end with Juan back in D.C.

"What's your situation?" Juan asked.

"The train arrived on time." The bitter wind burned Ares face. "I'm on overwatch."

"Any concerns?"

"Cut and dry as long as Russia holds off. Seventy-two hours, and we'll be golden."

"Worst case, you've scoped out the closest bomb shelter for Bravo?"

"Yeah, it's a block from the train station and our hotel. We would shelter in the subway station right there. We'll have our kits ready. I've ordered my men to carry seventy-two hours of supplies for operators and K9 including pee mats wherever they go."

"Good enough," Juan said. "Keep me informed. Out."

Ares stalled looking over the banister.

Hailey.

Even from way up here on the bridge, he recognized her graceful sweep of arms as she spoke with folks on the platform—greeting, directing, showing appreciation.

Efficient and in charge.

She fielded a line of folks coming up with their questions, pointing them to the right resource as she carried on with whatever her task was.

Ares would admit to himself that when Hailey came into view, he needed a minute to find a game face.

*Damn, she's beautiful.*

Her in his sphere was a gut punch.

He banged a fist to his chest to get his heart started. To force a breath.

The loss of their relationship roared through him, a flood of grief.

And he absolutely didn't want her to feel the same.

For anything about him to hurt *her*.

It could be that she'd fallen out of love with him. It could be that she still harbored feelings. Either way, she'd decided that his being in her life wasn't something she wanted.

His face, or Judge's, might be a trigger. And if that made her feel anything like what he was feeling now, he'd go to great lengths to protect her from this.

He'd stay off her radar.

He wasn't sure that was possible, but he'd try hard.

It wasn't that she'd be unloading today and gone on her merry way. Speaking with Kiyana at the Romanian TOC, Ares found out that they had to divide WorldCares supplies up over the first two days of transit. Half came in on this train. Half would come on the next.

A call to Remi told Ares that WorldCares was trying to work on the down low, slipping supplies into more than three dozen towns and cities.

Hailey would be busy checking the supplies and getting them moved to their destinations. She had some serious logistics to navigate with just her and what looked like a translator who was shadowing her.

It might feel like fate was putting a thumb on the scales to put them in the same place at the same time. But magical thinking wasn't part of Ares make up.

For a flash, Ares wondered if Hailey had moved on from their relationship to someone else's arms. He didn't want to know.

It was over three years since she'd accepted his proposal—the exact same amount of time that she decided their relationship wasn't something she could lean into.

Ares worked at not making that personal, at not thinking— dodged a bullet, when push came to shove she didn't trust me as a support. He knew that was antithetical to Hailey. The Hailey he had known. He hadn't a clue who she was now. If she were married, had kids…

He for damned sure hadn't moved on.

Hadn't really tried.

No one engendered images of permanence for him.

He hoped like hell that wasn't a lasting disability. Ares didn't know how to take his heart back after he'd given it away.

Drumming his hands on the rail, Ares thought, *Yup, no need to open wounds and let them fester. I'll try to stay off your radar.*

Judge, now, that might be harder.

When it came to Hailey, Judge always picked her side. Somewhere back in his three-year-old adolescent brain while they were in Hatari, Judge took up the idea that Hailey was his to protect.

And Judge wasn't shy about telling Ares he could go to hell for ordering him to do anything other than he wanted to when he was in "Hailey mode".

To be fair, Ares felt the same, and it saved her life.

That morning of the massacre, Ares had noticed that Hailey had forgotten her cell phone and wanted to make sure she got to the office safely. He'd flown a drone out to watch Hailey on her route to her station, using that as an exercise for the team he was training. Afterwards, Ares had planned to call Kibbi to let Hailey know he was bringing the phone to her at lunch.

What he saw was more than a bucolic ride.

There was a hurricane on the horizon.

They'd seen the militia riding hard toward the station.

Ares had never experienced that level of fear.

They'd tried phoning a warning, but for whatever reason, Kibbi hadn't answered.

Jumping into their vehicles, they'd crashed through the countryside, trying to get there in time.

While his vehicle was still in motion, Judge had leaped to Hailey's defense without a command. Ares shoved the gear into park, stood up in his seat to clear the windshield and taken the shot that killed the attacker who laid on top of Hailey with Judge biting the arm that had restrained her.

There's a saying, "A Green Beret can kill you twice before you even know you're dead." Ares thanked god for every second he'd spent on the training courses.

It was one and done for the militant.

Hailey, bleeding, with her face swollen and nearly unrecognizable, tugged off her ripped t-shirt and was trying to staunch Judge's blood, flowing from the machete slice that ran the length of his torso.

Judge, on death's doorstep, peeled his lips back, salivating and gnashing at the air, letting everyone know that he wasn't down for the count, and he would protect Hailey.

Moments later, as his brothers waded into the gore to destroy the invaders, Ares had Judge across his shoulders and Hailey cradled in his arms. He'd raced back to the vehicle and drove far enough away that he could perform field medicine.

He'd covered them with his body as the helicopter team lowered a basket for one and then the other.

Watching that heli take off for the hospital in Djibouti without him was torture.

But he'd turned the vehicle around and went full throttle back into the fray to support his team as best he could and to try to save other innocents.

But they'd failed.

Hailey was the sole survivor from the WorldCares station.

Yeah, Ares was going to have trouble managing his own emotions on this mission. And he'd have to manage Judge, too.

With that, there was a tug on Judge's leash.

Ares turned his attention to his dog who had pulled to the length of his lead and had his head pressed between the slits in the crosswalk balusters.

"Whatchyou got there, boy?"

Judge looked his way with a high-pitched whine.

A ball bounced out into the street, and Judge wanted to leap after it, was Ares first assessment.

But Judge's posture wasn't play; it was protector.

Ares scanned the scene.

A mother was talking to an organizer. They were both focused on an open notebook. The woman had a stroller off to her right and the kid, maybe three or four years old, was wriggling his way through the safety straps next to the busy roadway.

Ares cupped his hands around his mouth and yelled down.

The wind gusts snatched the sound of his warning and blew them back toward the city.

On the far side, a steady stream of cars raced the length. On the near side, a truck roared into view.

"Shit." Ares exhaled, sprinting for the stairs.

Judge was his shadow.

Ares held the lead out to the side as he vaulted, wide-legged, onto the handrails and slid. As the rail ended, Ares jumped, ran three steps, and leaped to the next railing and the next, leaning back and stretching his legs out to get as much velocity as he could muster.

Speed of action.

The kid was stepping off the curb.

Judge leaped the stairs just as they'd done in training and in combat.

"The kid! The kid!" he yelled in English. Russian just wasn't coming to mind.

As he slid the last staircase, his voice became more frantic. "Truck! Truck!" The two finally turned to look at him, spun to see what he was pointing at.

Their hands came to their faces, frozen in horror as the child stooped to pick up his orange ball.

The semi barreling forward, the driver scanning the pedestrians wasn't watching the road.

With a flick of the wrist, Ares signaled Judge to sit-stay, trusting their training.

A quick calculation told Ares there was no way to grab the kid and get back to the sidewalk before the truck got there.

The child was too short for the driver to see he was there.

Ares dove for the boy.

As his arms wrapped the child, Ares flattened himself to the ground. One arm wrapped over Ares's head, the other held his weight off the boy, keeping them as flat as possible.

Ares prayed that the driver stayed frosty enough to keep his wheels straight. If he tried to swerve, well they could easily be pancaked beneath the guy's tires.

The horn sounded long and loud as the truck drove over them.

Under the cab, Ares tipped his head up just high enough to assess.

Across the back of the truck, hung a curtain of heavy metal chains. They were meant to disperse static electricity.

At this speed? That didn't look survivable.

As the two sets of front tires passed beyond them, Ares put his hand over the child's face, cemented him to Ares's chest, and he rolled, using his elbows to keep his bulk from crushing the child.

As they hit against the curb, the second set of tires sprayed muddy slush over them.

The tires screamed as the guy stood on his brakes.

Lying on his back in a gutter filled with dirty melting snow and road salts, the kid sprawled, scared and confused, across Ares's chest. Ares, had his arms wrapping the kid, gasping for breath, his heart beating wildly in his chest.

The mother—wide-eyed, tears dripping, shaking like a damned chihuahua—tugged the boy into her arms, then collapsed onto the sidewalk.

Ares slowly lifted himself out of the road, keeping his eye on that truck.

Another block down, it came to a stop.

The guy looked their way, saw that everyone was alive, then got back in the cab and kept on down the road.

Ares turned to check on the child's well-being, looking up to whistle Judge to his side.

And there stood Hailey.

"You always did like the big entrance," she said softly. Her eyes scanned his body in front then rounded to his back.

Ares stood stock still.

"You have holes in your fleece. Your elbows are bleeding." Her hands started at his back, brushing slush from under his collar. Methodically she worked her way down. "Your uniform is made of weather retardant. Except the hole in your fleece, and the mud in your hair." She brushed his back. "You're coming out of that in pretty good condition."

Her hands swept over his ass. That used to be her territory, nothing new that she put her hands there.

Nothing new that his cock sprang to attention when she did.

She was crouching down to brush his thighs… and no, just no.

"Hailey." He stepped out of her reach. "My hotel is across the street. I'll just shuck these clothes and grab a quick shower."

Hailey seemed to realize what she was doing. She too took a step back, her face flooding bright red. Her fists, now pink with cold, pressed into her chest. "Sorry," she whispered.

"Hello," he said.

"Hi."

Their eyes caught and held.

For Ares, the world disappeared. The only thing that existed was Hailey's precious face.

Until Judge broke the spell.

Judge pressed into the space between them, standing on his hind legs and giving Hailey a thorough tongue bath, whimpering, and crying that he'd missed and loved her.

Damned lucky to be a dog.

When she saw Judge, Hailey's face pulled back into a mask of pain and grief. She wavered, and Ares was reaching for her, afraid she'd collapse.

"Just cleaning you off," Ares forced himself to chuckle and make this lighter.

Hailey wrapped her arms around Judge. "He's not cleaning you up." She pointed out.

"He doesn't love me as much as he loves you." That was a mistake.

Hailey spun as she dropped cross-legged on the cold, wet cement.

Her eyes slit and unseeing, she reached her arms wide.

Ares released Judge's lead, and Judge, crouched low to get into Hailey's arms, high pitched whimpers and tongue baths continued as Hailey squeezed Judge against her.

Judge loved Hailey. Was hyper-protective of Hailey. And almost lost his life saving hers.

Of course, Hailey—a woman with the softest heart and the steeliest determination to do good in this world—would collapse when she saw Judge whole and healthy in the flesh.

Ares had sent pictures of Judge's recovery. Hailey would send back a broken heart emoji. After a while, Ares stopped. "Salt in the wound" was how he decided his texts were received. He didn't want to force Hailey to relive those memories, to trigger anxiety.

Through the grapevine, he'd heard that Hailey was back on mission, trying to mother the world's population with food and medicine and what he'd come to term "Hailey magic."

And here she was.

People turned to watch.

Hailey hated to be the center of attention. Ares took a step forward then sent a fierce none-of-your-damned-business glare methodically around the circle of curiosity that was forming.

They peeled away and turned to go about their evenings.

Ares stood over Hailey as she sobbed into Judge's fur.

After a stretch, she closed her eyes, and rested her cheek on Judge's neck, hitch breathing. And after a longer stretch, her breathing returned to normal. "I love you," she said, eyes still shut. "Thank you, always."

Ares remembered the morning that she'd accepted his proposal. He remembered vividly that last time she'd said, "I love you," to him. This hurt like hell. Scorched him. Yet, he stood as stoic as he could force himself to be while Judge licked the last of the drying tears from her face.

Sniffing hard, Hailey put her hand down to push herself off the ground, Ares extended his hand, but Judge twisted to sit in her lap not ready to let her up.

Judge was far and away from being a lap dog. He'd lay beside Ares, he might even drape a paw over Ares's foot as they sat side by side. It was companionable but they were buds.

But Hailey was 'mama'.

She patted Judge's side. Ares knew she was looking for the scar from when Judge saved her. It was well hidden by his fur. But it was there. Ares didn't want her to find it.

This time when he spoke, Ares words were coldly mechanical. "Hailey, how about you check on the mom. Judge and I will catch you around. I need to get cleaned up."

"Oh. Okay." She pressed Judge away and stood. "Sure."

Knowing that a signal wasn't going to work to get Judge away from Hailey, Ares picked up the lead and said, "Heel to me," and he took off at a jog.

The mother yelled, "Thank you. Thank you!" to his back as he took the stairs two at a time.

From his peripheral vision, Ares watched Hailey turn and scuttled away with her head bowed low.

This scene left Ares off balance.

Hailey was safe.

Alive.

And once again working in a probable war zone.

## 9

Hailey

HAILEY STUFFED HER EMOTIONS DOWN.

She was here to save lives.

"Are you okay?" Jay'la handed Hailey back the folder that she'd pressed into her friend's hand as she'd gone to see if she could help with the child's rescue. Of course, Ares had it handled. That's what he did. It was who he was. *Sublimely* capable.

Right now, seeing him, he was able and probably likely to crush her heart. She loved him. *Loved* him. And the pain of it all was intense. Her emotions in this moment were a complicated whirl. Hailey reached up and scratched her hairline. She'd have to keep her distance if she were to keep her sanity. It wouldn't be long. Kiyana said that Iniquus would be out of the country with the Saturday train. Hailey would be leaving as soon as her stations were set up and humming.

It was a big world. There were billions of people. She could lose herself in the crowd again. And try to push her pain away.

"Hailey," Jay'la said sternly, "are you okay?"

"Fine," Hailey grumped.

"Do you know that man?" Jay'la asked, fanning her face. "He dove under a *speeding* truck to save that baby. And you rubbed his ass, cleaning him off like that." She bumped hips with Hailey conspiratorially. "Can't say I blame you. That man is as close to an Adonis as I've ever seen. Those muscles all bulging out under his fleece like that. That beard trimmed all sexy like that. You know I'm going home to my hubby. Love him. Love his dad bod, sorta." She lifted and dropped her brows. "I can't even imagine what it would be like to—"

Hailey picked up her speed as she walked on staring straight forward. Not giving Jay'la even a smidgeon of encouragement. Jay'la's words brought back images of Ares naked body. The length of his legs, those thigh muscles, the shape of his ass, like the underwear models in the magazines she'd found left behind in airport waiting rooms, the kind that made women pause as the curiosity ran through their systems and their imaginations made them wet. What would it be like to enjoy that?

Hailey knew.

It was *mind-bending*. The warmth of his skin. What it felt like to lie in his arms. To have him between her thighs. She shook her head and tried to pry those sensations loose and let the wind carry them away.

"Eh. Said too much, obviously." Jay'la's words were colored with curiosity. "I'm at work. I apologize. I'm going to chalk it up to the shock that I saw that rescue with my very eyes. Right there in front of my face. Crazy! And of course, that he is fine. And I mean *fine*."

Hailey pushed through the doors into the station. "There's Vlad. I need you to ask if he needs anything tonight. I have everything labeled for which floor. I'll be there first thing in the morning to direct the unpacking and setup." She tapped Jay'la's arm. "Tell him, please."

Her voice was harsh. She was trying to hold herself together until she could get to her hotel room.

Jay'la whipped out her impressive language skills, checking in with Vlad and translating back that his team would work through the night to get the boxes positioned on the correct levels. They'd be ready for Hailey when she got there in the morning.

Hailey forced herself to smile, hoping that it wouldn't come off as a grimace, gave a slight bow, and turned to Jay'la.

"Are you okay?" Jay'la frowned. "You look…bad."

"Thanks." Hailey was moving fast toward the front exit.

"I didn't say that to be mean." Jay'la raced after her. "I'm worried. You're kind of gray. Should I see about finding you a doctor? Do you need some sugar or something? What's going on with you? I've never seen that look on your face before."

Hailey stopped on the sidewalk, turning to her friend. "Look, I'm tired. My head is pounding. I need to go lay down is all. Pop some pain meds. I'll be good to go in the morning. Shall we meet at six for breakfast, kind of ease into the day?"

Jay'la was squinting at her like she didn't buy Hailey's explanation and she thought something fishy was going on.

"You need to get your own rest. We have the clinic set up to work. Then the second train is coming in to load up passengers. And my next six containers. That one's going to be more complicated because they all go to different locations."

They were staying almost directly across from the station, so it was an easy walk. They were pushing through the front door and nodding to the desk staff.

"Fine," Jay'la said fishing out her key card. "You go do what you need to to feel better. I'll meet you down in the restaurant where I will be drinking an entire pot of coffee. This cold and gray. Whew! It seeps into the bones."

And with that, the two colleagues separated to go to their own rooms.

Hailey tried not to think a single word.

Twice a day, she sat for meditation.

For twenty-minute stretches, she trained her brain to be silent.

Her mentor called it "meditation practice," because stillness was so hard to grab that that's what it was, a practice of watching thoughts form, working toward the goal of stillness.

Sometimes her practice was to let the thoughts come and label them: Past. Present. Future.

Sometimes, she tried not to have any thoughts at all by focusing on the sensation of air entering and exiting her nostrils, or by counting her breaths four counts in, four count hold, eight count exhale.

She was told, and sometimes Hailey found it to be true, that by doing this every day, she'd get better at it. That as horror rose from a memory, as her body ached along her incision scar, as all of the losses that she accumulated on that sultry morning at the station, when all the "why me? Why did I get to live when the others didn't?" thoughts burst into her present, that she could tame the monsters, if temporarily, with her breath.

Hailey worked on that now.

She focused on her breathing as she rode the elevator up and slogged toward her room.

When that wasn't working she switched to saying "In" and "Out" trying to make the words louder in her head than the pain.

After locking her door, she bumbled her way into the bathroom, stripped off her clothes. Standing under the shower, Hailey let the water beat on her head in scalding prickles.

But she couldn't push away the last time she'd spoken on the phone with Ares.

*Her* Ares.

Her hero.

They were talking about Hailey's group therapy session. Because of her job description, they'd put her in a circle with a bunch of guys that had seen some shit as contractors.

"Why, what did they say to you?" Ares asked.

She was walking in the park. The sunshine was merry, the flowers in bloom, and it was all so antithetical to the bleakness that engulfed her. "That, in war, we do things that would never be allowed in times of peace. They're a certain impunity to war. Next to the atrocities what's a little adultery or petty theft? Minuscule. But I think it hurts the soul. I think there's karma. That the universe sees clearly what others are willing to turn a blind eye to."

"Did you do something? I can't imagine…"

"I didn't do enough." Hailey walked a few steps as if she could gain some thinking space. The turbulence that whirled around her was filled with the debris of missed opportunities and their consequences.

Ares sat silently, watching on the video call as she twisted her body this way and that trying to get her bones and muscles to release the tension out of her. Hopefully, they'd be blown away where no one would walk through the cloud of angst and take it home with them, taking the pain and injustice along with them. Hailey imagined the sensations as the dry red African dust that smoked across her path with a gust of wind. Suddenly her clothes were powdered, the grit gathering along the elastic of her bras and underwear, abrading her skin and leaving a tiny row of blisters like the scarification that decorated the tribe's people's bodies.

Only hers was not intended, and not beautiful.

Still to this day, when Hailey lifted her breasts and looked at herself in the mirror, there they were. A scoop of scar tissues that showed that the underwire on her bra had been the wrong size.

The dots skipped along as a trail that had faded over time from hot red, to pink, and now white. Almost invisible. Almost forgotten.

But in the right light, still there.

Hailey leaned down to cut off the water. Reaching for the towel she'd thrown over the curtain rod, she mopped the moisture from under her breasts.

A little voice in the back of her mind reminded Hailey that blisters were the bodies way of protecting itself. The cushion of plasma was meant to keep the lower layers safe. They needed to be tended to so they would heal. But those scars were in no way protective. They were simply reminders of the time in the red dust, spattered in blood.

Hailey wrapped herself up in the towel and stepped from the tub.

Seeing Ares was lighting her up.

She'd been fine.

Pretended to be, anyway.

But now it bubbled back to the surface. Blistering once again.

Hailey had to get away from Ares.

He was soul friction.

And he hurt.

## 10

---

**Ares**

THURSDAY, NEZDOLANNYY

REMI GRINNED AT HIM, holding out a lidded cup. "I'm assuming you knew I was coming to chat because every time I sidle up to one of your men, they point me to you."

Ares accepted the coffee, feeling the warmth radiating from the thick paper, warming his hands red and stiff with cold. He'd just come in from a last potty break with Judge and was headed to meet with his team and go over their findings from today's reconnaissance. "Yes, ma'am. If I can be of any assistance, just let me know."

"You're going to ma'am me?" She tipped her head back.

Remi was a tall woman, just shy of six feet with her short black hair in a barely-there ponytail. Remi wore her personalized reporter's uniform of tactical leggings under a bespoke tunic that hid her secret survival weapon, a belly pack that she'd developed over her time in war zones. The things in that bag had made the difference in survival when she was trapped in a blown-up Beirut hotel room with T-Rex and the senator. But the way she wore it under her tunic, she looked about five months pregnant. Ares thought that was a different kind of protection. Remi worked in countries where women had little worth. Perhaps the men thinking she was pregnant gave her some kind of deference and safety.

"Honestly, I thought we were beyond that kind of formality." Remi smiled.

Ares pulled a hand down his face, trying to adjust. Today's face to face with Hailey had his armor up. Stiffly formal felt like a way to ensure he kept an emotional distance. "Sorry about that." His voice sounded warmer. "I'm in operator's mode."

She shook her head, "Nah, I've seen you operating before. I was the happy recipient of your skills. That's not what I was picking up from you."

"Speaking of seeing the team in action, are you staying in touch with T-Rex? How's he keeping?"

She held up her left hand. A gold ring encircled her left ring finger.

"Hitched? Congratulations. I'm happy for you. And the senator?" Ares nodded a greeting to the woman standing behind Remi then tipped his head toward the conference room inviting them in as he pushed through the door.

"She's doing better. Weak still. The senator says she's champing at the bit to get on the road again." Remi followed behind as Ares politely held the door. "I told her to fish a different journalist from the pool. I think she's jinxed."

"Ha! I bet she loved that. Yeah, Beirut was a difficult time. Glad to hear things righted themselves for you all."

Shutting the door behind the two women, Ares did a quick scan and headcount. The team was all present and accounted for.

"I'm curious why you said you're in operator mode. That

seems at odds with loading folks on a train." Remi came to a stop beside him. "Is there something more to this assignment? What's your gut telling you?"

Ares grasped onto that. Good enough, let Remi paint what picture she wanted. He'd play along, let her think his demeanor was about the assignment and not that his seeing Hailey had thrown him into head spin. Ares was thrilled that Hailey looked healthy and strong. When he was on the bridge, Ares thought Hailey seemed contented as he'd watched her work.

When she'd shown up at his side after the child's rescue, the pain of being near her scorched him. That he couldn't pull Hailey into his arms, couldn't crush her beautiful curves against him, taste her lips, read the love and lust for him that used to light her eyes.

Three years, he would have thought that the blow of seeing her in person would be softer.

Hell, Ares would go hand-to-hand any day against an enemy. But this was an internal fight. An emotional fight.

And he was losing.

Hailey made him ache.

Ares veiled his eyes, so perceptive Remi couldn't read any of those emotions. "My gut says we have a lot of people to get moved here in the next forty-eight hours. The first train out went smoothly. Those who left are our most vulnerable population. It's a good start." He looked over Remi's shoulder at the woman with a video camera dangling around her neck, the lens was like a cannon.

"So far, there's not much to report on," Remi said, "other than your street diving heroics." She tipped her head towards the videographer. "Cindy here caught it from the bouncing ball, to the slide down the hand rails, to the street dive. It's quite spectacular. Do you want to see?"

"No thanks, I'm good." Ares lifted his chin toward the camera woman, breezing by her last comment. "Who've you got with you?"

Remi shifted to allow the woman into their conversation circle. "Ares, meet my photojournalist, Cindy Au."

"Hi. Excuse me, I'm hearing Cindy Awl, is that the right pronunciation?"

"Close enough." She smiled.

"Do you mind spelling it for me?"

"Sure, it's A.U." Cindy winked. "I'm golden."

Ares had to reach back to Chemistry 101 to get her reference. Ares appreciated it when he had a mnemonic to help him remember names.

When he smiled, Cindy held out her hand for a shake. "Glad to meet you, Ares."

He liked her handshake; it was crisp and professional with just the right amount of pressure. Ares read a lot into people by how they shook his hand.

"Hey, can you do me a big favor? I deploy to some dangerous areas. My face on a public-facing video could cause me some damage along the line."

"Remi already warned me to obscure the operators' faces. I'll apply a blur filter on all my video footage. We don't intend to put your well-being on the line for a moment of glory. And, wow, was that a moment of glory. Even with my poor angle, it views like an action thriller."

When Ares didn't respond, Cindy continued, "Remi says you're the head honcho."

"No, ma'am." He bladed his hands on his hips. "I'm Tactical Search and Rescue Leader for Cerberus Team Bravo. I'm under Logistics control on this mission."

"Search and Rescue?" Cindy Au took a step back and turned worried eyes toward Remi, then back to Ares. "Why in the world would they send you in to Nezdolannyy?"

*Finesse it but tell the truth.* "Two-fold. We're working six K-9. Three of them, my dog here is Judge." He turned and pointed toward Ash and Mace. "And the two German Shepherds are trained to find munitions. We're going to keep a nose in the wind for anything that might go BOOM. It's an abundance of caution."

"Two-fold?" Remi asked.

"Why don't I introduce you to the team?" From the twist and pucker of Remi's mouth, he could tell that his sleight of hand move—look over here!—didn't work on her. She'd store that away to ask later. And he'd tell her. But he'd tell her away from the swarm. There was zero reason to jack people's emotions any higher than they already were.

"Cindy, ready to meet some pups?" Remi reached into the camera bag that hung from Cindy's shoulder and pulled out a microphone. "How about we do this in pieces that I can stitch together in an order that would make sense to the audience?" she asked Ares. "Maybe break things up into several segments." She nodded at Cindy.

Cindy had her camera up and was giving Remi a count down with her fingers up by her cheek. Three. Two. One. Finger point.

Remi faced the camera. "I'm here in Nezdolannyy with Ares, leader of Iniquus' famed Bravo K9 team. Nezdolannyy is an ancient city near the Black Sea. You might remember that Ares was one of the team members that helped find and save Senator Blankenship when she was suffering a grave illness entrapped in one of the buildings that collapsed in the Beirut explosion last year." She tipped her head toward Ares without turning away from the camera. "Ares, can you introduce the dogs you've brought with you?"

Before Ares could answer, Remi drew a finger across her throat to signal cut. When the red light was extinguished and Cindy lowered the video camera, Remi turned to Ares. "Let's meet the dogs, then I'd like to do a short interview about your role on this mission."

"Let's do it," he replied, extending a hand to direct them forward. "You remember Juan Ortega our Chief of Tactical Operations Center, he's in D.C." He dipped his head toward Remi. Remi and Juan had met in Beirut. "Our TOC is being run by Logistics in Romania. Our communications go through Mongoose who is also our support vet." From his six-foot-three height, Ares scanned the room. "He's not here right now. The K9s that are here were selected specifically for this event."

"Event?" Remi asked following along beside Ares. "Not mission?"

"Mission if you prefer." He lowered his voice. "Around our clients, we're careful with that word. It might sound military, or dangerous. This should be a train ride to a welcoming proximity country. We don't want to add to the stress levels."

"I see." Remi positioned herself beside Ares, shifted her shoulders back and focused on the camera. "Let me try a different intro."

Cindy did the count down and point; the red light blinked on.

"We're meeting the dogs and their handlers," Remi said into the camera. "This team is part of Washington D.C. based Iniquus Security. Cerberus Tactical K9 Team Bravo is renowned for their efforts in saving victims in natural disasters, traveling worldwide to lend their expertise. I had the privilege of meeting the team when I was covering Texas Senator Blankenship last year when three members of our group were trapped in a high rise following the explosion that devastated Beirut. As a matter of fact." She stopped and her smile was belied by the tears that collected along her lash line. She swallowed. "Excuse me." She smiled again. "I see my hero dog." She bladed her hand toward the blonde British lab who was lying placidly between Bear's feet.

Cindy spun her camera and adjusted the lens to zoom in on Truffles.

"Truffles, who is resting with her handler, Bear, tunneled through the debris to find the little survival pocket where the senator, her guard, and I were trapped. Truffles wore a communications collar that allowed us to speak with the rescue team. In that instance, as a human, desperate—and quite frankly terrified the building would collapse on us—it was very hard for me to release Truffles's collar and let her head back out to her handler. Truffles was a beacon of hope. More than a beacon of hope, we were days into being trapped. We were at the end of our water. We wouldn't have survived without the skill of Truffles and her team." She drew in a deep breath, turning to Ares. "Truffles's main job is urban search and rescue. From that rescue in Beirut, I, of course, recognize Judge."

She indicated Judge who seemed to know he was on camera, sitting up straight and looking very noble. It tickled a smile onto Ares's lips.

"Can you tell me a bit about this K9's specialty?" Remi asked.

Ares gave a subtle hand command to make sure Judge knew to stay on the X and not wander over to Remi for a scritch. "Judge and Jury is a six-year-old Malinois who has been operational for the past four years, starting his career with the Green Berets. Judge was trained in scent work to find explosive materials."

"For work in war zones."

"No, ma'am." Ares angled to both focus on the camera and on Remi as he'd been coached to do in one of the required Iniquus classes in communicating with the press. "When we move into situations like that one you experienced in Beirut, we have to make sure that we secure anything that might be combustible, be it a fossil fuel or a weapons cache. That's Judge's function. He keeps both the rescue teams and those in harm's way from further complications." Ares held back that Judge was also trained to chase and take down the bad guys. That shouldn't come up on this mission.

"He's trained to do search and rescue for people in the debris?" Remi asked.

"No, ma'am. In these situations, we have a protocol. We secure the area first. Once the area is secured, other team members are cleared to access the area." Ares lifted his hand toward his teammate. "Like Bear and Truffles. In terms of finding humans amongst debris in mass disasters," Ares turned to his left, "we have Knox and K9 Zydeco. Cocoa, for short, is a female bluetick coonhound. While most of the Cerberus kennel is made up of dogs specially bred for their jobs, Mace adopted Cocoa from a rescue shelter in Louisiana."

Remi pulled back the microphone for a moment to add, "Hence her name, Zydeco. Knox is your operator's work name. Like you're Ares. Does Knox's handle have an origin story?"

When the microphone was back in front of Ares's chest, Ares looked over and caught Knox's eyes, and with a laugh said, "Yes, ma'am. We call him Knox for his heart of gold." Then, Ares turned to nod toward Red. "Our other hound is Whiskey. She's the bloodhound there with her handler 'Red'."

"Let me interrupt your introductions and ask, why Cerberus would bring in urban search and rescue K9 for this event?"

Ares noticed she'd repeated his vocabulary and hadn't said 'mission,' and he was grateful.

"Our task is to get those who are associated with our contractor to a safe location until there's a better handle on what comes next in Nezdolannyy city. I'll give you an example. If a child were to wander off as they were getting loaded on the train, the parents could hand us a scent sample. Whiskey would track the child down."

"I know Truffles's reward is tugging a towel, though, I

promised her a steak when I was in Beirut, and I intend to pay up tonight. What is Whiskey's reward?"

"She gets a hot dog paycheck for a find. Though, honestly, Whiskey just loves the challenge, and she's great with kids."

They paused as Whiskey bellowed back at a dog barking in the distance.

"Loud," Remi said with a laugh.

"A blessing and a curse. There is no stealth mode when it comes to Whiskey." Ares pointed toward the team's two German Shepherds. "The red-haired shepherd, Hoover, is handled by Ash."

"Hoover?"

"He got his name because as a pup he used to run with the cattle on his breeder's farm. He seemed to like to dodge the cow hooves."

"So it's not that he vacuums up his food?"

"There is that." Ares nodded toward the other shepherd. "That big boy right there is Diesel. He's handled by Mace. To his left is Mongoose, or just Goose, our vet support."

"Tell me about that."

"When our teams are on missions or at events, our team vet manages the health and well-being of our kennel. As you may know, once the K9's are purchased, they go through a lifetime of consistent training to keep their skills on point. It's important to us that the dogs are in top shape to do the tasks asked of them, that they are checked and receive the best possible care, and that we prolong their field life as long as possible. And, equally important to us, that the K9 are as healthy and happy as possible when it's time for them to retire. Judge, here, has a lot of experience under his belt. He's calm amongst the fray. His skills are lifesaving. Building that into a dog doesn't come easily. It's time and patience. Their care has to be top notch."

"I've remarked on how tightly bonded the dogs are with their handlers," Remi said.

"Yes, ma'am. Judge is a piece of me. He's like another limb. If anything happens to Judge, it happens to me. We're that tight."

Remi stared into the camera without speaking for a solid count to ten, then she took a step back and caught Cindy's eye. "Good?"

Cindy scrolled back and watched her screen then gave Remi a thumbs up.

"That's a good start. That and the child's rescue. I like where this is going," Remi said as Ares pulled his buzzing cellphone from his thigh pocket.

He looked down at the screen, then said, "Will you excuse me?" He tapped the button as he took a step back and angled away. "Ares." He paused. "Yes. Let me call you right back." He tapped the red dot to end the call.

Turning and focusing on Remi, Ares said, "Hey, Remi, I have a favor to ask. You're friends with Hailey Stapelton aren't you?"

# 11

Hailey

THERE WAS a soft tap at her door.

Hailey pulled the cold rag from her forehead and went to peek through the viewer. Remi. Hailey pulled the door wide and gestured her in.

"Hey, I came to check on you."

"Somebody tattling?"

"Ares."

"Mmm." Hailey slogged back over to the bed, sat on the edge, then flopped backward, covering her face with her hands.

She heard Remi close the door and throw the safety latch.

"I figured out you two already know each other." Remi moved into the room and crawled onto the bed to lay next to Hailey. "And here I thought he was the perfect guy for you. I was going to set you up."

"Yeah. I know him."

"He thinks he upset you. He asked me to make sure you're okay." She looked her friend over. "You're obviously not okay."

Hailey opened her mouth to respond but no words came to mind, so she pressed her lips together.

Remi laid on her side with her boots dangling off the end of the bed. She propped her head up on her arm. "What did he do?"

"He saved a kid from getting run over by a truck. Dove into the street, rolled under the truck and, while it was still moving, rolled back out again with the kid clutched to his chest."

"Oh, yeah, well, I can see why you'd be pissed at him. The guy's obviously a shithead."

Hailey exhaled.

Remi reached out and tugged a piece of Hailey's hair. "Spill."

"We used to be engaged. You know, we never officially called it off, so maybe we still are."

"Wow." Remi blinked. "*Not* what I was expecting. When was this?"

"Ares was a Green Beret in Africa when I was at the Hatari station. I was with him the morning of the station massacre. He had proposed that morning. I accepted that morning. I was blissed out, so excited about…" She lifted her hand and dropped it, "everything. And then, the horses appeared on the horizon."

"Oh shit," Remi whispered. Remi's job was to report on war and massacres. She saw the destruction. She had survived some heinous events. How Remi kept her equilibrium, Hailey couldn't fathom.

Hailey patted at her chest and stuttered out, "They saved me, Judge and Ares. I would have been amongst the slaughter except for them."

"Ares seems to keep doing that, the shithead."

Hailey frowned. "You're making fun, but I'm upset."

"I can see that. And I'm sorry if I'm making light. That was insensitive. I apologize." Remi slid off the end of the bed and wandered into Hailey's bathroom. When she came back out, she held Hailey's brush. "Sit up. I'm going to help soothe you." She climbed onto the bed behind Hailey. "First, remember, it's over. You are in this moment and safe. You survived." She pulled her legs around to sit cross-legged behind Hailey, gathering her hair, letting it drape down Hailey's back in its natural, strawberry-blond waves. "You get to be in this world and continue with your good work. If you're wondering 'why them and not me' it's because of no reason." She sectioned off a handful of hair and started at the bottom, detangling. "There are two quotes that I use to keep me sane. I've even thought about tattooing them on my arms so in times of deep angst, I can pull up my sleeves and read them. Ready?"

Hailey nodded, closing her eyes and focusing on Remi brushing her hair, slowly and gently.

"The first is from Buddha. The Buddha said that 'All of the things a person goes through in life cause suffering, and they cannot do anything about it. Instead, they have to accept that it is there.'"

"Which means suffering just is."

"As ubiquitous as air."

"Okay. I see that in my work all the time. And I have to remind myself that I can't make it go away. I can't feed all the hungry. Shelter all the homeless. Suffering just goes on and on. Where I seem to be able to compartmentalize for my job, and focus on making one disaster better, to care for a group of people in the now, and then move to the next. It's not true for Hatari. I can't put the massacre away in a box."

"You've been meditating?"

"Yes."

"Good. That's a start. Here's my second stay-sane quote. Ready?"

"Yes."

"This quote is from Thich Nhat Hanh: 'The seed of suffering in you may be strong, but don't wait until you have no more suffering before allowing yourself to be happy.'"

Silence fell. Remi gave Hailey the space to process those words. After a moment, Remi repeated them, slowly and quietly. "'The seed of suffering in you may be strong, but don't wait until you have no more suffering before allowing yourself to be happy.'"

"Yeah," Hailey said, feeling wrung completely dry. "I want to be you when I grow up."

Remi chuckled as she brushed.

Hailey turned her head enough to catch her friend's gaze before turning forward so Remi could continue. The brushing was helping. Hailey would have to remember this. "It's true, though," Hailey said. "Your job is exponentially more dangerous and more vividly brutal than mine, but you slough it off. And, well you fell in love, you're happy. I haven't been happy since Ares proposed. I can't imagine feeling that again."

"Yeah. I get that. I'll tell you what, start with how you two met. Africa was…it was about three years ago?"

"Yes. Four in June. Judge was so wounded saving me that he was dropped from the military. Ares quit being a Green Beret. His job became rehabbing Judge."

"You met there, you and Ares?"

"Yes. We met the first week of my assignment. It was, mmm, fourteen months later that he proposed."

"I'm listening."

"Lots of memories." Hailey swallowed. "Really beautiful ones and searing excruciatingly painful ones."

"I get that. You can only do what you can do. It's a couple of days you're going to be here around him. I know Ares will give you all the space he can. I can pass him the message."

Hailey was quite for a long moment.

"So our 'how did we meet' story—" And just like that, in her mind, Hailey was back in the rubble heap that had once been a bustling village.

*It was her first assignment in Africa with her NGO. She was sent to learn the language and culture before she was reassigned. The name of the village was Hatari—danger in Swahili. Had Hailey understood the language back then, it might have given her pause.*

*The village had been a vibrant place, with solid homes built of cement blocks, a school, a clinic, a marketplace, and a church. There were businesses that sold necessities and restaurants that prepared traditional dishes. It was full of people on bicycles and on foot. A few cars. Bright-colored clothing in riotous patterns reminded Hailey of gardens in full swaying bloom.*

*She'd been out in the countryside with a WorldCares doctor who was doing a vaccination drive when the ground shook with such furor that they fell onto all fours, their fingers gripping at the dirt. Hailey had never been in an earthquake and somehow always associated them with California. To her, it was very unexpected, but Hailey later learned that she was stationed very near the East-African rift. Seismic activity wasn't unexpected.*

*When they called back to the Hatari clinic to check on things, no one answered.*

*They turned around, driving full speed until they found a group who were heading in to help. They were out of their trucks, standing where the road used to be.*

*A crack snaked long and wide, preventing further travel.*

*Hailey, nervous that the rift would widen, drove along the opening. It had to be like a riptide, she reasoned. In a riptide you swim parallel to the shore until you clear the danger. Then, you can turn and get back to safety.*

*Muttering under her breath that the whole world couldn't have been cleaved in two, she continued on and on. After about a mile, she was able to turn west again.*

*Hailey finally got to a point on the road outside of the village where the local military was blocking anyone who wasn't a rescue worker from entering the area. It was too dangerous. The village had collapsed.*

*Arriving amongst the destruction was surreal.*

*Her rooming house, gone.*

*The church was reduced to an angled cross amongst the debris.*

*Hailey turned in the direction that she thought would be the clinic. There, a mountain of a man was climbing behind his K9 calling commands, "Judge, seek!"*

*His Malinois traipsed, nimbly and surefooted, over the rocks, his nose searching the crevices. Hailey was mesmerized by their work.*

*The thing that pulled her away was the mewling of a kitten.*

*Though, Hailey hadn't seen a cat since she'd been to Africa.*

*She followed the sound. Lying flat on her belly and reaching into the crack, Hailey expected to feel warm fur. Instead, little fingers wrapped into Hailey's hands, clinging.*

*"Here! Here!" Hailey screamed out. Hoping to get equipment and manpower over to her. She was not going to pull her hands away from this child, lest the little one think that she'd been abandoned. And Hailey couldn't communicate in Swahili, yet.*

*"Here! A child!" Hailey hoped the man with the dog heard her. He'd spoken English. While she was calling, Hailey worked her other hand into a space, hoping to discover what lay underneath, and if the child had a pocket of protection or if that child was being crushed. But another hand gripped at her. Or the same child, Hailey couldn't tell.*

*There Hailey lay, arms beneath the destruction all the way up to her shoulders, clinging to a little life that somehow survived under the weight of the collapsed building.*

*A hand landed on her back. "What've you got."*

*"A child. Maybe two? I'm holding two hands. They're very small hands," she yammered.*

*"All right. Good."*

*Hailey saw nothing good about this moment. Except that maybe she was giving some hope to the little one. And that the man with the dog probably had some expertise to get the little one free.*

*The guy rattled into his comms.*

*Hailey tried to angle her head in such a way as to see who he was.*

*Hailey couldn't hear the response. The man patted her back and said, "I'll be back, stay put, keep hold of her."*

*He called the child "her."*

*Hailey too had thought of those hands in the rubble as a girl. It didn't matter, it was just a way for her brain to make a connection with the tiny human being who was hurt and terrified.*

*The man took off at a sprint with his dog at his heels.*

*Hailey lay there with her cheek resting on a sharp stone. The sun beat down on her back. Her skin crisped under the rays, praying, hurry, hurry.*

*As she lay there, Hailey thought about the elasticity of time. How the minutes and hours could stretch out, and when she wanted a moment to last, how time would snap into the tiniest of segments.*

*It felt like a long time.*

*Breathing in the cement dust, lying with sharp rocks beneath her, piercing her skin, the full heat of the sun baking her like bread. While Hailey was uncomfortable, she couldn't imagine what that child was going through.*

*Hailey began a game of squeezing the child's hands—two on*

*the right, and the child squeezed back. One on the left. Three on the right. Two on the left.*

*A crash pulled Hailey's gaze up. A rock tumbled from the mound of debris. Hailey tucked her face down, hunching her shoulders up, though that wouldn't give her much protection if it bounced directly in line with her head.*

*It caught just above her in a burst of debris cloud that showered Hailey with powder.*

*She couldn't see anything. Even though she was partially protected by her sunglasses, the dust caked her eyes. She coughed to clear her lungs. Lifting her shoulder, she tried to wipe at her face and gain some relief, but the last thing Hailey would do was let go of that child.*

*The warm hand was on her back, again. A rumble-voice was in her ear. "Were you hurt?"*

*"No, I don't think so." She turned her head so that when she coughed again it wouldn't be in the man's face. "Just, the dust."*

*"Here, let me help you." When he gently lifted her sunglasses off, Hailey squinted against the sudden glare.*

*"You've got her?" he asked.*

*Hailey squeezed the child's hands twice. The child squeezed back twice. "Yes. Are they coming?"*

*"It's a twenty-minute jog back to the unit's supply tent. They'll be slower coming back with the wench and supports. The knee jerk reaction is to start digging and pulling her out. I'm a structural engineer. It's better to wait and make sure haste doesn't make things worse."*

*"Yes." She coughed hard forcing the debris from her lungs. "Agreed."*

*"Let's get this dirt out of your eyes before you scratch your cornea." He poured water from his camel reservoir over her face, catching it in a cloth beneath her chin so she wasn't lying in mud. He used gauze from the first aid pack he had strapped to his leg to*

*dab her eyes. He was lying there next to her, his eyes so richly brown that they were almost black. So warm and intelligent. His biceps strained the fabric of his T-shirt.*

*"I'm Heath," he said. "You'll hear my team call me Ares." He put the lens of her sunglasses to his mouth and exhaled. Pulling his shirt from where it was tucked into his military tactical pants, Hailey caught a glimpse of his washer board abs, the top of a goody trail. He used hem of the shirt to clean her glasses, then slid them back on her face.*

*She'd licked her lips. "What should I call you, Heath or Ares?"*

*"Whatever you like." Pulling the hose from his camelback over to her he said, "If you're okay with it, I'm willing to share."*

*"Do you think I'm worried about swapping germs here?" she asked incredulously. Hailey was desperate for a drink. She was sure the child below her was, too.*

*Hailey let Ares toggle the spout open while she filled her mouth, swished, and swallowed. "Is there any way we can get some down to this child?*

*Ares looked the situation over. "I think it better to wait for the equipment to shore this up. My hose isn't long enough to reach. We're stable now. I don't want to go moving the wrong thing. This pile is pretty unstable."*

*Hailey didn't want to do anything that might cause that child any more harm.*

*She nodded and expected Ares to head on his way. But to her surprise that's not what happened.*

*Instead, he sang. And interestingly he sang children's songs— silly-sounding tunes—as he erected a make-do tent over her, protecting her from the violence of the noon rays, and a barricade against dislodged debris pulled down the pile by gravity.*

*A few minutes later, help arrived. Ares and Judge headed back out to do their work with an "I'll check in with you later, Hailey."*

. . .

"THEY GOT THE SISTERS OUT," Hailey told Remi. "Two little girls, four and six years old. They were sent in a pickup to the hospital in the city, and then were kept there because they'd been orphaned in the collapse. It was a miracle they survived."

"Absolutely," Remi said.

"Later, that night as we took breaks to eat, Ares found me to check on things. And…I just knew. He was mine. I was his. Meeting Ares was a second miracle of the day. Ares was with his Green Beret group training allied soldiers. We would have been ships in the night except for the earthquake." Hailey kneaded her hands in her lap. "That's the story."

"It's a good one. He's a good one."

"Yeah, he is." Hailey sighed deeply. "The best."

And she'd let him go.

## 12

**Ares**

ARES AND JUDGE pushed through the door heading toward the train track.

Judge needed a break.

That morning, they'd been inside the station where members of Iniquus Logistics were processing AgilitiCorp members and their families for today's extraction to Romania.

Just like yesterday, each person's face was scanned for identification. Each person checked to make sure they were wearing their correct tracking necklace. Each person and their bag had to pass a K9 nose test by one of the Cerberus munitions sniffers.

Judge, Diesel, and Hoover took turns. The handlers worked with their K9 partners, and then gave them a chance to relax. Shake off the stress.

Once their clients were cleared as safe, they moved to the waiting area.

Today was going to be the big push.

Logistics added more cars to the train and moved more people up the schedule to leave. Command indicated that the status for this area was climbing from orange to red.

This area was getting hotter by the minute.

Ares and his team would be gone on the last evacuation train the next evening.

Hailey would still be here, setting up the supplies that were coming in with today's train from Romania.

Did her NGO have a grip on what was heading their way? Would they ask her to stay even if she was at risk of being trapped in a besieged city?

Ares decided that he was going to have a very clear and direct discussion about what was coming next with both Remi, Hailey, and their teammates Cindy and Jay'la. If they decided to stay in country, it was imperative that they move further west. Inside a besieged city, there would be little they could do to help. They simply became liabilities.

Outside the door, standing in front of the empty track, Ares stopped to assess.

Today, the sky hung low. Gray with snow clouds. While it was cold, it was warmer than yesterday. The snow wasn't sticking as much. The roads were clear this morning when he and Judge had gone for their run.

Standing near the roadway, the scent of diesel fumes and wet dog assailed his nostrils.

He'd give Judge a bath that night, so he'd be fresh on the train. While Iniquus Logistics had set up several cars with shelves and crates for the evacuated pets (monitored by a local veterinarian they'd hired on), Cerberus Tactical kept their K9s next to them, always. No need to stink up the seating car for a fifteen-hour train ride.

Assessing the people on the platform, everyone out here were professionals preparing and organizing.

Ares nodded at the logistics folks who turned his way before focusing back again on their phones and clipboards.

Remi and Cindy were filming down on the track where the railroad staff had prepositioned the switch engine, ready to move the decoupled flat beds with the six WorldCares supply containers off to a parallel track via the juncture. Then off to a loading area to be placed onto flatbed trucks and distributed to the various points on Hailey's map.

Ares followed Judge's gaze toward Hailey who stood by the wall just out of the way of the bustle and noise, her translator was animatedly talking to some guy, then listening and turning back to Hailey. Ares had relied on translators in past missions, it wasn't the easiest way to communicate. You had to be pretty tight with your translator, so they weren't just saying the words, but they actually conveyed the message and intent of those words.

Hailey had on a tactical-looking winter coat. A thick hat was tugged down over her ears. Her hair was in a braid draped over her shoulder, ending in a little curl.

He noticed that today she had strapped a drop leg panel on both sides of her khaki tactical pants. A drop leg panel was threaded onto a web belt at the hip. The strap ran along the thigh to a bag that was then clipped into place just above hand's reach. This put her equipment right where it could be easily accessed. Ares wondered what she kept in those pouches. He'd never seen her wear that kind of apparatus before.

It was what Ares wore in combat. He didn't like the feeling in his chest at seeing her dressed that way. Though, no doubt about it, it was practical, and it was convenient.

But in Ares's mind, that kind of equipment was associated with battle.

And Ares wanted Hailey nowhere near flying bullets and mortars.

With her arms crossed under her breasts, Hailey certainly didn't look like that same woman he'd met lying in the filth, up to her armpits in debris, giving hope to two baby girls. She'd evolved in the last three years.

Leslie had told Ares that would be the case. That Hailey was a different person.

Ares didn't believe it. And that could be him being hard-headed. He didn't get his moniker for being easy to sway. But yesterday, he saw *his* Hailey shining through her eyes, until she shut it down.

*His* Hailey was in there still.

Glimmers of her.

He remembered. He could see her passion to help.

He'd like to get to know the woman she'd become, also.

Maybe seeing him again, seeing Judge fit and happy, *maybe* a seed was planted that it was emotionally safe to at least talk. No agenda.

Remi and Cindy turned toward Hailey, and Remi called something out. The wind blew her words away from Ares, and he couldn't make them out.

Hailey looked at the sky as if processing something before lifting a hand to her mouth and calling back.

Brave. All four of them. There weren't that many women (or men, for that matter) willing to go into places where there was little law and order. But the women faced dangers in a way that simply wasn't the case for most men. It wasn't equal footing, be it a battle or a natural disaster. The women had to be braver.

Sure, they all had the same level of comfort-deprivation and concerns about further degradation of the environment from the mass disaster or from those who took advantage of the chaos.

But the women had the balls to face more—capture, rape, slave trade… It made sense to him that the women who had the stones to show up in the destruction space would bond over their common experience.

Share tactics. Stories. Support. As well as share living spaces.

He'd always been proud of Hailey for her strength of conviction and selflessness.

Ares had believed that Hailey was his future. He'd projected a life out in front of them. A life filled with service, balancing evil with light. Violence with compassion.

Then, it all blew up. Reality and metaphor. A great big boom, and the future he'd been reaching for was gone.

He understood that.

He'd respect Hailey's boundaries.

He'd try to make this brush past as easy on her as possible.

Now, Remi was heading his way with Cindy in tow.

"Quite the look on your face."

Ares didn't respond.

"I checked on her the way you asked."

Ares scraped his teeth over his top lip.

"I got bits of your story," Remi said. "It's a shit situation."

Ares bladed his hands onto his hips and nodded.

She took in a deep breath, then pressed a hand to her heart. "I don't know what to say other than, thank you for saving her. She's good stuff. The world needs people like her."

*Yeah, this sucks.* "But she's okay? Seeing Judge and me?"

"Can of worms. Lots of wiggling confused emotions. I have no advice for you."

"I'm not looking for advice," Ares glanced Cindy's way, seeing she was involved in scanning a video with earbuds in place, he finished, "as much as I wanted to make sure someone who's close had an eye on the situation."

"I've got that covered, okay?"

His lips pulled wide as he pressed his lips together. He gave her a nod to buy himself some time to figure out how to move the conversation along.

Remi did that for him. "And I'm going to keep an eye on you, too. And to that end, selfishly." She smiled. "I've taken off the friendship hat. I'm now talking as a reporter."

*Thank god. That I can deal with.*

"I sat down with the footage I had from yesterday, the rescue and the dog introduction."

He sent a glance back to Cindy, who pulled the earbuds from her ear, then focused on him with a smile.

"Hi there. How are you?" he asked.

"Cold as shit, otherwise good. You?"

"Depends on what Remi says next." He swung his attention to Remi.

"Ha," Remi said. "I planned two different series—" She suddenly stopped. One hand shot up over her head, the pinky and index finger of her other hand were in her mouth, Remi whistled sharply.

A man's hand shot up, holding up three fingers.

The hand over Remi's head formed an okay sign, then tucked back into her pocket. She turned to Ares who was wiggling a finger in his ear, like she'd blown his eardrum with the shrillness of her whistle.

"Sorry about that, that's the coffee shop guy." She pulled her elbows in tight to stave off the gust of bitter wind. "I planned two different series of questions for you. Would that be all right?"

"That's fine." He checked his watch. "But ten minutes tops. Judge and I need to walk the tracks before the next train gets in."

The person showed up with a cardboard tray of drinks.

"Thank you!" Remi passed one to Ares, one to Cindy, and

taking the last one, handed the tray back to the guy to reuse. The server turned and loped off.

"The best kind of hand warmers." She winked then took a sip. "Mmmm. Hits the spot. I'm ready to start the interview when you are."

## 13

Ares

CINDY SCANNED THE AREA, then pointed to an empty space with a wall. "Can we head over there? The lighting is better, and there's probably less noise from the wind blowing on the microphone.

A moment later, Ares, with Judge at his feet and his coffee off to the side, was looking at the little red light glowing from Cindy's camera.

"We are speaking with Ares, the commander of Iniquus's famed Cerberus Tactical K9 Team Bravo. Good to see you, Ares."

"Thank you." Ares gave her a nod of acknowledgment. He forced himself to focus past the distraction of Hailey bent over the table, scrolling through a computer file. He had images in his head of her round ass, naked and wiggling an invitation his way, in just that position back when they were in love.

"Were in love" past tense was only truthful in that it was a plural. Ares was *in* love with Hailey.

How could he not be?

But he had become the bitter taste in her mouth. He was emblematic of pain and loss. Grief. When he was gone, he hoped she could put the ghosts back in the box, turn the key, and leave them untouched on her memory shelf.

Ares reached up and rubbed his eyes with his thumb and fore-finger, as if he could erase that thought.

"Ares is your handle," Remi said, "and you use that to protect your legal name." She turned to the camera. "In our interviews with Cerberus Tactcial K9, the men and K9s who deploy on missions as contractors into conflict zones have their faces blurred for their safety." She angled back to Ares. "You got your call name in the Army when you functioned as a Green Beret in Africa."

"No, ma'am, though I was a Green Beret in Africa, I got my name in Afghanistan a long time ago when I was learning my way around the battlefield."

"Green Berets are special forces like the SEALs and Delta Force Operators. The Green Berets have a specific role to play. Could you tell us about that?"

"Yes, ma'am. I am retired from the Green Berets. I was part of the U.S. European Command that covers Africa, Europe, and North Asia. I was with the 5th Special Forces Group stationed out of Fort Campbell in Kentucky. My role was as an engineer sergeant. I was a logistical planner and navigator. I helped to design structures in the field, like bridges, for example. While we were trained to build the structures, we were also trained in demolition and sabotage."

"You were last stationed in Africa. What were you doing there?"

"Training allies in the field. Green Berets are considered 'warrior diplomats.' Besides having an engineering degree, I went through a great deal of training to be an effective Green Beret."

This was a bit of a tiptoe. The Green Berets didn't like notoriety. They liked to go in silent and leave even quieter.

"Can you tell me what going from a typical soldier to a Green Beret entails?"

"The usual, basic soldiering, a selection process, a twenty-four-day stress test to pick those who can do the job, advanced schools including languages and cultures."

Remi looked at the camera and held still for the count of ten.

The light blinked off.

"Good?" Remi asked.

Cindy was watching the screen. Ares was getting to know the pattern for how these two worked together.

After getting a thumbs up from Cindy, Remi smiled at Ares. "Thank you. My next set of questions is about cats."

"Cats?" Ares laughed. "Okay."

Remi curved down like she was going to put the microphone between her knees. Ares reached out and took it from her.

"Thank you." She pulled the hairband from her ponytail and held it between her teeth as she said, "The wind." And put herself back together. She looked over at Cindy. "Am I okay?"

Cindy scanned Remi head to toe, then gave her another thumbs up.

Remi accepted her microphone back. "You look polished. You're fine," she told Ares.

They were blurring his face, Ares couldn't care less what he looked like, other than correctly in uniform.

Remi positioned, looked at the camera and Cindy held up fingers—Three. Two. One. Point.

"Ares, I see that there are a lot of animals here this afternoon. Cats. Lots of cats. I saw some hamsters. A canary. And they're all going on the train with the families that AgilitiCorp is evacuating?"

"Yes, ma'am. Families, extended family members. Pets."

"Can you tell me about that?"

"We know that many people will not leave their pets behind. They'll stay in dangerous circumstances so as not to betray their beloved companions. We see a lot of issues in the United States, as well. Not in war, but in natural disasters. If public shelters won't accept companionate animals, the pet owners will stay in the path of the category 5 hurricane. They'll wave the rescue boat on by if the boater says that animals aren't allowed onboard, staying in their flooded homes rather than put their pets at risk. Iniquus has a policy that has a hierarchy to it. Of course, human lives have precedence, but where possible and as part of our training and equipment, we save companion animals."

"In war-torn areas, as well."

"Fortunately, that hasn't come to pass here. AgilitiCorp is functioning out of an abundance of caution in moving their people over the border."

"But AgilitiCorp employees aren't the only people that Iniquus is helping to leave."

"That's correct. Going back to pets and conflict zones, psychological studies support the idea that people recover best physically and mentally when they have their pets with them. It creates a lot of unnecessary emotional issues if we force people to choose. The same with families. We won't take out mom and not her children and husband. That simply wouldn't work." It crossed his mind in that moment, did he handle his time in the military, and then transition to his retirement with relative ease because he always had a working dog by his side? Was caring for Judge the thing that kept him from internalizing the horror of the station massacre and his loss of Hailey from his life?

He'd have to think on that.

"You said to me earlier that Iniquus was functioning with 'an abundance of caution'. The war is not here. Are you expecting it?"

"The threat is there. The expectation is there. There is always an opportunity for Russia to change their minds and stand down."

"Has Iniquus got a time frame in mind?"

Whew boy, Remi was known for her pointed questions. That's why she was considered one of the best. Ares needed to be careful with his words. "We believe we can get everyone from our client company out before Russia strikes."

"Cutting it close?"

Hmmm. Nope. Not going to take the bait. Ares merely stood there.

Remi didn't take the hint and move on. "I'm speculating that that is why Cerberus K9 is in play."

No response.

Remi raised a brow.

Ares knew she'd cut the sections where he was silent. He wasn't worried about it.

Remi simply came in at a different angle. "I've reported from many an international crisis, be it conflict or natural disaster. Iniquus is hired by entities that have their people living and working in foreign lands. Iniquus signs contracts to be the boots on the ground when very bad things happen. Kidnappings. Natural disasters. Disastrous events like the port fire and subsequent explosion in Beirut. Civil unrest. War."

"Yes, ma'am."

Remi looked at the camera and counted ten. She turned to Ares. "I'm going to try that again."

He waited.

Cindy gave a countdown and a point.

Remi said, "Iniquus task forces work with the CIA, FBI, and other international groups to perform tasks for the United States government. On the private contract side, first, you go in and pull out those who hold contracts, be they schools and universities or companies, but Iniquus will also send in the teams as a charitable effort in mass disasters. That leads me, though, to my next question."

Ares lifted his brow.

"Your logistics team is one of the best there is. They train other groups around the world in how best to get their protectees out of conflict zones. I've reported this out on countless occasions. I have never seen the K9s attach in these extractions before."

She held out the microphone to Ares. Ares didn't shift his gaze from Remi's face and said nothing.

Tipping the microphone back toward her, Remi said, "Iniquus has its fingers on the pulse of the global heartbeat with international ties. Iniquus has a tight relationship with the Pentagon. And Iniquus has its own in-house team dedicated to understanding global dynamics so they can best fulfill their contracts. They must think that Russia will advance soon and move in quickly."

Ares canted his head.

"The K9s that I recognize here from my time getting to know your team in Beirut are all cross-trained. *Except* for Truffles, the one Labrador that you have with you on this trip. It's true that your team can choose between the K9s that each handler usually works with and others in your kennel?"

"That's right. Some Iniquus K9s are trained to work with Cerberus handlers on rotation so we have the best fit for the circumstances. Each handler has a K9 that creates a solid team. But we try for dynamic exceptionalism and that means connecting the right operator to the right K9 for the mission."

She must have sensed this wasn't going well, Remi shifted tactics. Ares got it; Remi was doing her job. He was doing his, representing Iniquus as he was asked to do. But he'd be damned if he was going to say on camera that they were prepared to look for their people in the rubble.

Nope. Not gonna happen.

"You're here with K9 Judge. Just like people in the military often earn their names in events, so do the dogs. Can you tell me how Judge came about his name?"

"I learned early on to always trust his instincts, for me, he is judge and jury."

"Nice. As I look around, I recognize some others. But I'm caught on Truffles. She is the standout to me because in the world of rescue, she is trained specifically for urban destruction. She likes to tunnel through debris to find live humans. There's a difference in the K9's training isn't there? Those that are scent trained for live finds and those that are trained to find remains?"

"That's a thing, yes, ma'am." Ares shoulders stiffened.

"Truffles isn't cross trained. I got to hang out with Truffles and her handler Bear for a bit after she saved my life." Remi put her hand to her heart and took a breath, then continued on with her "reporter's" voice. "Why, if Team Bravo is choosing K9 for this assignment, would your small team of what, seven?"

"Six handlers, yes, ma'am."

"Why would one of those dogs be specifically trained for squirming through debris to find people in rubble?"

"Each handler chose the K9 they would bring to this event."

"Event...not mission?" This time she was asking on camera.

"Every time we go out, ma'am, we consider it a mission. Mission often sounds tactical in nature. I don't want to sketch this as a military mission. It's better described as an event."

"Okay. Truffles?"

"Was brought because that's the K9 Bear handles on a regular basis, and there's no reason for him not to bring Truffles. Truffles is particularly good with children, and kids in stressful situations find her comforting to play with."

"So, are you telling me that you're not here in Nezdolannyy

because you think airstrikes are imminent, and you might be searching the rubble for the AgilitiCorp workers?"

She pulled no punches, that was for sure. "Our duty during this event is to provide whatever assistance we can to our logistics group."

"Thank you for your time, Ares." She made a slashing motion. and the red camera light went off.

Remi turned to Ares. "Off the record?"

"Are you recording?" Ares asked.

"I'm not." Remi turned to her coworker. "Cindy, are you recording?"

"Nope. You're clear to tell us the real skinny. War zone?"

## 14

Ares

"IT'S in no one's best interest to ramp up the rhetoric. Do I have advanced knowledge? It's probably the same as you've gotten from your other sources. This particular city is integral to Russian plans. Because of its geographical structure—"

"River leading to the seaport, highways that link east to west?"

"Exactly, in this part of the country, it's a transportation hub. Those are highly prized supply chain routes, necessary for any sustained action or successful occupation. That's why it's likely a first target for the Russian military, especially with mud season fast arriving. They won't be able to move tanks across the fields. When they come in, they're going to come in big, hoping to gain momentum. Hoping for shock and awe that will cow the populace. And more importantly, they're hoping for world complacency which has become the norm with Russian land acquisitions."

"Again, not on the record, but you were a Green Beret," Remi said, her brows pulled in tight. Her body held tautly. "You've looked at the satellite pictures, I'm sure, you've studied the tactics, what's their plan?"

"Russia's? This will be Syria all over again."

"Syria was flattened. Decimated. The populace starved and bombed into submission. The women raped, kidnapped, and enslaved. Children shot in the street trying to get water or food for their family. Chemical weapons…"

"Yes."

"Just like that? Yes?" Cindy was wide-eyed and unblinking.

"Yes, Syria was, in Russian eyes, a great success and a working template. It would be a mistake for any of us to see this war through a North American or European lens. That isn't the mindset of Russia. It hasn't been, ever. They have their own philosophy and worldview that doesn't line up gently with the West. They believe strongly in an "us/them" philosophy. They think the 'other' is subhuman, and the government is willing to wipe the 'other' out of existence."

"But the world is putting together economic sanctions packages."

"Which will do what?"

"Help the Russian people to act in their own interest," Remi said.

"We'll see."

Cindy frowned. "You don't think they'll work?"

"No. I don't. As long as Europe needs oil, it's a problem. If they converted to green energy? Yeah. Will Europe try to switch? Hard to do on a dime. The sanctions won't help that much. Mostly because Russia has some internal levers they can throw to relieve the pressure. It's going to take months if not years of sustained economic pressure through sanctions to have the kind of detrimental impact we'd like. Of course, there's the psychology of it. There's the possibility that it might make Russians curious why the world is turning against them. It's worth a try. Let's just paint me as skeptical." He dipped his chin. "These are my personal thoughts." He focused on Remi. "We're speaking as friends here."

"I appreciate that." She frowned. "My takeaway is that it's going to be bad soon, and it's going to be long and drawn out."

His nod was slow as the poignancy of the clearly concise words washed threw him. While folks at home would read about and hear all of this discussed on the news by reporters like Remi, it was an entirely different thing to walk amongst the devastation of a bomb strike, to find limbs lying in the streets without a body anywhere nearby. The stench of decomposition. The wailing from behind battered walls. The blood and the begging for help that simply wasn't available. The elderly with dust etching their wrinkled faces, the tears and gasps of mothers clutching their dead children's bodies.

War was hell on Earth.

And Ares—though given the name of the Greek god of war—strove for peace.

He'd seen too much.

His mission had been to help those who wanted peace to have the capacity to fend off evil. Now, it was to save the kinds of people he'd had to walk away from in the past.

"Will Russia win?" Cindy asked. "That would push them right up against NATO countries. NATO won't let that stand."

"It depends on this country's population, and the world response. Look, I don't need to tell you this. You've lived it, Remi, and reported on it, speaking to people far higher up the ranks than I am."

"We're off the record," Cindy said. "I'm looking for hope. Blow some sunshine in my direction, please."

"All right. One, the people are going to rise up and fight."

"Yes, I agree," Remi said.

"In urban warfare, it takes five aggressors to take down one defender." He used his fingers to show the contrast as he spoke. "The defender is fighting for their home, family, lifestyle and lives. The aggressor will fight for other reasons."

"Such as?" Cindy was wiggling her knees back and forth like she needed to pee. Ares was beginning to wonder if Cindy didn't normally cover conflict zones.

"They were conscripted and forced to come. They're mostly from Eastern Russia where there are few job possibilities and extreme poverty, and they want a paycheck. They were tricked into coming."

"How would you trick someone into going to war?" Remi asked.

"Following social media posts, the Russian people are being told that they are preparing for a typical military exercise."

"But they'd get here and be shooting at people," Cindy said.

"Eventually. But Russian commanders could say, here are your coordinates, show up there at this time. And once the troops and equipment are in place, then the leaders explain the objective. Which will be to annihilate everything. Remember, the Russians don't think of the people in this country as human beings, they are the "other." And the "other" must be destroyed and removed."

"How would not telling their conscripts that they were going to war in advance, where they were going, and what they were doing help anything?" Remi asked.

"No leaks?" Cindy asked. "No forewarning?"

"The world has plenty of warning. Satellites. We can see what equipment they're amassing and where. It's easy enough to extrapolate out next moves. It's a matter of timing."

"And keeping it from the Russian soldiers?" Remi pressed.

"Less whining from the Russian mothers who have a historic

place of reverence. If the mothers aren't complaining, it's politically easier. The Russian propaganda machine will be functioning at full force once shots are fired. I imagine that what the government wants is for a very quick win before the citizens find out what's going on. And I imagine they will stomp down hard on anyone who is opposed to the aggression."

Remi was looking past Ares's shoulder out at the heavy gray sky with a frown.

"Is that possible?" Cindy whispered.

"At first? Yes. As the days fall away, no. Russia is extremely good at psychological manipulation. Just look what they've done in America since the end of the USSR. They turned from cold war to cyber war. Their weapon of choice is algorithms. We've been at war with Moscow for decades, the only thing that's changed is where they choose to do battle."

"Whew!" Cindy exhaled. She looked at Remi. "This is a lot to take in."

"You were talking about the defender's reactions." Remi refocused on Ares.

"The defender knows the terrain. And frankly, it's hard to route someone from rubble. Once the buildings go down, the defender is entrenched. Russia doesn't have the numbers."

"But the cities in your scenario would have to come down," Remi pointed out.

Ares looked over her shoulder as he paused. Remi was married to a Delta Force operator. Surely, Remi had gone over this with him. And Remi had seen this stuff firsthand. Maybe having lived, stuck under the rubble for days on end, contemplating dying from lack of water made this real to her in a way that it hadn't been before, despite her long tenure in war-torn regions.

"The place where I take a sliver of optimism is the oligarch system," Ares said.

"Break that down for me, will you?" Cindy asked.

"Simple. After the dissolution of the USSR, industries were privatized. The industries were divided up. And they scrape all of the money out of their society and live large as the ruling class of Russia."

"We have a wealthy ruling class in America," Cindy pointed out.

"But we haven't degenerated to behave as an oligarchy. Not yet anyway. But there are similarities. Oligarchs are all about money. Money laundering. Money that buys influential governmental voices."

"So when the West puts the sanctions in place, the oligarchs will get mad, because that affects their bottom lines. There's a coup." Cindy shrugged like it was a no-brainer.

"Don't hold your breath," Ares countered.

"This country butts up against *NATO*," Cindy insisted. "Russia's threatening a nuclear bomb. A *launched* nuclear weapon, no matter the size has ramifications in Europe."

"Is that a real possibility or a threat? Posturing? Fear mongering?" Remi asked. "I mean, Chernobyl still impacts European health. That area is still incompatible with life."

"A possibility?" Ares rocked back on his heels. "Absolutely, Russia doesn't view nukes the way we do."

"Not as a reporter, but on a personal level," Cindy reminded him, "you were working toward giving me hope."

"It's a hard needle to thread to be honest with you and give you hope."

"Go back to the oligarchs and money. Money is power." Cindy's voice was getting frantic. She was grabbing at straws. "Do you think they'll unseat the Russian government, the oligarchs? Talk them out of this incursion to stabilize Russia? Once the Russians are pariahs, it will take a generation, at least, to come back from that."

"No, they don't have that kind of power. The West will make them squirm, I'd imagine. Take their yachts, make living their lives, and maintaining their lifestyles hard. The good thing about the oligarchs is that they're greedy, and that will haunt the Russian conscripts."

Remi shook her head, asking for an explanation.

"All the money that was supposed to go into troop readiness —MREs weren't purchased. They're probably fifteen years out of date. New tires weren't purchased. They're dry rotted. We're going through snowy freezing weather into mud season. Their tanks and heavy machinery will be stalled from disrepair and lack of readiness. And frankly, the middle and upper-class Russians don't have skin in this game. Like I said, their leaders cull the soldiers from the poorest areas of their country. Those soldiers don't want to fight. They want to be able to eat."

"Okay, Russian troops will be cold and eating crap," Remi said, "stuck in their vehicles on the sides of the road, is your prediction. Demoralized."

"Look, my prediction is that this is going to be war. And war is hell."

"Syria." Remi's brows were up to her hairline.

"Syria, yes."

"The women and children." Remi exhaled.

"Yes. But the West will stand up," Cindy countered.

"And fight?" Remi asked. "Surely not."

"No," Ares said. "They won't fight. That would be Armageddon. Potentially. If Russia was in the death throws, which it would be if it faced NATO, they'd take out humanity with their nukes. It's important to be careful what we say and how we say it. This is going to be tactically fragile." Ares skated a hand out, catching Remi's gaze. "This is friends talking. Friends who know what happens in war. I am in no way speaking from anything I specifically know from present-day military or from my employer."

"I appreciate this. It helps me to frame my choices," Remi said. "What will the allies do?"

"Send in the wherewithal to fight."

"Bombs and the like?"

Ares pressed his lips together. "Maybe. Hopefully. We'll have to see what happens with public opinion."

Ares looked out over the horizon. Like his grandmother could tell a coming storm in her arthritic joints, Ares could feel the rising conflict in his bones.

He just hoped to get everyone they could out in time to save their lives.

And that included Hailey.

*If she wouldn't talk to him, how was he going to convince her to leave in time?*

# 15

Hailey

HAILEY WAS in her hotel room, giving herself twenty minutes to lie down before she went to the restaurant next door for dinner.

She stared at the ceiling, thinking about Ares.

The night Hailey knew for certain that she loved him for life, was during a storm at the beginning of rainy season. Ares had accompanied her on some errand she was running for her NGO.

When the storm grew too wild, they'd ended up with her curled into Ares arms, lying on a tarp in an abandoned school.

He was solid. So damned solid and good.

Hailey had never heard him say a bitter word, never heard him disparage anyone.

"Everyone has their pain. I'm here to make things better not worse." In those words, she'd heard her babysitter Kerry and Kerry's parents taking photos of the tsunami victims. Her earliest mentors, her strongest influences, the reason that Hailey went to grad school to get her degree in emergency management.

She wanted that title on her diploma to be reality.

She wanted to manage the hell out of emergencies and protect people.

That night, through the broken windowpane, Hailey watched fingers of lightning reaching down to flick the soil. Close. Her nostrils tickled with the scent of ozone. The thunder was a sharp whip crack that startled her.

The boom of thunder that followed seemed impossibly brazen. Bigger than life.

She'd pressed herself closer to Ares chest, tucking under his chin, childlike and not ashamed of it.

When last of rumble sidled across the sky, she'd whispered, "Ares is the god of thunder. Can't you turn down that volume?"

He'd chuckled and dropped a kiss into her hair. "No, but I can protect you from it. Just stay tucked in close."

Hailey lifted their hands, twisting them this way, observing in the strobes of light how they interlaced. And she thought the tangle of their fingers was emblematic of the way they were weaving themselves together. She felt that way. Like the Hatari women who created the glorious artistry of their grass baskets, weaving stories and life into their designs.

Hailey had thought that was it. She'd met her man. She'd found her path to the happily ever after that her mother had indoctrinated her into believing was every girl's destiny.

It was not.

He was not.

Neither of them was at fault that they blew apart, seeds on the wind to plant a future elsewhere. It was just that she couldn't see past what came next.

Hailey remembered distinctly how her skin was goose-fleshed with cold fear from that storm. It was ominous.

An omen.

The portending of hideous things.

That thunder made her think of all the lives of good people going about their day and suddenly the blue skies and friendly sunshine were obliterated by the racing storm.

"I wonder what it's like not to feel fear," she'd whispered.

"I can't imagine," Ares had replied, his breath warm on her cheek.

Hailey lifted onto her elbow to stare down at him, seeing only the shape of his outline. "You are *never* afraid."

"Hailey, are you kidding right now? You think I'm a sociopath?" He sounded wounded.

She shook her head and tucked back into his arms.

"Here's the truth about that. Fear and I are friends. We walk together."

"What?"

"Back when I was in bootcamp, I was in my element. I loved all of it, the challenges. But, truth is, it was still frightening stuff sometimes. That voice in my head, man, that voice wanted me to stay small. You know? It said, it's audacious to think you're a hero. Put the word hero into quotation marks. By that, I meant that I could go into battle and be responsible for other people's survival. Terrifying. The voice said that maybe I could be a paper pusher or a bean counter. But I knew my calling was bigger than that. My friend Jimmy Warcloud told me I should take a walk and make friends with my fear because my fear would always be there, we might as well get along."

"Interesting."

"So we made a deal, my fear and me. My fear could come along on the ride, but it had to stay off to the side where it wouldn't trip me up."

"I had a female professor once, gave a lecture about women anxiety and 'imposter syndrome'."

"What's that?"

"Imposter syndrome? What you were saying. You don't belong here kind of thing. She said to give that voice a name, and when we hear the voice just say hi."

"What's your imposter voice's name?"

"Sammy Shithead."

Ares laughed. It was a wonderful laugh.

A meaningful night.

A night that Hailey thought she'd have for her entire life—that whole damned happily ever after lie.

# 16

Hailey

FRIDAY NIGHT, NEZDOLANNYY

THERE WAS A WORD IN GERMAN—GERMANS seemed to have a special vocabulary, that didn't exist in the English language, for some very complex emotions—the word was *Fingerspitzengefuhl*. She had no idea how to pronounce it. But she'd let the letters trip over themselves in her brain when the mood was right, and that was the only way she could express the sensation to herself. Hailey was told that *Fingerspitzengefuhl* literally translated to "feel of the fingertips." It meant to have an intuition about what was going on and an innate knowing of how to behave in a situation so that the outcomes were positive.

And now that Hailey thought about it, even a specialized word in German didn't quite convey what Hailey sensed.

She could feel it in the air, danger.

Checking her watch, Hailey took the last bite from her plate. It looked delicious, but Hailey found it tasteless. Stress.

It seemed she was the only person in that restaurant that felt that way. The room was filled with the murmur of conversations and laughter. People were smiling.

They shouldn't be, though.

For a while Hailey thought she had some special gift for knowing in advance that bad things were coming. It had happened too many times to name. But then, she was blissed out on the morning of the station massacre. Nothing tickled her conscious and told her there was any kind of risk.

But for a time, she had magical thinking.

It started, Hailey remembered vividly, back when she and her then-boyfriend, Stu, were heading to San Fransisco. It was years ago, when she was on Christmas break from undergrad school. They'd planned to spend a long weekend with Stu's parents to celebrate Christmas. On her way to the airport, Hailey had decided kind of on a whim to put a tourniquet in her coat pocket. She had them as part of one of her classes at the university.

Hailey had stalled, and on second thought, she'd put another tourniquet in her other pocket. She had no reason to do it, she also had no reason not to. Though mildly disquieted, about the choice, Hailey talked herself into thinking the reason she had done that was she'd just read an article in the paper about a "Stop the Bleed" class offered by the local library system.

Off she and Stu had flown. They were at the hub, changing planes when something in the air tickled her nose and she sneezed over and over. Stu reached into his pocket for a pack of tissues. When he did, a tourniquet fell from his pocket.

Hailey focused down at it. She'd felt her whole face harden as she stared at it lying there on the floor. Suddenly, the airport seemed as dangerous as any place she'd volunteered to provide emergency services.

When Stu came upright again, he handed her the tissues and shoved the tourniquet back in his pocket.

Hailey pointed.

"Oh, just a notion I had as I was pulling on my coat. No reason in particular."

Hailey reached into her own pockets and pulled out her tourniquets.

Stu blinked. "Do you always walk around with those in your pocket?"

Hailey slowly shook her head.

"Well, damn," was all he said, but both clung to the walls as they walked along, both of them had their heads on a swivel searching for cover.

They both adopted a quickened pace with a very short stride as if they were trying to glide along with both feet planted on the ground, lest something blow up when they were unbalanced on a single foot even if momentarily.

If security were watching them, they looked all kinds of guilty and dangerous.

Getting to California and out of public view relieved Hailey of her concerns. She thought they'd probably heard something on the news that had filtered through to their subconsciouses, and they'd both acted using what knowhow they had from their lives —Hailey from her training and Stu as a first responder.

But no, that wasn't it at all.

They'd both somehow tapped into the collective unconscious.

It was the day before Christmas when Stu's mom scowled over her computer. She was drinking a morning mug of coffee as she glanced over the papers. "Talk about a close shave!" she'd exclaimed. Her husband rounded behind her and pulled his reading glasses from the top of his head as he bent to read. "Wow! We'd planned to be there. The FBI finally did something right."

Stu and Hailey had caught each other's gaze and froze. Did they want to know?

"What's that?" Stu asked.

"For Christmas tomorrow, we'd planned—still plan if the FBI thinks it's okay—to go to Fisherman's Warf to walk around and see things. We'd wanted to show you around some of the tourist attractions while the turkey was in the oven."

Hailey clutched her coffee mug to her chest.

"Seems like there was going to be a terror attack. But the FBI caught the guy. Safe and sound." She looked up with a smile.

"Good job," Stu said. He'd turned to Hailey and reached in his pocket, pulling out the tourniquet that he'd moved to his pants' pocket today. "Wow," he mouthed to her.

Wow indeed.

Since then, Hailey had Remi talk through everything she did to keep herself safe. She traveled light, but every piece was practical and could make the difference when survival was precarious.

While Remi was always prepared, 24/7, Hailey didn't live the kind of life Remi did as a war reporter. Hailey took a slightly moderated approach. She'd made a list of everything Remi carried with her. She'd tried stuffing it into a backpack, but had discovered, as Remi had, that sometimes stopping to find the right thing—be it a chemlight or a tissue—meant time. And sometimes there was no extra time to be had.

Take those tourniquets that she and Stu put in their pockets, had they had them in the bottom of a backpack, someone could bleed out as they rifled past the things they'd stuffed on top.

But Remi kept her stash in a belly bag, and Hailey did too much stooping to talk to kids for that to be comfortable. Instead, she'd bought a leg platform bag and then she'd added a second. On her right, she thought of the things as her purse. Pen, pads, hand sanitizer, tampons…

On the left was survival. First aid kit, tourniquets, meal replacement bars, water packets…

She honestly hadn't planned to wear them here.

But that same tickle she'd felt heading to San Fransisco, had started in the same place of awareness along the hairline on the nape of her neck. Now, it had crawled up the back of her head and tingled her scalp.

A kind of constant warning system.

Was it triggered by seeing Ares and Judge?

Was she equating them with life or death?

Or was that an easy explanation? The preferred explanation?

Could it be that she'd landed right back in a war zone?

Hailey wiped her mouth on her napkin, then counted out the money for her check, and left the brightly colored currency on the table.

After she stood and moved through the front door, Hailey used her navigation app to turn right and started down the sidewalk toward the church, shoulders hunched up against the sudden sting of wind. Hailey ducked her chin into her turtleneck where the humidity of her exhale quickly made the wool damp.

She sped up her pace, listening to the peaceful monotony of a distant train clackity clacking over the tracks.

When she'd left for dinner, the AgilitiCorp extraction train was almost loaded for today. It took longer than Iniquus probably intended. There were a lot of people to get into place, pets to receive scritches as their owners tucked the carriers onto shelves in the animal car, luggage to be shoved overhead, children to be settled into their seats.

And there was a lot of clinging and crying, as one would expect.

This very well could be the final good-bye for so many.

Hailey couldn't imagine what that felt like.

She'd had a good-bye like that, but as Ares buckled her into the spider straps on the helicopter's lift basket, she was in the gray zone between conscious and unconscious.

Neither of them knew if they'd ever see each other again.

She could have died of her injuries. And she knew Ares would race back to the massacre to try and save more people. The guerillas could well kill him, too.

But here he was, the larger-than-life hero, diving under trucks and saving babies.

Yes, here *they* were.

Her emotions had been blocked for three years. Hailey hadn't realized the danger of her poorly constructed dam. Just seeing him, and it came tumbling down. Emotions flooded through her system, knocked her off her feet, powered her down a turbulent course.

She *loved* him.

She absolutely, deeply, *loved* him.

And she had no idea what to do about that.

Ares would leave on tomorrow's train.

So tomorrow, Hailey guessed, she'd know what those women felt as they waved good-bye. Possibly for forever.

Hailey rubbed her hands over her face and pushed through the heavy wooden door of the church.

Some of the people who were unloading and positioning the WorldCares equipment and supplies had asked to meet with her to ask some questions about what to do.

These people were wondering if they should send their kids to relatives in other countries. Should they send their wives and parents away?

Hailey didn't have answers for them.

But she didn't see anything good about saying no to showing up.

So here she was, doing her best to allay stress by giving folks actions…steps they could take.

A man turned her way and smiled, then gestured for her to follow him into the sanctuary.

After this question-and-answer session, Hailey planned to head down to the subway near her hotel to check on the set up that was going on there.

Busy was good.

Out of Ares's direct sphere was good.

Right now, volunteers at the mobile clinic as well as the six receiving shelters were busy unloading and stacking the boxes that had stuffed the eight trucking containers to capacity. They were following a schematic for each location that she'd developed and distributed via the mayor.

When possible, WorldCares stepped back and allowed the local citizenry to do most of the work. It was a psychological device for giving them a sense of ownership of the situation. They were strong and capable of helping themselves. The NGO's psychological studies found that this was a better route to moving forward, minimizing trauma.

It helped people feel like pro-active partners instead of weak and in need of rescue. It improved morale and maintained some semblance of internal locus of control when all seemed to be at the whims of the fates. And that sense of control often proved to make a difference.

Conversations ceased as she moved toward the priest who beckoned her forward.

Jay'la was already up sitting next to the podium, scrolling through her phone.

"Welcome," a woman said. "You must be Hailey Stapleton." She caught Hailey under the elbow and conducted her toward the front of the church.

Hailey's boots echoed against the ancient stones as she made her way toward the altar.

"Yes, I'm glad to be here. I hope I can be of help."

"You've done so much." She opened a hand toward the red carpeted steps up to the altar.

Igor, the representative from the government that Hailey had been working with during the course of her assignment, smiled encouragingly. He turned to the mic, giving it a two fingered tap. The muffled sound projected out. He addressed the attendees. Hailey would guess fifty or so sat with their arms across their chest, not looking particularly troubled.

Jay'la had stood and was in Hailey's ear with her translations. "Show of hands, who here understands English?"

Most of the hands went up.

"I think it best. How about if those five who need translation move to this pew over here, and Jay'la can translate what is said for you. I think that would be the least burdensome way to get the information across rather than having each piece translated back and forth. That takes time."

A woman stood. "What should we do? How should we prepare? We don't know if we will stay or if we will go. We don't know where to start."

"All right, well, my name is Hailey Sterl—" she caught herself. Ha! Funny that. She'd almost called herself Hailey Sterling. She'd only said that name at one point in her entire life and that was the morning that Ares proposed. Heath and Hailey Sterling had sounded to her like a Christmas tree lit up with tiny white lights in a darkened room. It had made her think of the clinking of glasses and laughter in the background. Yeah, she'd said it and imaged it. And it had been wiped from her memory.

The power of seeing Ares again in the flesh. Capable. Generous. Kind. Intelligent. Gentle giant that he was. She'd forgotten how it felt to be near him, grounded and whole.

That's not who she'd been for these last three years.

That version of Hailey seemed so far back in the past.

She cleared her throat. "Excuse me. I'm Hailey Stapleton, my translator Jay'la and I are with WorldCares, and we've come here this evening to listen to your questions and offer some insights that I've picked up in my ten years working in emergency zones. I must emphasize that I'm here speaking as an individual and not as a representative of WorldCares. Now, one thing I can say is that you have the benefit of time. I don't know how much time. Everyone I've spoken with seem to think it is very little. Days if not hours. But I've worked in many places with no warning whatsoever. People were going about their day and the earth shook and their world crashed around them. We're going to hope for days." She held her hand out. "We hope never. But knowing of the potential, it's best to prepare."

"Yes, thank you." Igor stood. "Will you speak about, how you say? Action steps?"

Hailey rubbed a hand over her forehead. "Okay, whether you plan to leave or plan to stay, one of the critical things that needs to happen is that you gather all of your paperwork. Your passports, your birth certificates, your medical records, your prescriptions, contact phone numbers, anything and everything that you might need to stay in touch, to prove your identity, to sustain. And take pictures of it and put it in the cloud. Give the passwords to a trusted person outside of the country if that's possible. That way you can access them wherever you are. Do that tonight. I don't normally suggest people forgo sleep. But if you have this time, I'd take advantage of it."

"Yes," Igor said. He let his eyes scan the room. "If you have issues with how to use a cloud, if you don't have a way to photograph, please let me know, I will help."

"Don't simply put it on our phone?" a man asked.

"I would suggest that you not have anything on your person that would identify you should someone, should a soldier, get it from you. If you have a cell phone, be careful about who is in your contacts, what pictures you have that might be used against you. Put them all in the cloud that you can access through your phone but have nothing on your phone or in your phone history that would flag the existence of your cloud account."

"Oh wow." A woman pulled her purse to her chest and hugged it to her.

"If possible, you need to accumulate the things you might need to support you for as long as possible. Start with for a day, then a week, a month… In the morning, make sure you've filled all of your prescriptions for as big of a quantity as the pharmacist will allow." She looked over at Igor. "I don't know the laws around that here."

He nodded.

"Think about having some bleach to disinfect your water. Start filling up jugs from your tap. The rule of thumb is a gallon of water per person per day. A gallon, that's about four liters. When I was working in Puerto Rico, which is a large island to the south of the contiguous United States, they went without water for a long time, almost a year in some instances. One thing that people did was clean out their trash cans—the very big ones that hold about two hundred liters—and filled those up with the garden hose, adding the proper amount of bleach to disinfect it. Many of you are in apartments, that might not be practical. I don't know." She looked from face to face, trying to gauge If they were understanding her words. "But…water is imperative. Lots of it."

"We have a creek near us, we can get water there. We can melt snow," a man offered.

Hailey shook her head. "Practically, those aren't going to work as well as stored water. Spring is coming, and there will be no more snow. The creek. I don't know how to say this delicately, so I'll just say it. In my experience, that becomes contaminated with people using it to go to the bathroom when their toilets don't flush. In natural disasters, there are often animal and human bodies that are decomposing in the water. I've known warring factions to pour gasoline into the water to make it unfit for drinking."

The heads nodded. People were scratching notes.

"Keep yourselves, your clothes, and your homes extra clean. If there's a break in the water lines, you'll appreciate that you have a few extra days to feel fresh." Hailey ticked off. "Cook now and fill your freezers with the foods that can be eaten cold when defrosted. Fill bags with water and shove them into every nook and cranny in the freezer. They will help keep your food cold if there is no electricity, and you can drink the water."

"My grandmother came from Germany in World War II," a woman said. "She talks about the things that affected her the most was that her family pictures and art were destroyed and stolen. Family heirlooms, gone. She stayed in Germany until well after the war. So this happened while she stayed in place. Of course, back then where could one go to flee the atrocities?" She put her hand to her chest. "I'm staying with my city. My family is staying. But I want to make sure that if the soldiers come that my things are safe. Have you any suggestions?"

"Yes, actually, that one I can help you with. In the United States, during our Civil War, I read about how—when the soldiers were moving through an area—women would put their silver and china down the well. This is true of women throughout history, hiding those things that are precious not only out of sentimentality," she touched her heart to give the word context, "but also pragmatism. They might hide money or tools that were needed for what came next. Removing these things from harm's way is what I'd suggest. Take large plastic bins that have locking systems to keep out moisture. In those place large plastic garbage bags. Now, the pictures and documents should be put in more plastic bags, you see? Plastic bags, within plastic bags, within a plastic bin."

She waited while pens scratched over pads.

"Next, secretly take these out to the woods or out to the

country and dig a hole as deep as you can. Put your treasures in the hole, cover them with dirt and debris. Now, here's a very important step. On your camera, you need to pull up an app that will imprint the GPS location on a photo. Take a photo of the site and load it up into the cloud with the pictures of your documents. If you have several bins, put them in different places. Don't tell anyone about them or what's in them. But your safe relatives or friends in a different country should know how to access that information. Okay? Now. Once you've taken the photos, make sure to remove the app from your phone. Your phone should be cleared of anything that you don't want the Russians to know about you and your family. Clear the histories, clear the photos, move all of that to the cloud. Also, if there is to be an invasion, you'll want to make sure that your location is kept secret. If you don't know how to use a VPN, ask a young person now. Also, the VPNs are expensive, but I know of an organization—" She turned to Igor, "I'll get you the contact information. The organization provides free VPNs to people in conflict zones."

She waited again for most of the pens to stop and most of the faces to look her way.

"About those plastic containers that you're burying, I forgot to add: You should take duct tape." She turned to Jay'la. "Can you say duct tape for everyone? I don't think that's a typical vocabulary word."

Jay'la looked up at the ceiling."*Kachyna strichka? Utinaya lenta?*"

It amazed Hailey that Jay'la might have that word in her vocabulary bank. How many times in a year does someone actually say duct tape?

Heads nodded. Pens scribbled.

"And tape along the edges of the box to keep out the moisture. It's the dampness that will harm your things."

A woman stood. "I think it's prudent to have a bag or bags

packed and ready by the door. If things become difficult, we can grab them and go."

"Yes, I suggest you do."

"Yes," she said, "but what should we bring? How do we decide?"

"If your precious things are in a safe place underground, then you're left with things to help you survive. From my experience, bring lots of underwear. You can keep wearing the same clothes over and over again if you can keep your bodies clean and have fresh underthings. Think about survival priorities. A roller bag and a backpack. Big water bottles in each of the net pockets on the backpack. Pack meal replacement bars. Nuts. Things you can eat that will give you energy and can sustain you for seventy-two hours."

"Seventy-two hours?" The man's wooly eyebrows shot up.

"That's the rule of thumb. Pack the most important survival things in your backpack, including your medications, for sure, so you have them safely attached to your back should you need to drop your luggage for whatever reason. Animals go into carriers."

"What goes in the roller bag?"

"Changes of clothing. Layering clothes are best. Shampoo etcetera weighs a lot and can be purchased once you're over the border. Lay everything out on the bed. Try to remove anything easily replaced especially if it's heavy."

"The children?"

"Children should have their favorite soothing toy and blanket. They will need things to keep them occupied and have a sense of normalcy. Cards, books, be careful of depending on anything that needs to be recharged or uses batteries. And having said that, let's talk about your attitudes as parents and how that will impact your kids. Your children don't know what's going on. They will look to you for clues. Choose your words carefully. It's important not to lie. They need to know that they can depend on you and lying breaks that trust. But that doesn't mean that they can handle adult information. You could, for example, tell them why you're leaving, your hopes for the future, what plans you have in place. If you have no plans and are just winging this—uhm , making decisions as you go forward—then tell them that you're on an adventure. Make sure the children know they are loved, and the family is fine."

Hailey well knew that this might be the case for the people who showed up in the church this evening, those who were trying to be proactive and prepared.

But the challenge of emergency work was that the emergency happened amongst lives being led.

People had different levels of capacity to deal with the situation. Different levels of physical strength, different levels of mental health stability, of disability, of wealth, and social structures.

She had learned to meet people where they were.

To find the need and fill it.

The first thing she asked people when they arrived at her station was, when is the last time you had something to drink? To eat? Slept? Do you have your medications?

Then, are you connected to your family?

Once those pieces were in place, they could get going on the harder stuff.

Much of what Hailey did was sit and listen.

So many trauma stories. So much pain and loss.

And here was the potential that it wouldn't be a village that flooded or a town that was shaken into rubble, but an entire country and her people were at risk.

"Let the children know some of the fun things that you're going to do once you've arrived at your emergency evacuation destination. For example, we're going to be meeting new friends and exploring new parks and playgrounds. Tell them that you're working as a community, everyone is doing what they can to help. That your job is making extra sure that everyone is safe. Right? How you frame this, what attitude you show them, that's what they will take to heart."

Those words were met with nods.

"Where I'm from, there's an old saying that 'children are resilient' the general idea is that kids bounce back, they process and move past things. It isn't what psychological studies prove. What we know now is that traumatic experiences frame events for a lifetime. Let me say that a different way."

Hailey had found that those who spoke English, spoke it very well. And her audience didn't have looks of confusion on their faces, they weren't looking from one to the other to see if someone was taking better notes.

"Children's brains are being constructed now. Their adult lives will be shaped by their childhood experiences. Anxiety, depression, phobias—we don't want to plant those seeds."

The audience leaned forward, brows pulled together, attentive.

"Be real with your kids but be hopeful. Watch your tone, your facial expressions. Work as a team to help each other. One more thing, you might want to visit the clinic that WorldCares is setting up," she looked to Igor, "you can direct them?"

"Yes."

"They have hospital bands there. You can have your child's name and contact phone numbers, medical needs, allergies and so forth put onto the band and placed on your child. Waterproof and very secure, they will stay on your children until they are cut off. An added precaution if you are somehow separated." Looking around, Hailey saw that she'd jacked everyone's emotions at the thought that they'd lose their kids. That hadn't been her intention. But she had seen it so often. They need to be warned. "Remember this mantra: One step and then another."

Just then, it sounded like there was a truck outside with someone leaning on the horn.

She waited for it to stop. When it didn't, she turned searching eyes on Igor.

"Air raid siren," he called. "Everyone into the crypt!"

Hailey froze. Did he say *crypt*?

# 17

**Hailey**

FRIDAY NIGHT, NEZDOLANNYY

HAILEY HAD HEARD warning systems before. They sounded different in middle-America where she was born and raised. A three-minute steady signal told everyone that there was a tornado on the horizon.

Homes had basements and saferooms all set up.

It was a couple of hours at most, and then, in her small town, they'd also send up a three beat 'all clear' signal.

Her parents had described it to her like "adult swim" at the local pool. You could be playing happily, the lifeguard blows the whistle, the children get out and wait patiently, then another whistle meant it was playtime again.

For Hailey, those sirens had been just that. She was never told to go down to their basement and feel fearful. Her parents also had some special toys and snacks down there that were only allowed when the siren sounded. Sometimes, as a child, wanting the normally forbidden BBQ potato chips, she'd look to the sky and hope for a tornado siren.

With the all-clear, people would pour out into the streets and look around, and when they found their neighborhood was intact, they'd turn on the news to find out if it hit a nearby community and did anyone need help?

In Hailey's town, most people kept an extra crowd-sized casserole or lasagna in their freezer, ready to pull out and heat up for whatever called the community together—a fire, a flood, a funeral. They'd head to the church nearest the event and provide food for the rescue workers or suddenly unhoused neighbors.

Disasters were terrible things. They caused enormous pain and suffering.

Still…

(And Hailey would only whisper this in the back of her mind.) There were the good parts. Communities were strengthened as people came together, working for a common good. The worst of humanity was rarely on display. Everyday people became daring. Bitterness and rancor were set aside. Yes, there could be joy amidst the debris when people banned together.

It was good stuff. It encouraged Hailey that the cream almost always rose to the top.

And then, there was the death and devastation.

But if Hailey focused on that, she'd go nuts.

She focused on the good. And while it had been repeated until it seemed trite, Mr. Rodgers was right when he said, "When I was a boy and I would see scary things in the news, my mother would say to me, 'Look for the helpers. You will always find people who are helping.'"

After hearing about the monster tsunami as a child, that quote rang true to Hailey. She wanted to live up to that ideal. To be the helper person.

That was why she was here in Nezdolannyy.

But with the air-raid sirens' shriek, Hailey wasn't amongst the white knights riding in to help; she was just one of the crowd.

Down, down they went into the bowels.

St. Olga's church had been built in the early seventeen hundreds, and this stairwell was dark and narrow. Made of stone, the spiral stairs were difficult to navigate. Hailey clung to the railing with one hand and gripped an elderly woman's hand with the other.

Along the way, naked light bulbs were attached high on the wall with the electrical wiring looping from one to the next.

"The church survived the Great War," the old woman said. "We'll be safe down here."

Ares, Judge, and the others on his team were probably moving into the subway station right near their hotel. Remi and Cindy were probably in there, too, interviewing folks to report out that this was the first air raid warning.

If she had a hand free, Hailey might cross her fingers that this was just a test of their system, giving everyone an opportunity to hear the noise and get used to it, to find their closest shelter, to figure out what they should bring with them in case this was ever the real thing.

*Please don't be the real thing!*

All over Nezdolannyy, people were finding their safe place.

And Hailey knew that not everyone would have a fortress of stone like she had today.

Many would be going to the basements of their apartment buildings, or the schools. Those spaces would protect people from shrapnel and flying debris. It would keep them safe from shock waves. But if a bomb fell on those places, they would be trapped.

With everyone hiding underground, would there be the good people, the helpers, who came to dig them out?

No. Not if the bombs rained down.

Entombed.

Wasn't that a horrific thought?

Hailey reached the last stair. She shuffled behind the others, moving into the underground vault. The ceiling in this space was a web of arches that made spooky shadows cast by the dim naked lightbulbs. It smelled damp and musty. Looking at the ceiling to make a quick guess as to the square footage, Hailey thought it would hold about two hundred. As more people flowed in, the smaller the cavernous room became.

She thought maybe there would be more people than space.

That they'd pack in like sardines.

She started thinking about oxygen flow, and her heart fluttered with distress.

That staircase looked like it was the only way out, maybe one of the side passages was a tunnel to somewhere else.

Squeezing the old woman's hand as a good-bye, Hailey set out to find Jay'la who had been a handful of people ahead of Hailey on the stairs.

Hailey thought about Remi last year. She'd survived because she was with the senator. Walking one room down the hall to help the sick senator was the difference between life and death.

Luck of the draw.

Fate.

Being down here, put all of that into perspective for Hailey. What would it be like if a bomb fell on the church, and they were stuck down here for days on end, dependent on someone outside finding them?

Ares would come.

He'd find her.

Judge would find her.

She had not a single doubt, after seeing the look in his eyes after she brushed him off after his death-defying dive onto the highway to save the child, that he would move Heaven and Earth to get her safe.

She would for him, as well.

She loved him. *Loved* him. And she wasn't sure what to do with that.

Thinking of the counsel she'd offered to the parents just before the siren about how brains were wired, she acutely felt that in her own life. In her mind, she'd tied ebullient joy with swiftly following horror.

She didn't seek joy, anymore.

She capped her good feelings at basic contentment. The taste of a chocolate tart, the satisfying bitter bite of black coffee in the morning, a soft pillow with a clean, smooth, cool case. Small bites of "nice."

Anything more was dangerous.

As she searched the growing crowd for Jay'la, Hailey wondered about Remi. How was she coping?

Hopefully, she was distracted by her work.

And Ares? Hailey would actually be surprised if he and Judge weren't standing at the church door when all was said and done, just to 'get eyes on' and make sure she was all right. Which was rather a silly thought since Hailey hadn't told him what she was doing with her evening.

"Miss Stapelton?" A gray-haired man with stooped shoulders hovered above her.

"Hailey, please," She brushed her hand on her pants, then extended it for a shake.

"Forgive me. Igor pointed you out. I was hoping to have a word with you about your provisions that WorldCares brought in." His English was quite good. But as it was explained to her, those showing up to ask questions were those who could gather the information and share it with their friends and neighbors.

"Yes? Are you with one of the teams that's doing the set up?" Hailey asked. She spotted Jay'la and raised her hand.

"No, my name is Fedir Moroz, I'm the director of the city's orphanage."

"Oh." She looked toward the stairs and wondered why he was here in the church basement. If there was an air raid siren, shouldn't he be with the children?

He seemed to read her mind. "The staff is with the little ones as they usually are at night." He looked up the stairs. "I live across the street."

"Oh. But you were looking for me?"

Jay'la saw her and waved back. She worked her way forward, leading with her shoulder.

"Igor said that you brought in supplies yesterday and today." Fedir sought Hailey's eyes to gain her full focus. "That there are three trains."

With Jay'la arriving at her side. "There you are! I was worried."

Hailey grabbed her hand and gave it a thank you squeeze. "This is Jay'la. She's my interpreter. And I'm sorry, I wasn't able to make out your name."

"Fedir. Fed-ear."

"Fedir, thank you." She turned to Jay'la. "Fedir is with the orphanage." She turned back to Fedir. "Is there some way I can help?" The two women formed a tight circle with Fedir. "You mentioned my bringing in supplies. The supplies I've prepared are all in the city now. Do you have needs for the orphanage?" That hadn't been brought up specifically by the mayor's office.

"I heard that you're taking people out of the country."

"I'm not, no. I was piggybacking—" *He might not know that word.* "Uhm, I was using the train that Iniquus Security had arranged. They are moving—"

"AgilitiCorp workers, yes." Fedir said. "Yes, that is what I want to talk to you about."

# 18

Ares

HE'D WAITED at the subway entrance to make sure that Hailey made it to safety. Judge panted as the people filed down the stairs. Stopping to sniff. Ares went ahead and gave him a signal to alert on any munitions scent. So far, nothing. No one was heading down with a gun or an incendiary device.

The people looked perplexed more than worried. A few were put out, checking their watches, looking up to search the sky.

The streets emptied, then the sidewalks, and no Hailey.

No Hailey…

With a last group filing down, he saw Cindy filming an elderly couple as they waddled to the subway, dressed in their pajamas and robes, their feet shoved into boots left unlaced, blankets around their shoulders. The man carried two folding chairs. The woman had a pillow under each arm. As they wobbled side-by-side they bumped against each other. Both of them needed a stabilizing hand.

Ares was about to step forward when a teen jogged back up the stairs. With a smile and a few words, she moved between them, grasping their arms.

Cindy caught Ares gaze, and not wanting to mess up her take, he mouthed, "Hailey?"

She nodded and mouthed, be right back.

This bitter cold wasn't what he was used to. He'd served in Afghanistan in the summer with a hundred-and twenty-degree days broiling his brains under his tactical helmet. He served as a Green Beret in Africa where the heat was an anvil that crashed down on his head. Now living in Northern Virginia just outside of Washington D.C., they had their cold days. They'd just gone through a snowstorm.

But the cold here was different. Damp, it seemed to wriggle and burrow into his clothes and to lay against his skin, now that the night was fully on them, and the wind whistled through the bare tree limbs.

It was no place for the vulnerable elderly to wander.

The subways weren't heated. No respite from the bite of cold would be found there. Perhaps on the subways themselves, without the airflow, and seats to sit on, the most vulnerable would be okay.

He imagined the impact on these citizens if the Russians took down the city's electrical grid. Ares knew that would be one of the first things the Russians would target. A survival impact, a psychological blow, Rusia would want resistance to crumble quickly, and no electricity would be a huge step forward in a besiegement. The city got its electricity from a nuclear plant. That was another point of concern. Would Russia attack a nuclear power plant?

Crouching down with Judge between his knees, Ares blocked

the wind from Judge with his body and was repaid by Judge's radiant heat. It reminded Ares of his early days as a boot, when he learned the benefits of "tactical spooning." For survival's sake, teammates would share body heat and layer their ponchos to ward off hypothermia.

Ares rubbed Judge's chest and spoke soothingly to him. "Hailey says cuddling up like this makes good hormones flow. Oxytocin, dopamine, and serotonin, are all stress relievers. I think she's probably right, in *some* cases."

Judge angled his head up to swipe a wet tongue along Ares's ear.

Ares lifted his shoulder to wipe off the saliva.

"In this case, though, I'm not sure I agree. You're going to give my ear frostbite, and you have rancid dragon breath." When Judge tried for another lick, Ares stood. "When this warning is over, it's teeth brushing time."

Cindy walked up the stairs far enough that she caught his attention.

"Hailey?" He called down.

"No hello? No how're you doing? Just 'Hailey'?"

"Sorry. Hi Cindy, are you doing okay? Have you seen Hailey around?"

Cindy laughed. "Yeah, I saw her eating dinner at the restaurant to the left of the hotel. I asked her to come to Remi's room to hang out, and she said she'd join us later. First, she was meeting with some local leaders at the church to talk about her experience with preparedness. They're going to spread the information around." She looked up at the sky. "Clear of bombs. Damned frigid, though. I swear the temperature is in a freefall. Could be nerves making me shiver."

"I think it's the temperature." Judge sat on Ares feet, keeping Ares's toes warm. "Which church was that? Did Hailey tell you?"

"Man, you've got it bad. Did you just meet her, and you're already in full-on protector mode?"

"We were in Africa together." He aimed to keep that information platonic. "She's in my operational sphere, loosely attached to Iniquus. I've accounted for everyone but Hailey and Jay'la."

"The church." Cindy turned and looked in the direction of their hotel. "When it was still light out, I could see the steeple." She gestured vaguely northwest. "I think if you follow the road and maybe turn right at the first corner, that it will get you there."

And then to pad the idea that he wasn't homed in on Hailey, but the general wellbeing of those working side by side, he added, "What's Remi up to?"

"She's doing interviews. Your team's taking turns showing off dog tricks, keeping people entertained. So, that's pretty cool." Reluctantly, Cindy came up three more steps, her eyes searching around. "What do you think?"

"I think that the emergency office might be testing the systems. I contacted my TOC, and they aren't seeing anything in their satellite images that made them think that tonight's the night."

"Gut?"

"It's good we'll be gone tomorrow."

"Well shit."

"Have you been trailing Remi long?"

"First time."

"First time in a conflict area with anyone?"

"Yes." She pulled her shoulders up to her ears. Fear or cold, Ares couldn't tell. But yeah, the way she'd been acting, Ares thought she was new to this.

"You'll get your sea legs quick. Listen to Remi. Use her systems until you can personalize them. You don't need to reinvent the wheel. Remi's been through some shit." He shoved his hands deeper into his pockets. "Listen to her, pick her brain, wear out your welcome. Learn. That's my best advice."

"Are you coming down here?"

"No, I think I'll take a walk. Look around."

Cindy nodded, turned, and went back down.

Ares had jogged past the church Cindy had described, St. Olga's.

St. Olga was one of the Eastern Orthodoxy's greatest saints. She was the patron saint of defiance and vengeance. Just that piece of information told Ares much about this culture.

The Russian bear wasn't going to find gentle ewes to devour; they'd be met by snorting rams.

St. Olga's was on the reconnaissance map that Bravo had developed first thing when they'd gotten here. And if that was the right place, Bear had said that he thought it was the structure that had the best potential for safety and for risk.

The safety? It was stone construction and hundreds of years old. Solid. It had survived World War II. It had a space deep under the ground that had once been a crypt. It should be warmer there than the subway without the wind. The crypt could maintain temperatures around sixty-five. That would be better for the elderly than the subways, but the stairs down were difficult for those with mobility issues to navigate.

As his pace fell into the light jog that was Judge's preferred cadence, Ares wondered what it was like to be confined to a bed in a hospital or nursing home, or even an apartment. To have everyone fleeing underground, and unable to follow, to lie there waiting for a bomb to fall.

Mental torture.

Of course, being above ground, with all its risks, could also hold benefits.

It might be easier to dig folks out.

The team had actually considered St. Olga's as their destination should the warning sirens blare. It had been rejected as their rallying point and the subway was adopted instead. One of the concerns the team had discussed—be it with the St. Olga's or some of the other potential spaces, the school down the street, the hospital—was that down was good but *not* the best.

Once you were in St. Olga's crypt, there you were.

And if a bomb fell on the church, that would be your tomb.

The rocks would be crushing. There was no way to get out. Especially if the city was hit hard and there were many sites to search and pick through.

Also, the church might be a Russian target. It was a cultural gem. And Russia disbelieved in this culture. They'd want to take out their emblems of pride first, along with their infrastructure.

If Hailey was down there, Ares wanted her out.

Better that she would have gone to one of her six staging sites or best to the clinic that she'd helped provision, or any of the many of the buildings here had underground passages leading from one to the other.

If he couldn't convince Hailey to leave on tomorrow's train, he'd make her a map of ranked safe spaces that Bravo had put together. He'd hand them to Remi, Cindy, and Jay'la as well.

As he moved through the city toward St. Olga's, Ares was largely guided by Judge and his super-canine night vision.

Ares wouldn't use any kind of light lest he be the reason a Russian pilot tapped the button and let a bomb fly.

The people of Nezdolannyy seemed to know what to do. The streetlamps were extinguished. Not a single window lit up. No one was peeking under the curtains to see who the lone runner was, beneath them.

With the moon in its dark phase, barely a sliver peeking through a thick carpet of clouds, it was hard to imagine that bombers would be active. Of course, the pilots could depend on computer systems to put them in line with their targets.

Complacency had no space in a potential war zone.

As Ares rounded the corner to the church, the siren blasted three times, an all-clear signal.

The city lights blinked then once again illuminated the dark corners of a city holding its breath.

Ares decided to stand there out of the way, and if Hailey came up, he'd walk her back to the hotel. He wanted to talk to her about tomorrow. About the dangers of staying here in the city.

Ares had no sway with her. He was out of her life.

And it wasn't like she was an unreasonable or stubborn person.

It was just that she was in helping mode. And she might not fully grasp what even a day's delay could mean to her survival.

If the Russians swarmed these streets in a siege, the best thing would be to be caught by a bullet. What the soldiers would do to the women would be grotesque.

He *had* to convince Hailey. He just hadn't landed on a plan.

People were making their way out of the church. Looking at the sky, then moving on.

Judge whined and stomped. There she was. She and Jay'la and some man.

Like the others, Jay'la and the man looked up at the sky.

Hailey looked right at him and nodded. "See? I told you. He's here," she said.

So she'd anticipated this. Anticipated *him*.

The man nodded and strode over with his hand extended. "Hello."

"Ares, this is Fedir, he's the director of the orphanage."

"If you have a moment, may I speak with you?" Fedir asked.

Hailey blinked up at Ares some tension, some expectation, and some confidence.

Ares was going to lean into the confidence she had in him, hard.

## 19

---

Hailey

WALKING with Judge pressed between them, brushing against each other as their arms swung, Hailey and Ares followed along side by side.

"Thank you for watching out for me," she said quietly so the conversation stayed private.

"*Always*. In this lifetime, I will *always* watch out for you."

"I know." No matter what had happened to her over the last three years, Ares was her safety net. She knew that if she were falling, he'd always be there to catch her. Even if that didn't turn out to be true—if he moved on to another woman, had a family of his own—she still liked to imagine that he was out there in the world and managed to still care.

Yes, as she brushed the slush from him in the street after he'd saved the child, she had looked for a wedding ring, telling her that the flame that still flickered in her soul for him still had wick to burn.

Hailey was adjusting to this new circumstance of him beside her, flesh and blood, larger than life.

Hailey tentatively let her left hand move a little bit away from her body and didn't swing it with her step.

Ares reached for her hand, wrapping it in both of his. She'd forgotten the size and strength of his hands. The callouses that spoke of physical work. She'd forgotten how he'd held her tenderly as if she were crushable like a flower petal. "You're cold." It didn't sound like a chastisement, simply a fact about the temperature of her fingers.

And yet, she felt ashamed.

"I have been toward you, yes. I've been cold. I'm sorry."

Three years ago, after the massacre, Hailey was taken to the American military base in Djibouti, then she was evacuated to Germany, and then home.

Ares, of course, was on deployment. And as with American military personnel around the globe, he missed important things at home. He missed the next steps of her recovery. They video chatted. He called. He wrote daily. With what resources he had, he'd done his darndest.

But in their separation a cleft formed. Each day the gulf widened.

It absolutely was *not* Ares fault.

It also wasn't hers. It just…was.

Hailey grew over time to dread the fact that Ares deployment was coming to an end and that she'd see him again in person. She was terrified of memories flooding back. She felt so damned guilty about Judge. And through Judge, Ares decision to leave the Army that he loved.

The blood in Hatari washed away the shiny goodness of "them."

Or so Hailey had thought.

But here he was. And she was surviving it just fine.

She had no nightmares last night. As a matter of fact, she probably slept better than she had in the last three years.

This morning, for the first time since Hatari, she didn't wake up with dread in the pit of her stomach.

And it seemed that his showing up at St. Olga's when bombs could be dropping from the sky, and holding her hand so gently, warming her fingers, that he didn't seem to hold the last three years against her.

In the bitter night, she felt her heart thawing.

They stopped a bit away from the others while Fedir fumbled in his pocket for the keys.

Ares squeezed her hand. "Tell me."

"I was thinking of Hans Christian Anderson's Snow Queen."

He looked up at the trees that lined the walk; they were magically frosted in glittering ice. "Yes, I can see why."

"Do you remember the story?"

"Vaguely," Ares said. "My grandmother used to read that book to us on snowy days when we came in to warm up in front of the fire. Something about a boy whose heart was frozen by the Ice Queen, and then it was melted, and he was happy again."

"His frozen heart melted because his playmate Gerda found him and kissed him."

"Ah, sort of a reverse of the Brothers Grimm's Snow White."

"Hmmm. I guess."

He squeezed her hand again. "Tell me."

"You are my Gerda."

"I'm reduced to being little girl playmate?" While he sent her a scowl, his eyes twinkled.

Hailey turned and gripped both of his hands, staring into his eyes. "My heart is healing just by seeing you." She pulled their hands to her chest and stepped forward. "It's been too long. I am so—"

Before she could finish, Fedir pushed the door open and called, "There! Welcome!"

And behind them Bear shouted, "Yo!"

Ares and Hailey turned to see Bear and Truffles jogging up the road.

Hailey pulled her hands back.

"Hey, good, you're here." Ares voice was thicker and deeper than normal.

Her words had affected him. Over the years, Hailey had hurt him. Her pain and depression, her horror, had made Hailey cocoon her emotions. Made her desperate to be out helping people, trying to assuage her survivor's guilt.

His texts and messages were patient as their relationship slipped soundlessly away. He was perfect—of course he was— there and steady. Available but not pushing an agenda. But she couldn't reach for him. She'd wanted to. Desperately. She'd paced her apartment so many nights wanting to pour her heart out to him. But there was something in her psyche that *couldn't*.

How many times had she erased that unsent text?

Deleted the email?

How many nights had she sobbed into her pillow with the pain of losing Ares?

It was a self-imposed punishment for being so filled with joy on that fateful morning...

But now that he was here, every cell in her body craved the oxygen of Ares.

Like a drowning woman finding air, she wanted to gasp him in.

She had to be careful here.

*Very careful.*

The last thing she wanted to do was hurt Ares more than she already had.

"We have a new wrinkle." Ares stepped to the side aligning his body with Hailey's.

"Yeah?" Arriving beside them, Bear's gaze moved from one to the other.

"Orphans," Hailey said, turning to join the back of the group to go in.

"We're going up to that guy's apartment to have a chat about the orphans." Ares caught the door and let Hailey pass through. She was careful to avert her eyes. She felt very protective of this first step that she'd taken toward Ares. And she didn't want other people to have any weight or opinion in the matter. This was between Ares and her.

"Which orphans are these?" Bear asked. "Come back here, Truffles, leave Judge alone. He plays too rough for a princess like you."

"Please," Fedir said from the steps. "I invite you all. A little hot chocolate." He started up the creaking stairs.

Hailey and Jayla, Ares and Judge, Bear and Truffles, followed along.

There was only a short entry hall, then the staircase. This looked like it had once been a wealthy family's home that was now converted into smaller sections. From the turn of the handrail, Hailey would say eighteen hundred. Old construction. Lots of stone. That might give the residence some protection. She realized that each building she went in, she was assessing for safety.

"Did Truffles do all right in the shelter?" Ares asked.

"Lots of people loving on her, I thought I'd give her a chance to shake off their energy."

"Which was?"

"Mostly surprise. As they settled in, there were waves of

stress. We did our best to keep the kids entertained while their parents were up against the walls worrying."

They trooped up the steps. The walls were painted a strange color of greenish blue that had been graffitied in white and purple. The doors along the hallways looked battered on the outside, but when Fedir opened the door, they walked into an apartment that was calm and neat.

"My wife, Zlata." She was short and wide with gray curls poking out from beneath a headscarf. She wore loose pants with a wool dress over the top, protected by a butcher-like apron.

"She wasn't in the crypt?" Jay'la whispered as the woman bowed and waved them in.

Fedir heard her. "My parents-in-law are not able to navigate stairs anymore. She stayed to care for them. I was only over at St. Olga's to find Miss Stapleton and see if I could elicit your help."

"Hailey, please."

Jay'la greeted Zlata and asked if she spoke English. There was a quick back and forth, unintelligible to Hailey, the woman retreated to the back of the apartment.

"Zlata said that she needs to tend to her parents, but greets us, and welcomes us all. She would like us to please let her know if she can get anything for us. There are cookies and hot cocoa ready in the dining room and the bathroom is there." Jay'la pointed to a closed door.

"Ah my wife, she is so good with knowing how to do these things. Good. Good. We can sit at the dining room table, and we can discuss."

"Please, apologize to Zlata for us, we came empty-handed," Hailey said to Jay'la.

Jay'la, in turn, passed the message with her hand on her heart and a slight bow.

In this part of the world, showing up in someone's home

without a present, a bunch of flowers or some chocolates, was considered rude.

Fedir caught Hailey's gaze. "Your presence is a gift, thank you."

Hailey unzipped her coat and shucked it off, lifting it onto a hook by the door, then bent to unlace her boots to leave them in the plastic tray, moving out of the way for others, padding into the living area in her pink socks with unicorns, a gift from her six-year-old niece.

Bear and Ares watched, then followed suit.

Fedir smiled at their care. "Thank you. And if you don't mind," Fedir moved toward his TV, "I'll just put the news on in the background. I would like an explanation of the air-raid siren." He pulled his cell phone from his pocket. "And if you would please make yourselves comfortable at the table, and help yourself to my wife's refreshments, I will just call the orphanage and check."

Instead of moving to the dining room, the five gathered in a semi-circle around the television. Jay'la quietly translated. "The unidentified planes flew into Nezdolannyy airspace. The military scrambled. The planes turned and returned to Russia. This provocation should be condemned by our allies and free countries around the world."

The image changed to that of two women, one looked like a reporter, polished and upright. The other looked like she had walked in from off the street, a bit windblown and off kilter. "This was a good opportunity to practice. Citizens of Nezdolannyy must know where shelters are to be found." Jay'la translated the news anchor. "It is imperative to make plans and develop their supplies. Tonight, we are announcing a project that will help our countrymen to remain safe." She held a hand out to the woman with the hat-crushed hair.

"Yes," Jay'la translated. "I am a software engineer. My senior team with homeland security has been working with a local American company developing the software for such a case." She held up her cell phone.

"American software? Does this have to do with AgilitiCorp?" Bear asked.

"They didn't say. Only 'American," Jay'la said. Then pointed to the TV to indicate she needed to listen. She translated, "This is available to you at the app stores for free. It asks for the name of the closest city. Then, in case of an air-siren, as the emergency manager hits the button for your safety siren, they will also press the button to push the warning to your phone. Right now, you might see either of two colors. Our engineers are working to develop two more. If the screen glows red you must seek shelter. When there is an all clear, this will glow green. While those in the city proper will be able to hear the sirens, as you move farther out to the countryside, this will not be the case."

"And the other two that you're developing?" the news anchor asked.

"Yes." The woman's face flushed a deep red. "Orange will indicate that we are under a chemical attack. Purple will indicate a nuclear attack."

"Nuclear," the anchor whispered. "Terrifying." When she seemed to realize what she'd said on national television, her voice changed to crisp and pragmatic. "Yes. Best to be prepared. Our government is working to safeguard our citizens."

"Ah, and to that end," Fedir said, pressing the button to turn off the TV, "I should like to talk to you about our orphans."

Ares pulled out his phone. "Fedir, if it's okay with you, I'm going to loop in the head of tactical logistics. On this mission, she's the one who has the decision-making authority."

## 20

Ares

WITH HIS PHONE propped up so that Kiyana via secured video app could be involved in the explanation of the orphans' plight, Fedir began, "There are many orphanages in Ukraine. You see, many of the children living in orphanages in my country have parents. They're simply unable to care for them. Amongst the other orphanages, my facility is specialized."

Kiyana leaned in. "Tell me about that."

Jay'la sat ready if translation was needed.

The dogs lay on their handlers' socked feet under the table that was covered first in a traditional cloth, then topped with thick, clear plastic to keep it clean.

Hailey blew on her hot chocolate, her pad and pen, pulled from her leg bag, were at the ready for notes. Her phone rested on her lap open to her contacts page.

"Many of the children have disabilities that the parents simply can't navigate. Especially those who are further out in the countryside without proper utilities running to their houses, difficulties getting their children the day-to-day care, physical therapy, speech therapy and the like, that the children need to have their best life."

"Who has custody?" Kiyana asked.

"Which means?" Fedir shifted toward Jay'la.

"Who has the legal authority to make decisions about these children?" Hailey said.

"We do." Fedir put his hand on his chest. "The parents, they love their children and visit, but they do not have the 'custody'. That belongs to the city. And I, as the director, have the parental rights to make decisions about these children. They are a segment of our most vulnerable population. There are other orphanages where the children are able to walk without walkers or to need life-saving medicines, those who can go into the shelters with ease and stay there for days if necessary. This simply is not true for my children. This is why I must get them out of the country until Russia is overcome."

"I see," Kiyana said. "How many children are we talking about?"

"One hundred and twelve special needs children aged three to eighteen."

Kiyana nodded as she jotted that down. "How many are ambulatory?"

"That is a criterion." He paused and looked at Hailey.

"Yes, criterion, a factor, a reason." She made sure that that was the word Fedir wanted.

Fedir nodded. "For our orphanage, they must be able to walk, though many of them use assistive devices to do so. We can put the youngest in carriages. Our older children can push them and help. Some of them are healthy enough to help. Just simply dependent on medications. We have several type one diabetics, we have several with celiac disease, others who are recovering from cancers, you see." He sounded like he was trying to sell them on the idea that this was going to be okay. Easy.

It wouldn't be.

"The carriages we use are…hmmm how do you say. They are the car seats that snap into a wheelbase?"

"These are the three-year-olds who need the carriages?" Kiyana asked. "I'm back to your children's ability to walk to, for example, use the bathrooms on the train."

"Those not yet in school we use the carriages. Twenty are under six. They can all go into a train bathroom."

Kiyana had her head down and was silently searching. "I'm looking at the train schematics. We would need an additional three seating cars to accommodate the added passengers." She leaned back, her head just in view on the cell phone screen. "Ben, before you head out," she called to someone off screen. "I need you to do me a favor. Can you figure out what it would take to put another three seating cars onto tomorrow's train? Thank you. Jerry, I need you to reach out to our contacts in immigration and find out what they would need in terms of paperwork for an emergency extraction of—" Her face came back into focus. "What is your caregiver to student ratio?"

"Four students to one adult," Fedir said, rubbing his hands together nervously.

"You have twenty-eight adults willing to go?" she clarified.

"Twenty-seven. I surveyed my staff and twenty-seven will go. I will be staying. But my co-director will be there. She has all of the legal authority that I do."

"What about your staff's families?" Ares asked.

"No. They stay. We think we will leave for the safety of the children. And we will regain our families after the threat goes away."

"One thirty-nine added people. Yes, three passenger cars."

She turned her face back to the camera. "Fedir, if we can get this in place, the train is arriving at sixteen o'clock and leaving at sixteen forty." Ukraine, like most of Europe, used the twenty-four-hour clock. "Our mission is to bring AgilitiCorp out of the area. We will not be able to postpone a day or even push that time frame. *If* we were able to get the cars attached in Romania, *if* we were able to meet the criteria for the Romanian government to bring you over the border, *if* we can jump through the legal and logistical hoops, it would be Iniquus's honor to be of aid. But there is a lot to put in place to move that many people in short order."

Fedir nodded in quick nervous bobs.

"The children have luggage, for example?" Kiyana asked.

"No. They have their school backpacks. We can put their medications and hygiene items in there. Maybe give them some garbage bags to put some changes of clothes. They do not have much."

"Hailey, what are your thoughts?" Kiyana asked.

"A hundred and twelve are a lot of children to keep track of. In these types of extractions, there is always the fear of trafficking. I have two ways that WorldCares could assist with that. One, I have set up a clinic in one of the city-center high rises. There, I have hospital wrist bands." She opened her hand toward Fedir. "I mentioned these at the church meeting. As they're waterproof and difficult to remove, as a minimum, it could identify the child, their birthday, blood type, and number that I can get set up as a secure portal that includes the children's medical histories that can be searched if properly credentialed authorities reach out to WorldCares. Also, we have allergy and medication bands. Should something happen that the children are separated from their care-givers, or they need medical interventions en route these might prove helpful."

"Yes, thank you, Hailey," Kiyana said.

"The other thing that I can offer," Hailey said. "I saw yesterday, as people were loading onto the train, that Iniquus provided those that are leaving with a tracking necklace."

"Correct," Kiyana said. "But those were issued in advance, and I haven't got the resources to provide that."

"Neither does WorldCares," Hailey said. "But thinking outside of the box, quite literally." She smiled. "When I sent the various boxes in to Nezdolannyy, I included tracking pods. While they aren't on necklaces, and frankly, I don't think I'd encourage them to be on the children as a necklace. However, I do have slender zip-ties. They could be added, as you all see fit, to the children's shoelaces or backpacks."

"Shoelaces," Ares said.

"Backpacks are easily separated from the child or left behind," Bear added.

Ares swiveled to face Hailey. "Tell me about those trackers. Who has access to that information?"

"I do. It's an encrypted database within the WorldCares server. We deal with all kinds of highly sensitive information. We're equipped to deal with that. To access the specific child's specific information, the request would have to be made by someone with a credential and a reason, then my NGO would share the file. A doctor in a hospital setting, for example. It sounds like red tape. But the process is quite streamlined. This is what we do. We know minutes can mean lives."

"Four to one ratio," Kiyana said, "That's probably not enough. With the Russian fly over tonight, that complicates things. Bravo is cleared to go into hazardous areas as well as militarized zones. My logistics staff are required to stay outside of these areas. I can't send support on the train and comply with Iniquus standards."

"Bravo will be on board. We can help. That's plus seven. Six. Goose will be tending the K9s." He turned to Hailey. "If Hailey and Jay'la would be willing to help these high-risk orphans, that would be two more sets of eyes and hands. An additional eight adults." Okay, that wasn't entirely cool on his part. He'd just put Hailey in a bad place, having to make a decision. Outside, she'd offered him a glimmer of hope. He may have extinguished it by advocating for his own position—Hailey needed to be on that train getting out.

In a perfect world, she'd leave, and they could reboot.

This was *far* from a perfect world.

Bottom line? He didn't give a flaming shit. He needed Hailey out. Safe. And he needed her out *tomorrow*.

Bravo's commander, Juan, had been damned clear on his call from D.C. yesterday, Iniquus was pressed up against the edges on this mission.

While Juan and Kiyana were moving forward as planned, they were only about seventy percent sure that the train would run tomorrow.

The Romanian engineers had already drawn the line. They would not be driving their trains into a war zone.

The moment a Russian boot stepped over the border; the contracts were severed.

Bravo would be on their own getting this last group out.

Logistics had already sent the contingency plans to Ares.

He hadn't looked them over, yet. He was going to gather Bravo tonight to start weeding through and making decisions based on what they'd seen here on the ground.

"All right," Kiyana said, "this is the plan. It's late, and I'm not sure what I can affect tonight as everyone's gone home for the day and offices are locked up. However, I will work the phones. Thus far, my counterparts in Romania have been amazing. This, however, might not be within their sphere of influence. I don't know. We'll have to see. But for now, let's act as if. Hailey, if you would please follow through with gathering the equipment needed. This is what I need to have in place: One, Hailey if you can get the children's medical information loaded into the World-Cares site, get the children's identification numbers, initials and last names, blood type, allergies, and any imminently dangerous conditions, like the type one diabetes, onto the armbands. Two. For Iniquus to transport the children and the staff, we need security checks on the adults. Fedir, I'm sure that's something that the orphanage requires."

"Yes, I have all of the social services and police reports," Fedir said.

"We'll need that. Ares, if you would please enter that into the evacuation system that will start the ball rolling. I'd like to see us implement the trackers that Hailey offered. Those, too, need to be loaded into our control system, so that they can be tracked into Romania to their final destination. Where that is will be something I need to discuss with my counterparts here. Right now, from my experience with boots on the ground, I can almost guarantee that the children will be routed to a different country until this is resolved."

"I've got it handled," Ares said.

"From there," Kiyana continued, "I suggest that you all get a little shuteye. Fedir, in the morning Bravo team needs to take pictures, front and profile for our system, that should be quickly accomplished if the children's information and tracking numbers are all ready to go. The children at that point can have their wrist bands put on, the trackers attached to their shoes. Move in groups so that while some children are going through intake, others are packing their backpacks and whatever bags you can scrounge at this point."

"Yes, that can be done."

"Hailey, as this is your bailiwick, and I know you have your own ongoing and very important projects underway, but your expertise would be appreciated should you have the time."

"I'll make it work," Hailey said.

"Good luck then, let's see what we can get done before that sixteen o'clock train." The screen went black.

As they stood to leave, Hailey asked Fedir, "You've decided not to go with the children? Will you try to evacuate to the countryside if the Russians begin bombing?" With Ares holding her elbow, she stepped into her boot and tied the laces.

"My parents-in-law will not leave this apartment. My wife will not leave her parents. I will not leave my family. I will pick up arms to defend them and my country."

The man was in his late sixties, arthritic and stooped, but there was conviction in his eyes.

Russia had no idea what they'd be coming up against.

## 21

Hailey

Using the van borrowed from a friend of Fedir's, Ares had accompanied Hailey to collect the equipment.

They'd driven to the orphanage where they'd found Bravo, with their dogs sprawled and sleeping around the room, was reviewing the security documents, and adding the names to their database.

The building was large with dorms and school rooms in one wing, the other wing had the kitchen and dining hall, and offices on the bottom level. They were told the children had recreation spaces, upstairs.

Everything seemed clean and comfortable if sparse and worn.

Once Hailey and Ares were on scene, they broke into task groups and worked efficiently to process the data and prepare the tracking pods and bands for each child, prepping if they got the green light.

Now, it was two in the morning.

Hailey was cross-eyed with fatigue.

"The children wake up each morning at six to get cleaned up and fed," Fedir said as they gathered their coats to leave.

"What do you think is best, Fedir, as far as the morning goes?" Hailey tugged her hair from inside her coat, then zipped it closed.

"The dorm monitors said the children are having a hard time sleeping, frightened as they were by the sirens. Perhaps we let them wake up and start their routine as normal with dressing and breakfast. If you come at seven thirty, I think we can start. Packing them will take little time. They haven't much to take with them. And the rest, well you all have that organized and ready. We are good. We just wait for word from your people."

Ares drove Bravo and Jay'la back to the hotel. Hailey, Judge, and Fedir stayed in the van to drive Fedir back to his apartment building, where Ares handed back the keys for his friend.

After saying their good-byes and admonishing Fedir to get some rest, Judge, Ares, and Hailey walked the short distance toward the hotel.

"He's getting tired," Hailey nodded toward Judge.

"Long day. It means a lot of snoring tonight."

They let the silence and exhaustion wrap them in a blanket as they walked beneath the dim illumination of the streetlamps, the streets so quiet that their boots echoed with each step. The snow fell lightly on their shoulders.

As they approached the hotel, she stopped.

"Hailey?"

Turning to Ares, Hailey laid her hands on his chest, standing toe to toe.

She didn't know how to go forward; all she knew was that she didn't want to step back. She wanted to keep that shard of ice in her heart melting away.

Ares waited for her to speak with that patient curiosity that she'd always found endearing about him.

"I remember us."

He held his breath.

"I was hoping you'd kiss me," she admitted.

Ares cupped her face in his palms, letting his thumbs brush over her cheeks. He looked deeply into her eyes as she tipped her head back. Blinking against the snow, she let her lashes rest on her cheek. Finally, the soft pressure of Ares's lips.

He kissed her and pulled away.

When she opened her eyes again, he'd rolled his lips in and was rubbing them against each other. "Electricity," he said.

"We still sizzle and snap, don't we? Even when the kiss is gentle."

He wrapped her in his arms. "What do you want to do, Hailey?"

"There's not a lot of time before we need to be back at the orphanage. Would it be okay if I came to your room? I... Could I rest in your room with you?"

Without another word, they headed through the doors into the lobby, with Ares's protective arm around her.

As they headed toward the elevator, Hailey thought about Remi and all her brushes with death and horror. Yet, she focused on that Thich Nhat Hanh quote, "The seed of suffering in you may be strong, but don't wait until you have no more suffering before allowing yourself to be happy." Remi had taken that to heart.

She'd forged a relationship with T-Rex.

And even though the two were often on other sides of the world, they'd found happiness in their marriage.

Truth was, Remi was happier than Hailey had ever remembered her being.

It was possible to allow that.

No amount of angst on Hailey's part would bring back her friends.

Their stories had a beginning, a middle, and an end. A horrific end. But an end, nonetheless.

Living miserably, had that helped anyone?

No.

"Don't wait until you have no more suffering before allowing yourself to be happy." That was a radical idea to Hailey. She'd have to spend some time thinking about it.

But one thing she decided in the here and now was that she wasn't going to let these next four hours go to waste.

She was going to embrace them.

Twist the knob, let the door open, and see...just see. No agenda. No end goal. Just four hours with the man that she'd loved and ached for all these years.

"Hailey, I need to take a quick shower. Do you want to go first?" he offered.

"No, thank you. You go ahead. I'm going to hang out with Judge."

"All right then. Make yourself at home." He moved into the bathroom but left the door ajar.

After a moment, the water was running.

Ares would be in there, naked and soapy. Hailey had to stop herself from going in to watch him. That seemed...too sudden. But that didn't stop the movie that was playing in Hailey's mind.

She pulled off her boots and socks and stuck them in the corner. "Can I borrow a t-shirt?" she called out.

"Top drawer."

When she tugged the knob, Hailey found a pair of sweats and a t-shirt neatly folded. It was what he liked to wear to bed on chilly nights. She pulled them from the drawer, taking the bottoms to the bathroom. Holding them in her hand she stuck them through the crack in the door. "Do you want these?" She waggled them.

"I was going to put on a uniform. But if those are okay with you, yes."

She couldn't quite reach the sink from outside the room, so she gave them a gentle toss onto the vanity.

Peeling off her own clothes, she tugged the shirt over her head.

Ares's t-shirts were huge on her. The short sleeves fell past her elbows, the hem came to her knees. She checked herself in the mirror, and yes, her nipples jutted out with anticipation.

*You can't blame a girl. Ares is mere feet away and naked.* And Hailey's body remembered.

He strode into the room, rubbing a towel over his hair.

His sweatpants rode low on his hips. His goody trail looked delicious. "Find everything you needed?"

Hailey just stood there. This was a lot. *He* was a lot.

Judge was on the carpet lying in a little beam of light from the nightstand, belly up.

Hailey followed Ares's gaze. "He's worn out, poor guy. And as predicted, snoring."

"Me, too. Worn out that is. I don't think I snore. At least, Judge has never complained about it." Ares pulled the comforter off the bed. Hailey didn't like to touch comforters in hotel rooms. He moved it over to the luggage rack. He must have remembered.

Hailey crawled onto the bed, tugging the shirt low, so she didn't flash Ares.

The room was overly warm, or maybe it was just her system. She laid on top of the blanket, her arm under the pillow, curling on her side.

Ares laid down next to her. "I'm setting the alarm for six." He tapped at his phone then set it on the nightstand. "Lights off or on?"

212 | FIONA QUINN

"On for now."

Ares rolled onto his side facing her and reached for Hailey's hand. "Good?"

"I'm a little wigged out to be honest. I don't want to be here."

Ares looked at the door and sent a questioning glance back her way.

"I don't mean *here* here. I want to be here, or I'd leave. I mean in Nezdolannyy."

"Where are you in your project? When were you and Jay'la heading out?"

"The six subterranean stations are fine. The clinic, as you saw when we went to pick up the bands, has a ways to go. They can take people in now. But in terms of providing medical care, I think that's another three days or so."

"I want you on that train tomorrow."

She bit down hard.

"Seriously."

"Personally?" Hailey asked.

"Yes. Extremely personally. To the point that if you don't get on that train tomorrow, I won't either."

"To save me again?"

"As many times as you need in this lifetime."

She interlaced her fingers with his. "I was shocked to see you here."

"I was lying in the streets when you happened onto the scene, I can see why that would be shocking."

"You weren't."

"Shocked to see you? No. I knew you were here."

"Iniquus told you? How would they know to do that?" She pulled his hand, and he scooted a bit closer to her.

"They didn't. I saw you when I was standing on the bridge."

"Ah." Hailey pivoted and threw her legs over his hips. "Is this okay with you?"

"A little closer." He tugged at her hand until he was lying on his side, and she was able to put her feet on the mattress behind him. This was how they used to like to lay and chat back in the day. It was relaxing for her. She pulled a pillow under her head, tipping her head up enough that she could see his face while they talked. His dick was hard against her thigh.

Those sweatpants were the only thing between them.

"We did some good today," Ares said, his hand painted over her knee and down her leg and back again.

It felt so damned good. Being here with him was so *damned* good. "I hope your logistics folks figure this out and all of our prep tonight wasn't in vain."

"Kiyana didn't get to her position because she takes no for an answer."

Hailey laughed. "Yeah, I picked up on that when I was trying to arrange my deliveries down from Poland. I'm good at what I do." Hailey yawned long and loud behind her fist. "She's fabulous."

"If you want to sleep, Hailey, I'll rub your back and help you relax."

Hailey stalled answering. Sleep was not what her body was humming for.

"It's going to be a lot of moving parts tomorrow." She ventured. "Sleep would help keep my mind clear."

He nodded and started to turn, reaching out for the light.

Hailey caught his hand. "It's going to take more than a back-rub, though, for me to relieve my stress and wind down."

He tipped his head.

"If you wanted to."

He said nothing.

"It's okay if you don't." Wow, that thought hurt, that he'd turn her down.

He didn't say anything, but his eyes were burning coals. And his cock pulsed against her thigh.

"Do you remember my little hut?" Hailey asked. "The mosquito netting was romantic, I thought. Do you remember how we used to lay like this and how we'd have slow sex? Would you…could…is that something…?"

He pulled her hand to his lips. "Hailey, I don't have a condom with me. But if an orgasm would help, we can do other things. I could hold you while you masturbate, or I could do it for you with my hand or mouth."

Oh, *yes* he could. Ares had a magic tongue. The memory made her squirm.

"You know Remi would have one in her survival bag," Hailey said. "If I were certain she was in her room, I'd go bang on her door."

Ares snapped his fingers. "Ha!" He slid his arm under Hailey's knees and lifted her legs, then rolled off the bed.

He strode to the bathroom, his cock pointing the way. When he came back, he was naked with a foil square in his hand. "After Remi showed us her EDC." He used the initials for every day carry. "We all started putting an unlubricated condom in our own kits. Remi gets flowers for this." He popped his brows then sent her a grin.

Hailey laughed. "She'd want an explanation. Maybe we just keep this to ourselves."

The laughter fell off Ares's face. He stilled and braced. The mood changed.

He turned to the nightstand and laid the condom next to his phone.

"What's happening here?" he asked, finding his place exactly where he'd been before his "ah-ha! I do have a condom" moment. Only thoroughly naked and pressing up against her bottom. "Hailey, I love you. There is nothing more I want than to be inside you, bringing you pleasure. But…these last three years have been hell on me, I'm not going to lie."

"I'm sorry," she exhaled, then glanced toward the door. "I can leave." She held her eyes wide and unblinking. The last thing she wanted was to go. And it had nothing to do with having an orgasm so she could sleep. Or having an orgasm at all. It had to do with, "I still love you," she whispered.

"Same." He reached his free hand to lift a strand of her hair and twiddled it between his fingers. "But out of self-preservation, I think it would be a bad idea for me to make love to you, thinking that it meant we have a tomorrow. Slow?"

"No." She shook her head against the pillow.

"No, then." He gave her a tight smile. "Okay." Grief replaced the ardor in his eyes.

"No, *not* slow." She shifted around agitatedly. "*No*. I am not going to wait to feel safe and sane and well before I allow myself to be happy, damn it!" She shoved her elbows into the bed to prop herself up. Hailey looked at him through the haze of tears. She was so *pissed* in that moment at the three years of happy that were robbed from her by those guerillas. Those *dead* guerillas whose rampage was *still* causing destruction. "No, I'm not going to hold your affection hostage on the off chance that I can be brave. I *can be* brave."

"What?"

"Nothing." She all but yelled, thoroughly vexed. "Heath Sterling, put that condom on your dick. Put your dick inside my body. And don't you *ever* ask me to go slow with my feelings for you again, do you hear me?"

Ares threw his head back and laughed, long, and hard. "There's my Hailey!" He rolled back over, crushing her into his arms and kissing her hard. "My god, but I've missed that mouth of yours."

"Ares?" She lifted her brows. "The condom?"

## 22

Hailey

HAILEY CURLED ONTO ARES. He was holding her hand over his heart. The sweat that had slicked his skin had evaporated, and he had fallen into a post coital sleep.

Hailey had friends who hated how orgasms put their partners into a near-coma. They were awake and wanting bonding time. Like them, Hailey found that sleep evaded her right after sex. Some throwback, she'd read somewhere, to caveman days when this would be her genetically provided opportunity to escape into the night.

Hailey had zero desire to leave Ares's arms.

And she'd never been jealous of this sleep.

In some ways, it was a sense of pride. Like, look how being with me destressed my man.

Not that Hailey was feeling stress at the moment, either.

Ares had worked all of that out of her system, as usual.

218 | FIONA QUINN

Yes, this was the time Hailey liked to have all to herself. She could stare at his face, and glide her hands over his muscles, she could think "he's mine, I am one lucky girl" thoughts. She could dream of their future.

She could just be.

For all the meditation that everyone kept encouraging since Hatari, Hailey had never felt good at using her breath to reach for calm. Possibly because she'd never used her breath to reach anything like this state of peace. This was as close to Nirvana as Hailey thought she could attain in this lifetime.

She rolled her head to press a kiss onto Ares's chest, leaving her lips there, she inhaled his clean scent. She brought her hand up and traced his tightly clipped beard. He hadn't had this in Africa. She liked it.

As she rubbed her fingers through his whiskers, Ares reached for her hand, kissed it, and brought it back to his heart. "Tickles," he murmured.

Hailey smiled.

On the floor beside the bed, Judge sounded like a freight train with his snores. Every once in a while, he'd wake himself, adjust his position, and start up again.

Could anything be more wonderful that this moment in—

Hailey jumped with the sudden blare of air-raid sirens.

Ares was instantly awake, reaching for the lamp. "Again?" He seemed more put out that the sirens had awoken him than to actually be afraid of what they could mean.

She'd messed up.

Hailey had let herself push past her strict limit of contentment and had imagined herself happy, joyful even.

That endangered everyone.

Her whole body shook.

"Come on, Hailey. We're okay. We have a minute. Get dressed. The shelter is right across the street."

Hailey shook off her first knee-jerk reaction. That magical thinking of hers, that somehow the bad things lurked in the shadows, waiting for her smiles, feeding off her joy to give evil power was really not rational. Or even sane. Hailey remembered the conversation she'd had with Ares about imposter syndrome. This was really the same thing, right? She didn't belong here in this relationship. She didn't qualify for happiness. "Shut up, Sammy Shithead," she mouthed, dragging on the clothes she'd left on his low boy, shoving her feet into her boots.

"Calm, Hailey. That air raid siren covers the whole region."

"I'm doing my best. It's unnerving." She picked up her phone, swiped the air-raid app. It glowed bright red. "This is why Remi sleeps with her shoes on and a survival bag around her waist. I bet she has her clothes in a bag on the end of her bed. She hears the siren and scoots out the door."

"After Beirut," Ares had his head tucked down as he tied his boots, "I'd imagine she was one of the first down in the subway system." He looked up. "Ready?"

With Judge on a lead, they gripped hands as they made their way down the hall.

Hailey stopped at the elevator to wait for a car with the others who were tumbling from their rooms. Ares dragged at her hand and headed them to the stairs.

Yeah, he was right. The stairs in an emergency.

"If a bomb falls or a Russian boot hits the soil, the train isn't coming. We'll be on our own to get the client out," he said as if to himself. "So I damned well hope this is another harassing fly over."

"Clients not orphans?" Hailey was pushing to keep up with Ares long stride. For every two steps he took, she had to take three. Normally, he adjusted his gait to match hers, but his hand was tugging her along. He meant for them to be covering the distance just shy of a jog.

Judge was excited by all this activity. He'd gone from snores to go-mode in the blink of an eye.

"That's not part of the plan." The stairwell door kachunked as Ares pressed the bar handle. "But once I've done my job. And we know what the ongoing situation is, I'll do my best to help them, Hailey." He stopped for a moment to catch her gaze. "I promise."

**23**

Ares

SHOWING up in coats slung on over pajamas, kids crying sleepily on their parents' shoulders, the people slogged down the steps of the subway for the second time in twelve hours.

There was a single toilet that had been there for the subway workers, there was now a long line. They were allowing the children, the pregnant, and the elderly to the front.

There was a lone light on over by the ticket booth. It had an electrical strip and people gathered patiently as cell phones were charged.

A few families set up pop up tents along the wall. They must have gone home after the earlier siren and made plans.

The tents would help cut the wind, anyway. And give them a bit of privacy if they needed to change, or just a safe cocoon for their kids. A way to keep their pets with the family.

In front of the tents, shoes lined up neatly outside the zippered door

Around them, some held up blankets while others changed their clothes, having arrived in pajamas and winter coats.

An elderly man sat in his folding chair, propped up against a column, a cat wrapping his neck and a hand crocheted afghan tucked around them. His head was tipped back as he snored. Asleep already. The noise didn't seem to bother him.

Ares guided them to a wall that had a post in front. He figured it would give them some protection from people accidently trodding on them, stepping on Judge's tail.

He spread the blanket he'd grabbed on their way out.

Hailey said it was best to let everyone get down, stake out a spot, and take a breath before they started checking on people to see if they could lend a hand.

Remi wandered over.

"You're not taping?" Hailey asked. "Join us." She patted the comforter.

Remi plopped down beside them, pulling her feet up to her hips and leaning back against the cold subway wall. "Not much different than the first air-raid siren. I need a new angle."

"I've got one," Ares threw out casually. "Orphans."

Remi rested her cheek on her knee. "Yeah, I talked to Mace about that when he was out letting Diesel go to the bathroom."

"You need to follow that story," Ares pressed. "You started with taping us, might as well let that story have a beginning, a middle, and an end. The orphans are a good plot twist."

Remi lifted a brow. "You got the go ahead from the Romanian government?"

"Not yet. Kiyana was working the phones."

Remi was silent.

"Look, Remi. Serious here, okay?" Ares said. "It's going to be a siege. You need to get out or you won't be reporting the story, you'll be the story like that murdered reporter in Israel that Auralia is investigating."

Remi turned so her forehead rested on her knees and she was looking down at her hips. "Give me a few minutes to process that thought."

Not good enough. One, he felt like Remi was a friend. And despite her job, or maybe because of her job, she needed to leave. Two, and probably of equal importance, if Remi and Cindy were leaving, Ares had a better chance of getting Hailey to leave with the train and not wait an extra day or two while she finished her work.

"You need to get out." He pointed his finger for emphasis. "Remi, I'm talking to you."

She turned her head to look at him.

"They come for the press first. I know you know, but I'm stating it again so you can hear my argument. They'll come for the press first. It will be imperative to Russia that they maintain control of the narrative. They've been working on this for decades. They have control of the airwaves. Anyone who says anything about this being a war—not even saying that they stand against the aggression—just telling the truth will go against Russia's narrative. If you tell the truth, they will hunt for you, and they will kill you to shut you up and to frighten others away."

Hailey pressed into him harder.

Judge crawled from between Ares's legs and went to sit on Hailey's lap, draping his jowls over Hailey's head. She looked like a Davy crocket with a dog for a hat instead of a racoon. Comical, yes, but not the time for humor. Ares needed to keep the pedal down on his pressure campaign to save Remi's life.

"Yeah, I hear you," Remi said. "I was watching a newsfeed in my room, waiting for my editor to call me back. A Russian woman was arrested for standing up with a blank poster. A white piece of cardboard, no symbol, no color, no words. She was dragged to the police van, and she's disappeared. No one knows what's happened to her. Her family, her lawyers. She's gone."

"Right. Here's how I see what happens with that," Ares said. "Any images that come out of this area will be discounted as fakes. False flags. Paid crisis actors. They will say that America wants more power, and this is a power grab. They will say that NATO is creating the fakes to make Russia and her people look bad. That the images are doctored, altered and untrue. It will get harder for them to maintain this. They'll crack down. How?" Ares asked rhetorically. "They will stop social media, and they'll hunt for the journalists who are gathering the pictures."

"Mores the better that I should be here, Ares, and quite frankly, thank you for everything but that's the extent of your responsibility for me."

"I'm just saying get on the train today with the orphans and finish the story, then make a decision. Stay outside the perimeter of any besieged city. You can look in and report."

"No, I can't."

"Think. Hunted, raped, shot, thrown into a shallow grave, how will that serve anyone?" He scratched at his forehead. "Another thing you have to take into consideration is Cindy."

"How's that?"

"This is her first gig she told me."

"She's a seasoned videographer. She survived getting shot at the protests last summer."

"Protests aren't war. Rubber bullets not hollow point. She has no skills. You need to leave with Hailey."

"Wait, leave with Hailey? Hailey isn't going anywhere. Hailey needs to be here serving these people as things go from bad to worse. Hailey has the expertise." Hailey blinked her lashes. "And why am I speaking in the third person?"

"You most certainly do not have the expertise for this Hailey," Remi said.

*Thank you, Remi!*

"My supplies…"

"Are not connected to you," Remi said. "They have the supplies, they have your schematics, let that be enough. You'll become a liability when this city is besieged."

"You don't know that's going to happen." Hailey wiped her forehead, then reaching for Judge's collar. "Judge, you're drooling in my hair."

"What am I?" Ares asked.

"A dog handler," Hailey said.

"Okay, fair enough. I am a K9 handler, but I was also a Green Beret. I spent my time teaching militaries how to defend themselves. We got a briefing on this area before we came. I saw the images of the movement of their military. The Russians are poised to quickly encircle this city. With the rails running east to west, they can get on site and shut down the road systems in twelve hours, quicker if they've trained specifically for that move. Why this city? They need it for several reasons. The most benign is that it's the jumping off place to take the coast and give access to their ships."

"And the not benign ones?" Remi asked.

"Psychology."

"You're going to have to be more specific."

"The Russians use horror as a tactic of war." He watched the blood drain from Remi and Hailey's faces. He hated to give voice to this—but this was the reality; it had to be faced head on. "Remi, you and I talked about Syria. This is going to be worse. Why? Because when people look at pictures of Syria, it's hard for them to understand. The location looks like something out of a space movie about other worlds. The people's clothing and speech are unrelatable to the average westerner. When people who speak like you do, who look like you do, who have the same kinds of clothes and houses and experiences as you do are attacked, it feels

226 | FIONA QUINN

more personal. That's what I've observed in my conversation with folks. Now, when these people are viciously attacked, when the assaults are inhuman, it will be terrifying. Terror saps will—emotional and physical. Russia will want this over quickly, in a matter of days."

"How many days do you think they're aiming for?" Remi asked.

"What I think they're projecting in taking the entire country? A hundred hours."

"That's oddly specific." Remi curled her lips until deep lines formed from nostril to chin.

"It's the amount of time of the ground war in Desert Storm. I can see how the Russians, after their disastrous time in Afghanistan, might want to meet or beat that time frame. A source of strength. Shock and awe."

"Do you think they have the capacity?"

"It all depends on what the citizens here decide is right for them. If they stand and fight the West will stand with them. If they don't give a good showing, we will turn a blind eye. Without the West helping, no matter how brave they are, they can't win."

"That's harsh," Hailey said.

"We're talking about realities here. I'm calling it like I see it."

"This will be over in a hundred hours?" Hailey asked.

"No."

Hailey gripped at his arm. "But you said…"

"That will be the goal. If the citizens stand up the way I believe they will, the Russians will have a hard time of it. Their equipment is crap. They put a lot of their security resources into psychological warfare and propaganda. They were working under the idea that the only war they needed to prepare for was a nuclear war."

"Nuclear," Hailey exhaled. "Do you think they might use a nuclear bomb?"

"I have no idea. No one does. And if the order was issued, would it be carried out? I don't know that either. But if the Russian president is cornered, all bets are off.

Hailey started crying. The tears fell silently as her whole body shook.

Remi filled her cheeks with air and blew out slowly.

"There are too many variables to go through and that's not the point. The point is, the Russians aren't going to get what they want in the way they want it. They will try to squash any reporting out of the area so their citizens only hear the propaganda stations.

"There you are." Cindy came over.

"Plenty of room on the comforter. Sit," Hailey said. "Have you seen Jay'la?"

Cindy plunked down then craned around the column, looking toward the dark of the tunnel, then tipped her ear that way. "Down there. She's chatting with some of the local men. Seems they're getting a team together to prepare Molotov cocktails." She looked pointedly at Ares. "They know you're here and they're going to ask you some advice on how to use them effectively."

"All right."

Remi looked at Cindy and winked. "You know what we need to do to distract these people? Get Bravo dancing."

Remi obviously wanted to change the subject.

"The dog tricks yesterday kept everyone happy," Cindy said, turning to Hailey. "Bravo did two dances with the dogs in the choreography. It was awesome." She looked at her watch. "Given the time, we could pretend the nightclubs haven't shut for the night. Crank up some music on someone's phone. Bravo dancing would change the mood. It would change mine. I'd like to see Bear bust a move."

"What's that?" Hailey asked.

"Rule of thumb," Remi said, "distractions are good, otherwise people sit around looking at their belly lint and thinking morbid thoughts. On disaster sites, though, I bet everyone is so exhausted from trying to survive, they just work, eat, and sleep. But in war zones, when nothing's happening, it can get pretty bad when people catastrophize, imagining the worst possible outcomes." Remi canted her head. "You've seen Ares dance, haven't you?"

Hailey sent Ares a bemused look.

To be honest, after the shit he'd just handed these two women, it wasn't bad to give them a reprieve so their brains could sort through it, process.

The look in Remi's eyes said she was doing just that, processing, but she said, "True story, this man can dance. Did you take dance classes as a boy?"

"Not as a boy, but at Cerberus."

"Dog handling and dance?" Cindy shifted around and sat cross-legged. "Is there a correlation?"

"Cerberus Team Alpha started it and the training sifted over to Team Bravo with time."

"Dancing?" Hailey wriggled her fingers in Judge's fur as he splayed across her thighs.

"Sure. I like most things athletic, and it's a good challenge. Alpha is led by a guy named Ridge. He came to Iniquus by way of Delta Force."

"Okay." Cindy posted her elbows on her knees, her chin in her hands.

"One of the habits that started way back at the beginning of Delta Force as a military experiment was that they'd end the day with a game of volleyball."

"For a specific reason? Building glute muscles from jumping?"

"Right, but team cohesion, fun, blow off steam. It's a good habit."

"And the dancing?" Hailey asked.

"Ridge brought the Delta Force culture to Team Alpha. Volleyball isn't readily available when they're deployed to an event. He decided on dance routines. It started off as capoeira."

Cindy pulled out her phone. "Spell that." As Ares said each letter distinctly, she put it into her search. "The Brazilian government, afraid of an uprising made capoeira—am I pronouncing that right?"

"I think so."

"Made it illegal. Huh…let's see. Brazilian martial arts…fear of ex-slaves revolting…Jail…disguised as a folk dance."

"Sounds like Irish dance," Hailey said. "Except for the martial arts part."

"How so?" Remi asked.

"A friend of mine in college was on the Irish dance team. It's kind of crazy what they can make their feet do. From the hips up though, they got points taken off for any kind of movement. Her arms were rigid and held ramrod straight. If she picked them up off her thighs, she lost points. No bobbling of the head, it was all footwork. She said they don't have a clear reason why, but speculation was that dancing was against the law. If anyone looked through the window, it would look like someone was simply standing there, when in fact they were dancing their hearts out."

"Interesting." Cindy looked back to her phone, muttering, "I like this topic. It's distracting, and I could use a bit of that right now."

"You said Cerberus started out as Brazilian martial arts routines," Remi asked, "and then what?"

"Is this for a story?" Ares asked.

"Cindy, do you have tape of them dancing last night to entertain the kids?"

"I most certainly do."

"Then yes, I can turn this into a human-interest story."

"Okay. From there, we add more dance moves. Some of our dance is martial arts, some for fun."

"I'd imagine you're also building flexibility, and stability of lesser-used muscle groups. Being light on your feet, able to move from off the X, as you guys like to say, in any direction." Remi looked at Cindy. "How did I miss out on this?"

Cindy pulled her camera around and queued up the video.

Hailey and Remi had their heads over the screen.

"Now that I'm seeing this as a thing," Hailey said. "I can imagine if the team came in at the end of a stressful day, and they were dancing and smiling, it might help their morale from all the bleakness that is part and parcel to their mission. We used to do that back in the Hatari Camp. The villagers would gather to sing and dance." She paused and frowned, then with a sniff pushed on. "Ares didn't dance back then. He sang, though. He has a beautiful voice, rich and resonant." She sent Ares a soft smile and that made his heart stutter. "He liked to sing slow songs, ballads for the adults, lullabies as the kids in the camp were going down to bed. Songs that sounded silly—even if the children couldn't understand the English words—when he played ball with them."

She stopped breathing.

Ares could imagine Hailey thinking, "they're all gone, now" thoughts. He reached out and waggled her knee to pull her back from that picture. "There's joy amidst the sorrow in my work with Cerberus. Dancing at the camps while we're on a mission. It helps people. It gives them a break from the sad. We all need a break from time to time."

Aries was used to death and destruction.

And Hailey was, too. But for her, it was Mother Nature who inflicted the pain. For Ares, he'd grown used to the—or maybe just developed a way to cope—when the pain was created by one human who wanted power over another.

"Dance as a coping method?" Cindy said, tucking her phone into her pocket. "Cool."

"Of course, our biggest morale boosters are our fur babies."

"Fur babies." Hailey snorted. "Hear that Judge? Ares thinks of you as a wittle bitty baby. Are you down with that?"

Whining noises came from the back of Judge's throat as he crawled forward pressing his nose under Ares's hand. Ares smiled down at him and gave him a two-handed scrub under his chin. "I was thinking more of the hounds and labs. Judge here is a fur missile. Respect."

"Hey, Ares?" Cindy leaned forward and whispered.

Ares caught her eye.

"Why two air-raids so close together?" Her eyes were held wide. "Do you think this is it? Do you think the Russians are coming over the border?"

# 24

## Hailey

IT WAS two hours later that the app turned from red to green, letting everyone know it was safe to emerge.

Up the stairs, they heaved out into the city.

A quick shower and change of clothes, and the team jumped into hired cabs to take them to the orphanage where they spent the morning finishing up the intake.

Everything fell into place. There was only one hitch.

"Anything on the okay from Romania?" Fedir asked.

"Not yet," Ares had said. "We'll just keep moving forward."

It had gone smoothly. Too smoothly? Hailey felt like when things happened too easily, they were jinxed. Smooth, in her experience was the inverse of "in like a lion out like a lamb."

The teachers had the kids outside playing. They wanted them burning off energy in case they were about to be on a long train ride, and it kept them from asking too many questions about why their things were in garbage bags with their names written on tape.

One of the teachers stood next to Bear, Ares, and Hailey.

"What does your dog do?" she asked.

"Truffles is a search and rescue dog, but she also likes to think of herself as a therapy dog."

The woman lifted her chin toward Truffles. "I read about a woman who trains rats like your dog."

Yes?" Bear asked. "To do what?

"She puts tiny rat backpack on and sends them into buildings which have collapsed in earthquake. When rat finds alive person, they press a thingy, a switch, a level? Level is the word?"

"I understand what you're getting at."

"Okay, yes, so they find person, they make signal, rat run back to handler for getting treat."

Bear turned to Ares. "Sounds like an idea. Should we start a new team? The Rat Pack?"

"Ha. Yeah. I think we should bring that idea back to Juan and see what he thinks."

The men fell over laughing.

"I…this is true story." She frowned.

"Yes, ma'am," Bear said. "We're laughing because our commander freaks out—that is, he is frightened by rats. There's a whole story of him being trapped in a sewer to hide from some terrorists."

"This is terrible and yet you laugh."

"There's a phrase for that in English," Hailey said, "gallows humor."

Ares's phone rang. He looked down at the screen. "Kiyana." He stepped back, tapping the line open and stuck a finger in his ear as Whiskey started trumpeting. "Ares."

Fedir started over to them his face a mask of stress.

Hailey stepped over to Ares and put her head toward the phone. Ares didn't shoo her away.

"What is that?" Kiyana asked.

"That would be a bloodhound."

"You're a go. We've secured a hostel that's located near the hospital for temporary housing. The government is assisting finding next steps. It's a little bit of limbo, but at least there won't be air-raid sirens."

"Thank you," he said with a grin.

"Out."

Ares tapped the red dot to end their conversation. Turning to Fedir, he said, "We've been green lighted."

"This means we can go, yes?"

"Yes. We can get you on the train to Romania as a first step out."

"Did they say where they're going from there?" Hailey asked. "Last night, Kiyana mentioned England."

"England has this in blood," the teacher said. "They *should* help. When London was bombed by Nazis, the parents pinned notes to kids' coats, stuck them on trains for countryside and crossed fingers that families who lined up to help were going to be good care for their children."

"Different times," Fedir said.

"Still, England should remember necessity of removing kids from harm's way and step up."

"What's that look on your face, Hailey?" Ares asked in her ear.

"Tension. I've been doing this for over a decade, things don't normally fall in place this conveniently. It seems to be going too smoothly."

"Iniquus built its reputation on making things glide easily."

Hailey bobbled her head. But that was a way to deflect that particular conversation from continuing, not an actual agreement.

The teacher turned and blew a whistle, then nodded at the other adults who looked her way.

"Hell of things," Fedir said as the teachers helped to get the children into a line and head toward the first of the three buses provisionally lined up. He gestured toward the blacktop where the children had been playing. "We're lucky for this opportunity. There are so many children who must stay. Yes, many have left city already for friends in the countryside, or a different country. But many don't have the means. I've been speaking with other schools. They say that today they paint word in big white letters see from the sky to say 'Children.' We will do this. No kids here, but we want to keep our buildings safe for their return. People will use our basement for a bomb shelter. We ask that they paint here, too."

Ares scowled. "I'm not sure how to advise you about that."

"You don't think that will work?" Hailey asked.

"I'm skeptical—the Russians aren't great at respecting red crosses. White hats. From my studies of their tactics, that might be a bullseye as much as anything else." He reached across to scratch his left brow. "I'm not sure if that's a safety blanket or an easy target."

"That would be against the Geneva Convention—that would be war crime," Fedir said, suddenly ashen.

"Yes."

"Yes?" Hailey's whole body tensed. "Just 'yes?'"

"What do you want me to say, Hailey? It *would* be a war crime. That has never deterred Russia before. Look, the Russians want to come in fast and furious. They need to."

"Why?" Her words were a mere whisper.

"Because they've been to Afghanistan, and they know what it is to get bogged down in urban warfare. The peoples of Nezdolan-nyy, having spoken to them, they'll fight. Hard. Does Russia know it? Someone sure the hell does. The Russian government doesn't want the fight. They want capitulation and fear. What is more frightening than an enemy that flouts norms and laws? An enemy who targets the vulnerable? Who is willing to harm and kill children? The pregnant? The elderly confined to nursing homes? The more atrocious they are as an enemy, they believe, the faster the people will beg for mercy."

"Is that really what you think?" Fedir asked.

"I think that if this goes down, the atrocities will be mind-bending. I also think that, if the enemy is that cruel, it will gird your citizens to fight back. And the world will be forced to confront the situation. The terrible thing is that Russia has nuclear bombs, and unlike the rest of Europe and the United States, it is within their ethos to use them."

## 25

**Hailey**

Saturday, Nezdolannyy

Team Bravo was back in their cabs, heading once again to the train station to do what they'd been doing for the last two days.

The three munitions sniffers—Judge, Diesel, and Hoover—would be keeping close tabs on the rails and the stations. They'd process the people associated with AgilitiCorp as they loaded on.

Ares said that since there had been the air-raid sirens, this all seemed much more real to folks, that those on the contingency list would want out.

Those who hadn't at least checked the box as last-minute deciders, weren't in the system and could not be accommodated.

Ares said that had all been explained and paperwork to that effect had been signed.

Hailey was both concerned for those left behind, but she was thrilled that Iniquus wasn't changing their minds and kicking the orphans off to make space.

In her mind, there was still a chance that Russia was saber rattling.

Anticipating this, back in Romania, Kiyana hadn't just added three cars for the orphans, but enough cars to clear the list. There would be plenty of seats for Remi and Cindy as well as Hailey and Jay'la.

After a check in with WorldCares, Hailey and Jay'la weren't given the choice to stay. They were ordered out of the country. Jay'la started crying with relief. Hailey let the decision sound like it came from their NGO, but the truth was, Hailey had planned to make sure the two of them were on that train, regardless.

Ares had said if she wasn't on the train, he wouldn't be either, and she wouldn't risk him or Judge, let alone Jay'la and herself.

Remi and Cindy, too, had had time to assess. They were going to follow the Cerberus Bravo story and the orphan evacuation story to its endpoint and then make their next determination. They'd meet at the train.

Now that it was all decided, it was just a matter of time. Less than two hours and they'd be chugging away.

Hailey and Jay'la caught a ride on the last school bus heading to the station, then dismounted, and went to get their things and check out of the hotel.

At the train station, the women were directed to seats in the car behind the pet car. That's where Bravo would be seated. The two went ahead and put their bags in the overhead bins and left their hats on their seats to show that someone was already sitting there.

They peeked in to wave at Goose, who was attaching the pet carriers to the shelving units. Ahead of them, people streamed to their places.

Goose asked if he could borrow Jay'la to help him communicate with the pet owners. Hailey patted her arm and said, "You hang out here." She looked out at the orphans to see if their care-givers needed any help. "They've got this pretty streamlined. Why don't I go get us some snacks?" Hailey asked. "Want anything, Goose?"

"I'm set."

"Jay'la?"

"You know what I like. Anything with chocolate. And defi-nitely coffee. Tall and black."

"Got it." With a smile and a wave, she dropped back to the platform and started for the coffee shop.

And just like that, this adventure was nearing its end.

Hailey smiled as she passed the last group of children, nodding at their caregivers.

There was a clatch of three women, standing by the trash bin, eating from paper trays. Their wheeled bags beside them, their backpacks piled on top. Hailey could understand wanting to wait until the last possible moment to climb on the train. It would be a very long trip.

Remi sidled up to her. "Set?"

"We're in the car behind the pets."

"Us, too. Coffee run?"

"Yes, where's Cindy?"

"Taking footage. She wants me to get her one of those dough-nutty things we had yesterday." She checked her watch. "Ten minutes. Hope there's no line."

Hailey saw Ares and called, "I'm getting coffees, want anything?"

"No, we're good."

"Where is everyone?" Hailey called.

"On the train, settling the K9s with Goose, checking the passengers."

"You?" Remi called.

"I'm last man on." He pointed a finger at them, reminding them that until they were on the train, he wouldn't be getting on either.

Remi lifted her hand with her fingers splayed. "Five minutes, I promise."

Hailey's hand landed on the doorknob as a siren sounded in her pocket. She pulled out her phone and it glared red.

The city-wide siren began its wail.

"Get on the train!" Ares yelled. "Get everyone on the train!"

As he and Judge dashed for the front of the train, the train started to chug forward.

Hailey and Remi, rushed to the other two doors that were loading the children.

Remi reached for a child lifted and tossed them to outstretched hands. "Run," she yelled to the others.

Hailey followed suit. "Run, run," she called to the kids. She picked up the slowest child first, the fairy child with her wispy black hair and over-big brown eyes. She handed her off then the next and the next until all of the kids near her were on the train.

The little one stuck her head out, screaming and reaching. An adult's hand held her wrist. The little one was stretching her arm, her foot hovered in the air as the train gained speed. Her fingers splayed wide. Her screams of desperation rose with the blast of the train whistle.

Hailey turned toward where the child was focused.

An old well-loved rabbit lay on the platform.

Hailey snatched it up and gave chase. She knew from her own past what a rabbit could mean to a child. Possibly the last connection this child had to her parents. She sprinted.

The train was gaining speed.

There was zero chance that Hailey had the body coordination and strength to get herself on that train. But she could maybe accomplish this.

With an extra push, Hailey got close to the little hand waving out of the open door, the tear-stained face with the unblinking eyes. Hailey pushed harder than she'd ever pushed herself before, her feet barely pressed against the ground propelling her forward. She reached her arm out as far as it would go as she wished she were elastic. The little fingers wrapped the foot, the child tugged her rabbit free. Pulling it to her chest and tucking it under her chin.

A high-pitched whistle dove from the sky.

A blast rocked the platform.

And Hailey felt the world whirl. Her arms still stretching out, her hands hit the pavement, her body rolling with momentum toward the track.

And skating in beside her, Ares scooped at her waist and twisted violently away from the churning wheels. There was a tangle of limbs as their bodies fought physics.

Hailey wanted to help herself, help Ares but she was straight-jacketed by fear as her brain put together the impact scene.

She sensed Judge was there, his teeth biting into her coat, dragging her.

Hailey just wanted her body back, to be able to move. She hated "freeze" more than most anything.

Ancient in its attempt to save her, Hailey had no control of when it restrained her, when she lost her body to paralyzing fear.

That sensation was a vast swirl of horror in Hailey's system. Every time, it thrust her back to the massacre. She didn't have any idea of what she did or didn't do.

What if she had done nothing to save the children?

What if she'd just stood there frozen with her mouth hanging open like a skeleton in a Halloween display?

Ares was on top of her, yelling.

Finally, her body thawed. She scrubbed at her face.

"Hailey! Are you hurt?"

"I hate freeze."

He pushed his hips back so he knelt on either side of her thighs. "It happens to the best of soldiers. There is no off switch." He was patting over her body, checking for himself that she hadn't broken anything in that fall. "The brain is the brain. We hope like hell it doesn't happen when our brothers and sisters need us to be functioning. We train muscle memory in the hopes that when the brain shuts down, our bodies are still functioning." His voice had a soothing quality. He was trying to talk her down from her skyscraper of angst. "There's no guarantee no matter your level of training. You know this." He scooped under her head and gently sat her up.

"Intellectually, yes." She let Judge lick over her face. "Thank you, buddy. You helped, didn't you?"

Another blast sounded at a distance.

The air raid sirens shrieking.

Her head swam.

"Are you okay?" Remi's words were muffled sounding like they arrived from underwater "No. Your head is bleeding."

"Remi," Hailey's voice shimmered with surprise, "you're not on the train."

"Yup, looks like we missed our ride." She nodded over at the three women standing like statues, food trays in hand, luggage at their feet. Hailey wasn't the only one to freeze.

Those women hadn't even tried to get on the train.

The six watched from an otherwise empty platform as the caboose disappeared into the dark of night.

Hailey screamed after them, *Get safe! Go!* then realized that she hadn't moved her mouth, simply winged her wishes forward as if with the power of her mind she could shove that train farther down the track, and the children would be safe. All of those children. All of those people. Cerberus was on that train. The dogs!

She swayed. They were left behind in a war zone.

Ares was dragging her arm around his neck. "I've got you. Lean in."

# 26

Ares

"KIYANA," she answered her phone with the kind of brisk efficiency that engendered trust.

"Ares here, we have a situation."

She listened to him explain that with the air-raid siren, the train engineer had put his train in gear and taken off down the line like a bat out of hell. And that he was right to do so. Bombs were raining down.

"And you're not on the train? Where... Okay, I have you up on my screen, you're near the train station still."

"I'm on the steps down to the subway shelter. I was on the platform making sure the last of the passengers loaded. We got all but three from AgilitiCorp on the train. Also, I have Remi Taleb and Hailey Stapleton with me."

"Six, then. I assume Judge is with you?"

"Affirmative."

"Your bags and equipment?"

"Headed your way with the rest of my team."

"Same with the others?"

"Those three women from AgilitiCorp have their roller bags and backpacks, Remi and Hailey are always prepared with survival equipment, but their suitcases are on the train."

"All right. We have to get you out of the city for starters. I have the satellites up. Yup I see the train. It's dark out now, as long as they aren't using their lights, they should be all right."

"Let's hope so, that would be a hell of a tragedy."

"Remi and Hailey can hold their own. What about the other three?"

"From a visual, they're mid-thirties, they look active if not athletic, they were dressed properly for the weather and are wearing hiking boots."

"Panther Force is in Northern Africa. I'm getting them in the air. Mmm. Four-hour flight time once they're boots up. Might as well have them heading your way in case you need help." Her voice faded as she turned away from the phone. "Jerry, get Titus Kane on the line. I need him to spool up for an emergency extraction. Details to follow." She was back. "Stay on the line, Ares. I have a call coming in from Mongoose."

Remi and Hailey moved up the stairs toward him.

He wished they'd wait inside. But this was tenuous. He had a duty to the three women who didn't make that train. And Hailey and Remi were free agents.

"Where are the others?" he asked.

"Ines is in line for the bathroom. Polina and Katka are just below us, hoping you have a plan."

"I'm working on it."

"I had to come up," Remi said "The shock is wearing off and

this is usually when reality settles in and the wailing begins. I hate that sound. It vibrates the bones."

"Life is a string of little deaths, isn't it?" Hailey arrived at his side and pressed her forehead into his bicep. "Even if everyone survives this bombardment, the lives they've led up until now are done. They'll have to grieve that."

"Grief is powerful. And surprising. You never know from day to day. You never know from minute to minute, the thing that will spring up and catch like a burr, poking and pricking, impossible to ignore, impossible to remove." Remi patted her stomach where she kept her emergency supplies under her tunic.

It seemed to Ares that double check was reassuring to her. Her system was in place, she had things that could help her stay safe.

He noticed Hailey reach down and do the same. Ares was glad she'd bought leg platforms that were made for war. Durable. They'd survived the tumble just fine. And except for the abrasion on her forehead, she'd come out of the nosedive okay. Maybe a few bruises would show up by tonight.

When Hailey reached down, Judge thrust his nose under her hand. Hailey, absentmindedly, scratched him between the brows.

"Sometimes I like grief," Hailey said. "That pain reminds me of how much I miss someone, how much I loved. How I had plans and hopes for time together." She held up a finger and looked at Ares. "Though I don't want anyone to grieve me when I'm gone."

Remi stroked a hand down Hailey's arm. "You're right in a way. We tell people not to grieve us, but they should rejoice in the lives we'd lived." She stopped to take a breath, looking out over at the darkened hotel across the street. "I'm not sure it's the truth. Personally, I think I'd be vexed if I died, and people really rejoiced in my life without at least a little bit of grief. It kind of reminds me of Velveteen Rabbit." Remi turned to Hailey. "I saw you save that kid's rabbit. Since the train was going too fast for us to jump on, that was a really kind gesture."

It might have been kind, but Hailey had come damned close to rolling under those churning wheels. Ares crossed his arms over his chest, leaning his shoulder into the wall. He swung his head as the whistle of a bomb fell and exploded on the other side of the city. He was used to the sounds of war. "It's old home day with these kid books. Hailey and I were talking about the Ice Queen yesterday and now we're on to Velveteen Rabbit. That's another story grandma used to read. I'm thinking back...the rabbit was in sorry shape because it was so well-loved that it had become threadbare? Or am I mixing that up?"

"Yeah, loved until his eyes fell off. And that's how it became real. That's love isn't it? I mean honestly." Remi scrolled through her phone. "It's one of my nephew's favorites. Here let me just find." She tapped search words into the bar. "Here. Okay ready?" She caught Hailey's gaze and waited for her nod.

Remi read:

*"What is REAL?" asked the Rabbit one day, when they were lying side by side near the nursery fender, before Nana came to tidy the room. "Does it mean having things that buzz inside you and a stick-out handle?"*

*"Real isn't how you are made," said the Skin Horse.*

*"It's a thing that happens to you. When a child loves you for a long, long time, not just to play with, but REALLY loves you, then you become Real."*

*"Does it hurt?" asked the Rabbit.*

*"Sometimes," said the Skin Horse, for he was always truthful.*

"Sometimes," Hailey repeated.

*"When you are Real you don't mind being hurt."*

Ares sent a searching gaze to Hailey's face. She lifted her eyes to meet his. He loved her enough to take on any pain. Could she read that in him? Did she understand that?

*"Does it happen all at once, like being wound up," he asked, "or bit by bit?"*

*"It doesn't happen all at once," said the Skin Horse. "You become. It takes a long time. That's why it doesn't often happen to people who break easily, or have sharp edges, or who have to be carefully kept. Generally, by the time you are Real, most of your hair has been loved off, and your eyes drop out and you get loose in the joints and very shabby. But these things don't matter at all, because once you are Real, you can't be ugly, except to people who don't understand."*

Physically changed as you loved someone? Ares thought, sure that was a thing that happened in long-lived love. His parents had aged together; their bodies battered by the life they'd led side by side. It could happen for the good or bad. It could just happen as a consequence of being together. In Hatari, when he'd returned to the fight, Aries had gone hand to hand with a drugged-up machete-wielding brute. Ares got tattoos to hide the deep slice scars on his arms and chest so Hailey wouldn't see. She had enough grief and self-recrimination. He wouldn't add to it.

Unlike the Velveteen Rabbit, Ares had kept his hair and his eyeballs. That was a plus.

"That book was never comforting to me." Hailey held out a hand. "Not to say it's not a beautifully poignant book. It just—portended the pain of loving. And being loved. That's not something I want to do to someone, love them ragged."

"I can't follow that," Ares said. "First, we love whom we love. I'm not sure we have a choice in that. Unrequited love is painful. Denied love is probably even more painful."

She scowled at him. "Agreed."

"So how do you make that work in your head?"

"How indeed," Hailey asked.

They paused as another bomb shook the city. Yet none of

them made their way into the relative safety of the subway. Somehow that staircase seemed like their place to be.

Remi put her phone away. "Jean Baptiste was my Velveteen Rabbit. Worn to shit from his life. Just as ugly as can be, but *so* loved. These blasts are making me think of him dying in the Beirut hospital while I got to live through the blast."

"I'm so sorry for your loss," Hailey said softly. "It's incredible that he survived Syria only to be lost in a terrible accident."

"I was supposed to be there." Remi dropped her hands between her knees.

"How's that?" Ares put a hand on her shoulder to stabilize her. "You were at the hotel getting ready for bed. Visiting hours at the hospital were over for the day."

"Yeah. No." With a deep inhale, she stood again. "I was in Ethiopia reporting on the coup alongside the FR13 team. When they got a lead in Syria, they invited me along and I accepted. I was supposed to have been there when ISIS captured the team. The only reason I wasn't was that my boss forced me back to the states to go to the National Journalism Awards Ceremony."

Hailey scowled. "Oh, wow."

"It's different you know, war reporting on strangers and the experience of knowing that it was a loved one. Completely different. I mean—" She caught Hailey's gaze. "My therapist specializes in survivor's guilt." She tapped Hailey's arm and sent her a significant look.

"Was your therapist able to say anything helpful?" Hailey whispered.

"She's said some things. Helpful? No, not really. Some of them were trite to the point of being insulting. 'Allow yourself to grieve.' 'Remember this is common.' 'Practice self-forgiveness and selfcare.'"

"But you did nothing to forgive yourself for," Hailey said.

"Apply that to you. Can you do it? Separate out from the fact that you survived while loved ones didn't?"

Hailey swallowed and looked at the toes of her boots.

"You were there in Africa with Hailey," Remi said. "Do you experience that, Ares?"

"Survivors' guilt? No. We're taught to focus on outside factors that led to the event. We make it external. Outside of Hailey, I didn't have a lot of contact with that village."

Hailey looked up.

"Now, if I'd failed Hailey, I never would have forgiven myself. So I'm not going through what you are. But I can damned sure imagine what that would feel like." Quietly he added. "I dream about that night. I dream that Judge and I are running forward but the ground is like a people mover and rotating in the wrong direction. No matter how hard I run, I can't get there. The whole scene plays out as I experienced it firsthand, only Judge and I never arrived."

"Sounds horrible," Remi said. "How do you handle it?"

"We get up and go for a real run. We run damned hard. And a very long distance. Sad to say, Judge loves it."

"And you?" Remi asked.

"It's hell."

"I need a beer," Remi said.

"Once we're over the border. I'll buy the first round." His phone vibrated. "It's Kiyana."

"Hey, we need you out of there stat. We're not waiting for this bomb shower to stop. We think the Russians are trying to keep heads down while they're moving tanks on roads and rails. And they're parachuting in. Even though it's safest in the short run to stay in the subway. Your options are narrowing. I say get out while you have the best chance of surviving."

"Shit." He caught Hailey's gaze. "Russians are on the ground."

254 | FIONA QUINN

"Grab your protectees and stand in front of the hotel," Kiyana said. "I bought you an exfil vehicle. It'll be there in thirty minutes. They'll hand you the keys. This is your window. I'm texting you directions to your guesthouse. I'm getting you as far out of the city as I can before daylight."

"Wilco. What kind of vehicle am I looking for?"

"It's a piss yellow septic tank cleaner's truck."

# 27

Ares

Ares had left the women behind with Judge while he did a quick run to the police station where they'd done the intake for some of the Iniquus civilian soldiers' supplies.

As he ran, he debated what to bring out. He wanted everyone in bullet resistant plates, but if they were stopped, and those plates were found, they'd be considered soldiers. In the end, he left that equipment behind. But he did get transceivers in case the phones went down, and he got night vision technology so he could drive with his lights off, and he'd picked up a small set of binoculars with night vision settings for Remi and Hailey, since both of those women had been trained to use them in the field. That was the most he was willing to risk.

Back now, he'd gathered his group. They waited under the awning at their hotel for Kiyana's gift.

"Piss-yellow truck with a picture of a plumber unclogging a

toilet? This is us." Not that there was anyone else out on the streets right now to confuse them.

The bombs continued to rain down on the city.

"Serious?" Remi laughed. "This is marvelous."

"How marvelous?" Ines asked. "It's piece of shit. Literally. Shit."

"Yes, it's the irony of driving away in this truck that I was referencing." She stepped away from Ines.

The driver dropped down to the pavement. "Name?"

"Ares."

He tossed Ares the keys, looked at the sky, then raced down the steps into the subway.

"Okay then, mount up."

The front had a bench seat, he put Hailey and Remi up with him. He had tasks he needed performed.

Judge jumped in and nestled on the women's feet.

His three protectees went into the back on jump seats.

Not particularly comfortable.

But this wasn't a luxury cruise, this was fleeing for their lives.

He handed his phone to Hailey. "You navigate." He handed Remi the night vision binoculars. "I need you scanning for anything that might be a concern."

He lifted his chin to address the women in the back. "Safety belts, please."

Ines muttered under her breath. "Safety belts as the bombs drop. Like that would help."

Dimming the interior lights on his dash, with his night vision snapped into place, Ares headed down the road.

Just outside of the city limits, his phone vibrated.

"This is Hailey on Ares phone the speaker is on. He can hear you," she said.

"Kiyana here, you all holding up? I see you're on the move. Any issues so far?"

"There's a clogged toilet painted on the side of this van." Ares laughed. "You bought this thing?"

"And paid five times market value for it. Don't scoff at my gift, Ares. Would you as a soldier be interested in searching a sewer van?"

"Point taken."

"We have our eyes in the sky. I have a box on your van. If you're to leave that van, you need to let me know. I also have Ines, Polina, and Katka's necklaces pinging. As long as they have those on, we're tracking them. I'm tracking phones of Remi, Hailey, and you. I need you to turn on Judge's collar."

Ares snaked his hand down to the floorboard by Hailey's feet and flicked on Judge's tracker. "Good?"

"Not necessarily good, but I have your dots on my board now. The train is making remarkable progress toward Romania. That conductor is hightailing toward the border."

"Everyone's safe and healthy?"

"On the train, yes. Also, Panther Force has a private jet moving toward you. The goal is to get you to the seashore where they can effect a pickup and move you to Romania. We keep moving forward. Call me when you get to your guesthouse."

"Wilco. Out."

Silence followed.

Remi and Hailey took turns in fifteen-minute intervals scanning the countryside as Ares powered them down the road.

They had a full tank, he'd have to keep his eye on the gauge, the last thing they needed was to be stranded on the side of the road tonight.

Hour after hour, the tension rose and fell like ocean swells.

Hailey squeezed Ares leg, lowering the binoculars. "What's happening up there?"

Ares slowed to a crawl then he stopped. Opening his door, he stood on the running board and focused. It took him a moment to figure out the images. Then he reached into the van for his phone.

"Kiyana, we have a problem."

"You're only twenty minutes from your guest house."

"Yes, ma'am. The bridge is out, and there's a stream of people who look like they're evacuating on foot. We're not getting across."

"Turn around and start driving back. I'm sending you new coordinates for the contingency guest house. I'll let them know you're on your way. They're English speaking. You've added an hour to your travels, do you have the gas?"

"So far this shitmobile is getting surprisingly good mileage."

"Keep your eye on that. Not that there's much to be done about it at this hour."

Ares climbed back in the cab, pulled the door shut, and snapped on his seat belt.

The phone pinged.

Ares tapped the screen. "New destination," he told Remi who was taking her turn at navigation while Hailey used the binoculars.

"Why? What's wrong?" Ines asked.

"Bridge is out. We're fine, just sleeping in a different bed is all."

This new road had seen some action.

A car had been run over by a tank and sat at an odd angle in the street. Ares wondered if someone had been inside the vehicle when that happened.

"Heads on a swivel," Ares said.

Another car angled at the crossroads, as they passed, Ares saw three bodies sprawled in the road. He was glad Hailey was looking in the other direction, no one else in the van would be able to see what he did.

Ares wondered if his Russian would kick in if it was required.

Thankfully, it wasn't required. The last thirty minutes of their drive there wasn't even a cow in a pasture. All was quiet.

Pulling to the side of the road, Ares called it in. "Kiyana, I can see the farmhouse. Is it safe to approach?"

"I'll call you back."

It wasn't a minute later that they were given the all-clear.

A man signed with a broad sweeping arm that Ares was to pull into the barn.

There was a group of people sitting on logs around a campfire.

"We've arrived," Ares said. "We should be safe here."

## 28

Ares

SATURDAY, THE COUNTRYSIDE


"COME SIT." The host gestured toward the fire.

After closing the barn door, the elderly man quick stepped to catch up with Ares's group. The three women pulled their luggage with them. Remi and Hailey had nothing.

"Tell us the news." A man patted the log next to him.

Ares caught them up on what was happening in the city and what had happened up the road to the bridge.

"We heard an explosion in that direction."

"Can you show me the bathroom?" Ares asked.

The man looked at him and was savvy enough to understand.

He took Ares inside where Ares told him about the cars and dead in the road. The man wiped a hand over his face then patted Ares on the shoulder. "Vodka?"

"No, thank you. I appreciate it, though." They headed back to the fire where their host said his wife was finishing up fixing their rooms.

"You've had a difficult day today," the man said. "Let us relax a bit. Who is hungry?" He looked around the circle. "No? Maybe some apple cider? We make it ourselves with apples from our own orchard. We heat it on the fire, and it warms the belly on such a cold night."

"Thank you," Remi said. "That sounds lovely."

The man pointed at each person in the circle and waited for a yes or no, and with five fingers held in the air, he disappeared into the house.

The woman sitting across from Ares, tipped her head. "Ares. You are called Ares?"

"Yes, ma'am."

"Your mother gave you such a name?"

"No, ma'am, my mother named me Heath."

She tried to pronounce that back to him then gave up.

Remi looked his way. "I don't know the story behind that name. Army name?"

"Eventually. In boot, I was called Lorraine."

"What?" Remi laughed.

Ares lowered his tone to explain this much. "Yup, some guy at boot heard quiche when I said Heath. Some older guy replied, 'real men don't eat quiche' — that was the name of a book back in his time, defining masculinity for yuppies. Young up and comers I think is what it stands for. Coke lines, yes, egg pies, no."

"Huh," Ines said with a wrinkled nose. "Heath—are you from England? Your accent sounds American."

Ares turned his head as their host came out. He got up to help him with the tray of empty mugs. The man turned and went back in the house. Ares put the tray on a small folding table. "Heath—my mother was absolutely sure that I was going to be a Heather. She bought everything in pink and ruffles.

Which was fine for my sister when it came to hand-me-downs. Now, mom just tells people that my baby pictures are really my sister."

Hailey smiled; she had always loved that story. The idea of massive Ares being dressed the first year of his life in dresses and lace tickled her to no end.

"Your mom dressed you in the clothes anyway?" Polina asked.

"I don't think I cared much what color I wore when I was an infant."

The host came back with a metal pitcher that he set in the coals. "Soon, yeah?"

"Thank you," Hailey said.

"I ask hims about why they call him Ares," the woman said. "He's going to tell us his Army story."

"Yes, well, I was fighting in Afghanistan."

There were ten of them around the fire now that Ares's little clan had arrived. The people here hadn't offered their own names, though they were talking about his. That was something that happened in wars. No one liked their names to be on the tips of anyone's tongue, lest they were captured.

"I was in Afghanistan, we were talking to a tribal leader who was… unique, let me put it that way." He grinned and cleared his throat. "In Afghanistan, it was my job to negotiate an agreement to allow safe passage through a certain area a canyon that was a set up for a death alley. The guy signals and then holds up his finger that I should wait. I sipped my tea, wondering what was happening. This guy brings a massive ram. He got it from a tribal chief who brought it as a prize from Tajikistan." Ares used his hands to animate his story and help his hosts with comprehension. "Massive horns that swirled. Proud. Majestic." He threw his shoulders back and puffed out his chest. "This was a breathtaking beast. The kind that you find in art as perfection. Yeah." He blew out through his lips with a shake of his head that made Hailey laugh.

"What happened?" Polina asked.

"The tribal chief said that he would listen to the winner of a contest. If I won, he would clear the pass and allow the convoy through. If the ram won, it was a sign that he was to be tough and not allow this to take place." Ares looked around the circle. "Everything was riding on this mission."

"Riding?" the woman asked. "Did he want you to ride the ram like the kids do at the American rodeos?"

"I wish. No, we had to butt heads."

The woman lifted her hip and patted her behind. "Butt…?"

"No, ma'am." He got up to act this next part out. "They put the ram up on a flat rock to bring our heads closer to the same height, then I had to lower my face."

"Your face?" Her lips pulled thin, showing her horror.

"We were forehead to forehead and this ram was pushing me backward. As this ram was shoving at me, I could feel the vertebrae quivering in my neck." He ran a finger down his spine from his skull to his shoulder. "As I pushed, he got excited about the competition and hunkered down to give it his all."

"How much did you think he weighed?" Katka asked.

"Weight? Maybe three hundred pounds?"

"What?" Remi was laughing.

"But a lot of that weight was his wool coat. They didn't shave this guy. They thought that it would sap him of his virility." Ares popped his eyebrows at Hailey.

"Very Samson and Dalilah," she said back.

"Okay, I have a clear picture of you in my head," Remi said. "What happened? I can't imagine you winning. I mean, honestly, the ram has genetic coding that tells him to butt heads and you, one would assume, have genetics that specifically tell you that's a bad idea."

"I punched him in the throat, and he fell off the rock."

The men in the circle roared with laughter.

"So ram—Aries like zodiac?" Katka asked.

Ares sat down. "We already had a guy name Scorpio in our group. They thought having an Aries with an 'i' was too much. They went with Ares, no 'i'."

"Not a ram." The woman who begun this story with her question looked disappointed.

"Hardheaded at least," Ares said.

"A good thing or bad?" Remi asked.

"Depends on your point of view. The Tyrik ram wasn't too pleased. The women and children who got their food and medical supplies were glad that I gave it a go liked I did."

"Oh man, I'm embarrassed," Remi said. "You led off with the reason for the contest. It just seems like a bro thing to do—a hold my beer kind of viral-wanna-be antic."

"No beer. This was in the tribal lands of Afghanistan."

"With every sentence I'm feeling small. I apologize."

"Nah, no need. It all worked out. And a guy on my team had started off as a chiropractor, so he snapped everything back in place."

Hailey winked at him. "Rammed you back together?"

She and Remi high-fived that one.

## 29

**Hailey**

THE CIDER WAS PASSED.

The people spoke in undertones in their native language. Questions back and forth. Stories. It was nice to hear, like white noise. Hailey appreciated not having to listen or participate.

While Remi was tapping out a story on her phone, Hailey sipped the luxurious silkiness of her hot apple cider. She lifted her mug to their host and nodded with a smile.

He sent her a thumbs up and a grin.

Ares was also on his phone doing…something tactical.

She got to look at him, his olive skin glowing in the firelight.

He was a beautiful man. Glorious to look at. He turned heads wherever he went. But Hailey didn't love him for his looks. She loved him for his heart.

While they had met the first time at the disastrous earthquake.

She'd seen him again at a different rescue. The area had days of aftershocks. While they were smaller, their impact accumulated.

Her team got a call to go and help when another village crumbled. The roads were destroyed by the sides of the hills shaking their rocks loose.

All these years out, all of the rescue work she'd done since, she couldn't remember the particulars or why things unfolded exactly the way they had. But she remembered that she was there doing what she did—the paper and pencil things, the pointing and shouting things, the organizing and herding things.

Ares and his team were out using their bodies and minds to save people.

She remembered watching him work on building a structure so he could get a child out from under a delicate area. When he pulled the child, a baby really, maybe five or six years old from the rubble. Dressed only in her panties, the rest of her clothes left behind as she was pulled from her pocket of debris that had allowed her to survive the crush of the building, he lifted her so gently, so protectively, with such focus on that child.

That baby most certainly wasn't another notch on his belt.

Yeah, Hailey had met some rescue workers like that. Sometimes it was about swagger and bragging rights—but that was never the case with Ares.

Hailey knew that there were no roads left, no ambulances waiting.

Ares scanned the horizon planning his next steps when their gazes caught and held. She was unable to breathe. It was as if in that moment the world stopped on its axis, that the whole of humanity gasped and held its breath. The sounds stopped, the smells disappeared. It was as if there was a sensory eclipse, everything slid into darkness except for his gaze. And then just as suddenly, everything popped back into clarity—the bright copper penny stench of death and decay, the rubble dust that swirled its smoke into her nostrils, the jack hammers and commands from the team to her right.

"This way," she called and without hesitation, that mountain of a man, cradling the child with her whisper thin grasp on life, bent his knees to be the shock absorbers as he clambered out of the debris and did a long-legged speed walk next to Hailey as she ran.

It was three miles to the medical tents. All the while, he murmured that the child was such a good girl, that she was so precious, that the world needed her beautiful heart.

Three miles without cease he spoke to that unconscious child with her head nestled between his bicep and chest, so it didn't dangle and bump.

Her skin was pearl gray from the plaster dust except for the single line of creamy brown skin, exposed by the rivulet of tears that flowed from her hooded eyes.

Hailey never knew what happened to that child.

That image came to her from time to time and swelled her heart with the kindness that existed. Hailey worked in bleak areas with desperate people. Sometimes she just needed a touchstone—an image of goodness that she could readily pull up. That scene helped Hailey remember that the world was populated with people like Ares.

Ares looked over at her, catching her eye, and sending her a smile.

The spell that swirled between them broke when he turned to the woman emerging from the house.

"Come, I'll show you to your rooms," she beckoned.

The hostess showed the weary group upstairs, opening the door to the first room with twin beds. She pointed to Ares and Hailey. "I only have two rooms with the single beds, so I put the couple in the queen bed down the hall."

Hailey followed her pointed finger with Ares trailing after her.

The others were adults, they could figure out their own sleeping situations. Hailey would just get out of the way.

The room was lit by a single low-watt lamp on the bedside table.

The bed was a mattress with no head or footboard, but it was covered with a cheerful handmade quilt and really, at this point, Haley would sleep on a rock.

Hailey immediately started pulling off her boots and clothes as Ares settled Judge with a horse blanket their host had provided for him.

Chilly in the night air, Hailey slid, naked, under the covers, holding out her arms to Ares.

He tucked the covers around them as he joined her.

There, he ran his fingers down her neck. He painted the pads of his fingers lightly over the fine bones of her clavicle, brushing lightly back and forth over the slight bump where the bone didn't heal quite right after she'd fallen from the jungle gym at the park when she was five. He moved his fingers to the divot in the center. The slight pressure of his thumb could crush her windpipe so easily. But she didn't have a moment of unrest. His thumb there was a sacrosanct. It was like being anointed. A baptism. A blessing.

He lifted his hand and replaced the weight in that place of vulnerability with a kiss. So gentle. She wrapped her hands around his head to hold him there. To prolong the magic.

"I love you."

He tipped his head. Their gazes met. "I am powerless to stop loving you, Hailey."

And Hailey sent up a silent prayer that they could get out, get home, get on with a life that allowed for them to be.

# 30

Hailey

THEIR GROUP STOOD on the hoarfrost crispened grass. Their hostess was cooking oatmeal in a large pot on the fire. Since last night's bombs, there was no electricity.

Ares had gone to fill up the gas tank, though Hailey thought that the pumps needed electricity to function. Maybe there were hand pumps available. Ares was an engineer, he'd figure it out, Hailey had no doubt.

Filling an earthenware mug with black coffee from the pot resting on a metal grate above the glowing coals, Hailey watched as Ines was kicking at the rocks and sniveling.

Hailey made her way over to the distraught woman. She rubbed her arm without saying anything. Sometimes it was best to just sit and hold space for someone in an emotional place. Hailey simply said, "I brought you some coffee." She set the cup on the stump next to Ines, then Hailey sat on a section of rock wall beside it.

"It's insane that my husband is fighting the Russian army," she told the trees. "Absolutely insane. He has no training for this." She exhaled as she turned to the road where a farm tractor chugged along. "He has blisters on his hands." Ines turned to Hailey, holding out an empty palm and tracing circles on it with her index finger. "Terrible blisters bigger than a quarter. Do you know how he got them?"

Hailey shook her head with a frown.

"By being a guy. And doing stupid guy things. He was out in the yard cleaning up the debris from the storm, and he decided to burn it. Did he put it in a fire pit? No. No he didn't." Her voice became hard, edged with something like anger. "He was burning it with a blow torch, of all stupid things. Then he looks down and his pants are on fire. I said, 'So you stopped, dropped, and rolled the way you're supposed to?' 'No,' he said, 'I had the torch burning in one hand with nowhere to set it down. My pants were melting into my leg.'"

"What? No!" Hailey exhaled.

"Exactly. So I'm looking at the burns on his hand and ask him, 'So you patted it out with your bare hand? That's how you got the burns?' Yes. That is how he got the burns. Did he come tell me? No. He knew I'd want him to go to the doctor, and he wanted to finish burning his rubbish."

"The pain must have been terrible."

Ines lifted the mug and placed it on the ground. She plunked down on the stump, wrapping her arms around her legs, leaning her forehead onto her knees. "He said he felt no pain at all—that must mean they were third-degree burns, right? I mean, you don't feel pain if you burn through the nerve endings?"

Hailey didn't know.

The stone wall, jealous of Hailey's body's heat, sucked at her warmth, making her bones ache.

The angst on this woman's face made Hailey's heart ached.

Hailey was miserable in body and soul. "I'm sorry. I don't know the answer."

"The man caught his pants on fire with a blow torch. The fibers melted into the skin of his hand. You can see the gray from the fibers. He. Melted. His. Pants. How can he survive against the Russian army? How can I ever see him again?"

Hailey had seen too much for shallow platitudes. This woman was conflating two very different ideas. She was suggesting that her husband's creative, albeit unsafe, way of dealing with the garden rubbish was associated with survival. There were the memes all over social media—pictures of men who rigged up a system of ladders with a buddy as a counterweight hanging at improbable heights to accomplish a task. The memes would read something like, "and this is why women live longer than men." People laughed.

And yet...

So he was trying the "creative" way to deal with a situation. Or, who knew, maybe the guy was just out there having a little pyromaniacal fun and things got away from him. It didn't matter. Systems were in place to try to counter danger. Systems weren't fool proof. In fact, Hailey had learned, only fools depended on systems.

The best they might do was to better the odds.

In a disaster, survival was often just sheer dumb luck.

Look at Remi. Remi was one of the bravest people that Hailey knew. She had worked to develop personal systems to give her the edge. Hailey had learned from Remi and in the field often applied similar techniques.

Did the fates honor that by helping Remi survive? Divine intervention?

The senator that Remi was covering was sick and confused, and Remi helped the senator back to her proper hotel room. Apart from that, Remi would be dead.

Though Remi was a strategist, her strategies would have failed her.

No, this man who burned the shit out of his hand, with fibers from his pants melted into his skin, was not in danger because he was in his wife's words "a moron." He was in danger because the world was dangerous. And he would survive like everyone else who made it from one day to the next intact, by sheer dumb luck.

By his guardian angel not stepping away to refresh their coffee.

*Wow, was that cynical.*

Well, this woman was supposed to be on last night's train. She was supposed to have chugga chugga choo chooed her way to what was statistically a safer place. There, she'd worry and pray over her husband.

And with a little good luck, they'd reunite soon. Hailey patted her knees then stood up. Ines's mood was infectious. And Hailey knew the dangers of that. She meandered over to stand with Remi.

Remi tipped an ear toward Ines. "Everything all right?"

"Emotions," Hailey said. Using a piece of leather set out for just such a task, Hailey reached for the coffee pot and poured herself a mug. She lifted the pot in the air. "Need a refill?"

"I'm good," Remi said. "Hey, where did our fearless leader and his doggo take off to? I saw the truck heading down the road earlier."

"Gas," Hailey said.

"That man." Polina sent out a low whistle. "He is what you call 'fine specimen' yah? You know, I would like to wash my clothes on those abs of his."

"Stop!" Hailey said.

Polina's brows went up. "You think I'm kidding? You are a very lucky woman." Then she waggled her brows and swished her hips.

Remi started laughing.

Hailey swatted at her friend for egging Polina along.

Ines came over. "I've decided I'm going back to my husband."

"Good luck to you." Remi turned and accepted a bowl of oatmeal from the farmwoman. "Thank you." She swirled her spoon through the hot cereal topped with honey and cream. "You know, I'm a war correspondent, let me lay out what's going to be happening. This is the truth without filters. Ready?"

Ines and Polina scowled.

"If the men stay in the city and aren't amongst the fighters, the Russians will find them and shoot them in the back of the head," Remi said dispassionately. "The women will be raped. They will be starved. When the Russians hit the food distribution and the water supplies, people will be out gathering snow to boil. The snow will not last long—in a week, that resource will be gone. People will die. Disease, famine, dehydration, hypothermia, violence, guns."

Somehow Ines had only caught on the problem getting water. "Then comes the rains, the mud," Ines countered. "It will bog down the enemy."

"In the countryside? Sure. But that won't clear things up where you are in the city. The Russian soldiers will be comfortable in Nezdolannyy. They'll take all the supplies they need, leaving nothing for those who are besieged. They'll move into the apartments, killing the men and keeping the women for sex and chores."

"If you go back," Polina told Ines angrily, "you're only a

burden and a worry to your husband. He can't fight as a soldier and be home trying to protect you. Your husband will fare best when he knows you're safe. And that's just the reality of these things."

# 31

**Ares**

Tʜᴇʏ ᴡᴇʀᴇ ᴍᴀᴋɪɴɢ progress heading for their X, when the call came in.

"Kiyana here. You have a problem."

"Listening."

"The Russians have set up a check point five klicks ahead. They're setting up a check point at the crossroads you passed twenty minutes ago."

"We're caught between the two."

"With no other routes for me to send you. I want you to stage the van off the side of the road as if it was broken down. Then get into the woods to the east. I'm sending you a topographical map of the area. Your job is to keep everyone moving toward the south. I'll help you link up with Panther Force as soon as we have the protection of night."

As instructed, Ares staged the van to look like it was broken down a while ago.

Abandoning their vehicle, Ares stalled their group at a boulder outcropping about two hundred meters away. Through the binoculars he watched as a vehicle of Russians found the van and searched it.

"They're on their radios," he muttered. "We're going to hunker down. I don't want any movement to pull eyes our way. They have their binoculars out."

The women pressed between the boulders, pulling their limbs in tight becoming as small as possible.

"More people coming."

Remi crawled up beside him and reached for the binoculars. "It looks like they're forming a search party."

"My thoughts."

"But the soldiers also don't look like they know what they're doing."

"Also my thoughts. But even the worst of soldiers sometimes get lucky." Ares accepted the binoculars and laid still as he watched and assessed.

Three men turned and headed toward a farm up the crossroads. Two stood guard outside the van. Others were going through the luggage that the three AgilitiCorp protectees had left behind.

The air split with the crack of rifle fire.

"They're shooting the tires and the engine," Ares told the women.

He climbed off the rock, handing the binoculars to Remi. "Can you keep watch? I need to have a conversation with my protectees."

Crouching down beside them, Judge between his knees, Ares asked, "Is there a reason why the Russians might be tracking one of you?"

"Why would you ask that, Ares?" Hailey asked.

"It seems like there is a lot of coordinated effort on this stretch of road. Why? There are a couple of farms. No other traffic."

Katka moved restlessly. "I…might be paranoid. But I think they may be following us and trying to find me."

"You?" Ines asked. "Why you specifically?"

"I am the mayor's daughter. He had a list of people within the city's government that he thought might be Russian sympathizers. Not a long list by any stretch, three maybe four names. My father could do nothing about it until the war began. He had a plan though. With the first bombs, they would all be held until the incursion was resolved, and then they'd be put on trial for aiding and abetting the enemy. I don't know if that happened or not. This is secret, though."

"You are married to an American?" Ares asked.

"Yes."

"He was on the train out?"

"No." She shook her head violently, kneading her hands. "He stayed to fight. His fighting doesn't have to do with bombs and bullets. He's a computer person who provides cyber security for AgilitiCorp. He knows how to hack, so he can help shore things up so Russia doesn't get hold of our grid to interrupt electricity in the middle of the winter. People need to be able to cook their food and heat their homes. When they aren't hiding in the subways and underground."

Ares ran his hand down his face. "Targeting you for capture makes sense on both counts."

"How so?" Hailey asked.

He opened his phone and pulled up a file to a map. "This is the city. This area all around it is Russian border or Russian annexation. In these annexed areas, the Russians believed that as soon as they made a move to take over the country, that all of the

Russian speaking peoples would rally to Mother Russia, raise arms and fight."

"That's not going to happen. In the last thirty years we've made too much progress toward a European-styled life," Ines insisted. "We like it too much to consider going back to the ways of Russia. They take all the money and live large while in rural areas only about a third of the people even have access to cold running water while we have made so much progress."

"There are a few that are pro-Russia, like at my father's office," Katka said.

Hailey leaned in, looking at the map, listening intently.

"Looking at the troop formations and equipment that Iniquus picked up through satellite images, Iniquus made the call, rightly, that our contracted firm was in immediate danger should Russia decide to advance hostilities. The reason to get everyone out the way they did was based on the analysis that Russia would besiege Nezdolannyy."

"To what end? To swallow us up? There are many small cities and villages for them to take."

"A nuclear power plant that provides electricity for a third of our country," Polina said.

"They'd go after a nuclear plant after what happened in Chernobyl?" The color from Ines's face drained. "This is not possible."

"My father said that our city is at high risk because of proximity to the border, and the nearby nuclear power station," Katka insisted. "It's important to maintaining electricity to the country. Without it, how's the morale? How's the capacity to fight?"

"Another Chernobyl situation?" Ines shook her head emphatically. "The world would come down on them swiftly and emphatically. It will be world war three. But I can't see anyone standing with Russia under those circumstances, except perhaps for North Korea."

"Okay stop." Hailey held up a hand. "This whole conversation started when Katka said that we might be in trouble because of her father the mayor. Surely, the Russians wouldn't be putting this much effort into finding her because her husband has hacking skills."

"I agree with Hailey," Remi whispered down. "People can put up with a lot as a personal decision. Or even an executive decision. It's a whole different equation if someone thinks their loved one is suffering."

"Suffering how?" Katka whispered, turning to Ares.

"I don't mean to frighten you with speculation."

"That's…please."

"Let's say they had a hero mayor standing up against the Russian bear. He rallies the citizens. They are all doing their best under devastating assault. Then, privately, that mayor hears that his child has been captured. He is sent, I'm sorry, disturbing photos of her treatment, perhaps even videos."

Katka stared unblinking.

"Exactly," Ares said. "That thought you're having, that's it exactly. I can't allow that."

Polina scowled. "But how would they be following us?"

"A tracker in your clothing? In your luggage?" Ares threw out.

"I can—could we search for it?"

Ares shuffled a heel under his rump for stability as Judge leaned into him. "It's easily disguised, it could be anything or anywhere. In the heel of your shoe, in your smart watch—" His sentence fell off.

Hailey caught his eye. "What was that?"

"Just before we were deployed, they confiscated our phones. I have a new phone. One of the men on our team picked up a stalker, and she planted malware that infected the phones he called. Mine for example."

"People can do that?" Katka asked. "I have face recognition. No one can access my phone."

"You've had trouble with your battery draining," Remi said. "How long has that been going on?"

"I don't know. A month? I had my husband look at it. He thought maybe it was a dud."

"Would he have thought to look at it for an external tracker?" Ares asked.

"No." She shook her head vehemently. "Of course not. Why would he? I'm a stay-at-home mother. I walk the dogs and go to the grocery. I have nothing to do with anyone."

"Except people who work with your father," Remi said. "The ones who are concerning enough that they were put on a list."

"To stop them from internal sabotage. Their families are all living in Russia. Some of them are in the upper levels of the military."

"What was your father concerned about them doing?" Hailey asked.

"That they might harm him and take over the government, give the Russians a key to the gates, if you will."

"I see." Ares held out his hand. "Your phone please."

With shaking fingers, she handed it to Ares.

Ares swiped the phone and held it up to Katka for facial recognition. He opened her security, her tracking permissions, her apps. Then handed it back to her. "Look at this list, are all of them familiar to you? Did you put them all in place? And as you're scrolling, take the time to look carefully. Make sure there's not a little change that you think is correct but might be a lookalike." He glanced around. "Would you all do the same? I know you'd like to have your phones on you, it feels safer. Let's give them a scan. And then, we'll take the batteries out until we need them."

"Batteries out? Not just airplane mode?"

"I'm told that some apps can run GPS even in airplane mode.

I can't say that with a hundred percent certainty. I'm saying it's a precaution that we'll be taking."

"This one." Katka leaned in and pointed at the light blue icon. "I don't recognize what that is."

Ares used his own phone to search the name. And there was none. "Ines, you bought your phone locally?"

"Yes."

"Can you look up this app?"

She stared at Katka's phone then typed into her own. "My hands are shaking. I'm terrified that each second we sit here trying to figure this out, someone might be tracking us. I have the same make of phone and same carrier. I'm not able to access that app."

"All right, let's play a game and see what comes of it." He accepted the phone.

"Everyone, stay down and out of sight," Remi called. "There's a truck on the road."

The angst ratcheted up.

Pulling a poop bag from Judge's zippered vest, he asked, "Remi, do you have duct tape?"

With his gear in hand and an idea in mind, Ares crouch-walked to the bank of the river with Judge at his heels. Making sure the phone was on and operating, Ares dropped it into the camouflage poop bag and tied it shut with a tight double knot.

Tipping a short log up, Ares used a length of the hundred-mile-an-hour tape that Remi had handed him from her survival kit, to wrap around and around the circumference, trapping the weight of the bag. Then he hefted the log down the slick slope, dropped it into the swift current, and watched it bounce away.

Ares jumped from a low hanging branch and swung himself up in the oak.

With Judge in a down-stay amongst the roots, limb by limb,

Ares clambered up into the highest branches that might hold his weight. He lifted the binoculars and watched.

The vehicle backed up to the crossroads and turned on the street that ran parallel to the river.

Bingo.

They'd been followed.

And nearly captured.

Quickly, the truck would overtake the log, then they'd figure out the ploy.

Now, Ares had to get his group headed in a different direction.

They had to move on to Plan B.

And fast!

He called the situation in to TOC.

"Ares, I don't see a clear route for you on the satellite images. I'm going to suggest you get yourselves hidden in the woods. Night is your friend."

"Agreed."

"Panther Force has an electric exfil boat. They'll be using night vision as soon as it's dark enough. We're on course following your GPS coordinates. We can get to you, pile everyone in and get to the sea by dawn. Within hours of sunrise, you'll be along friendly shores. We'll arrange pick up there and move you to accommodations."

"We'll work that plan."

"Everybody okay?" Kiyana asked.

"Minor wounds. Cold. Everyone's pulling their weight. Complaints are minimal."

"Good. Hunker down. We're coming to you. Out."

Ares scuttled up the hill, back to where he'd left the group. And there they stood in a cluster, hands on their heads and a rifle aimed at Hailey's heart.

# 32

Ares

As thunder rumbled from Judge's chest, his lips peeled away exposing the viciousness of his teeth and jaws.

Ares signaled him to silence.

They threw themselves to the ground. As long as they weren't seen they could act.

But this guy looked young and nervous. That was a deadly combination in a war zone. Ares pulled his blade from his pocket, his second-best weapon. He had Judge with one hand and his binoculars with the other.

He first checked the guy's trigger finger. So far, so good, it lay alongside the guard.

That gave Ares options.

Sweeping the area, he found another guy with a gun.

In the field was a tank with and open turret.

The distance between the two soldiers complicated things.

Hate it as he did, Ares was following the plan in his head. The main thing was to keep everything as calm as possible.

Ares pressed into his knees and elbows as he backed down the hill.

Low and slow, he moved, and Judge was his shadow. Here was where training was paramount. If Judge did what Judge wanted to do, go in to save Hailey, that automatic rifle would mow everyone down.

In a wide arc, Ares raced. His boots barely touched the ground before they were pressed forward. They slid up to the tank. With Judge in a down stay, Ares climbed on top and peeked into the turret. Empty, but lots of blood.

Ares would guess that these soldiers had lost their team and were on the run.

That explained their nerves.

The soldier that held Ares's group, was shouting for help.

This guy looked like walking back behind that boulder was the last thing he wanted to do. He wagged his body this way then that trying to gin up some courage.

As he pulled his rifle around, Ares leaped from the top of the tank on top of the guy. A hand around the gasping mouth, kept him from signaling the danger.

With other hand, Ares tugged the soldier's knife from its sheath, in one swift move, Ares slid the blade into the Russian's carotid.

The soldier dropped to the ground, clawing at his neck, trying to staunch the blood.

Ares took his rifle and signaled Judge to him.

The soldier down the hill, was growing more agitated when he didn't hear his buddy call back.

He was screaming at the women.

Ares could see Katka saying something, then all of the women sank to their knees.

Ares got Judge's attention then gave him the signal. A loop around the back and a bite.

Judge took off like a sizzle of electricity. A brown blur against the winter landscape.

Coming full speed down the hillside, he leaped through the air.

The women turned their attention to Judge. And as they did, the soldier looked around.

Too late.

Judge sank his teeth into the man's wrist.

The soldier threw his head back with a scream as all two hundred and forty pounds of bite pressure from an angry, protective Malinois defended his Hailey.

Ares raised the rifle to take the shot, but the women piled on the soldier, with fists and rocks they beat on him, with Judge keeping that weapon arm inoperable.

Ares got the man secured with Remi's tape.

A farmer arrived in his tractor, hooking up the Russian tank.

Ares handed him the bleeding, beaten prisoner. Maybe eighteen. His plate carrier had car magazines in the front and back instead of ceramic plates. He was cold and scared and hungry.

This wasn't his war. He was a pawn. A very scared pawn.

## Monday Zero Dark Thirty, The Countryside

THEY HID in amongst the trees for hours.

The Earth made its slow rotation around the sun.

Finally, the call came in from Kiyana, "Your boat is arriving."

Panther Force was black against the stygian night.

In silence, the exhausted group climbed into the tactical raft.

"You're okay. We've got you now," Titus said. He clapped each person on the back as they climbed in, counting them off. "Six and a K9. All present and accounted for," he mouthed into his comms.

Silently they shoved off the shore, into the choppy river, down to the sea.

They bounced over the waves to freedom.

# EPILOGUE

THAT NIGHT, Ares said he'd be very late getting in, not to wait up.

Hailey had sat out on the sleeping porch on the second floor of their newly-purchased eighteen-eighties house that they'd bought when Hailey moved to Virginia to work under Kiyana on the Iniquus Logistics team. It meant that when Bravo deployed to humanitarian efforts, there would be a good chance that Hailey would be there coordinating their response.

Ares had given up his dream job with the Green Berets; Hailey could make adjustments for their relationship, too.

On this glorious night, Hailey had curled up on the wicker couch, reading and listening to the breeze whispering secrets to the leaves of an ancient magnolia tree. It was like being a child and sleeping in a tree house.

She must have fallen asleep, rousing when she felt Ares kissing her.

"I have something I want to show you, Hailey."

There was no watch or clock to check, but a robin made the first tentative peeps, calling in the new day.

Sleepily, she took his hand and stood. "You're dressed just fine," he said as she opened the closet door.

She was in her long nightgown, made of billowing white cotton. She found it old fashioned and romantic. After slipping on a pair of sandals, Ares tucked her in the car and drove them to the park.

Hailey could not imagine what this was all about.

The full moon hung just out of reach, a glowing peachy shade of pink.

Holding Ares's hand as she moved over the dew damp grass, they walked down to the edge of the pond and out onto a wharf where a wooden rowboat was tied.

The bottom of the boat had a plastic mattress like one used in a crib. Ares had covered the top with a quilt and throw pillows. Ares got Judge settled in the front then helped Hailey climb in. Ares sat on the bench seat at the back, lifting the oars and sliding them into the midnight black waters.

"No life vests?"

"It's only waist deep from here to where I'm taking you."

She nodded.

The night was satin as it brushed her skin.

Ares moved the boat into the path formed by the reflection of the magnificent moon.

The tree frogs chirped, and Ares was playing her favorite cello music, the one that she'd told him massaged her soul.

Hailey adored making love to Ares to this piece. To her, it was slow Sunday mornings in bed. "Bach's Air on the G string. A lascivious title if ever there was one," Hailey murmured. She let her fingers drift in the water as the boat gently rocked.

Ares paddled them out to a sea of lotus leaves.

"I've never seen a pink moon before. I'm glad you brought me out here to see this."

"The Strawberry moon," Ares said.

"Mmmm. Perfection."

Ares rested the oars in the locks. He slid to the mattress, pulling Hailey back so she was sitting comfortably between his knees, her head resting against his chest.

He reached in the basket behind him and pulled out a bowl of strawberries.

"Cute," she said.

They listened to the music and floated in perfection, nibbling on the sweet sun-ripened fruit.

This was bliss.

Absolute magic.

She contentedly drifted in and out of sleep as Ares stroked his fingers through her hair. The birds roused her. "The moon is setting, the sun will be up soon," her whisper was tinged with regret, Hailey wanted this to go on forever.

*Mmmm* was the most Ares said.

Peace was to be treasured, and Hailey absorbed this into her very being.

Little by little, the tree trunks became shadows, then she could see more forms. The stars twinkled a last goodbye.

She closed her eyes, not willing to let go of the moment.

"Hailey." Ares nudged her. "Look. This is why I brought you here."

Blinking her eyes open, Hailey watched the miracle unfolding. All around her the lotus buds that had been closed tight for the night yawned awake. And now she and Ares were floating in the periwinkle morning amongst the splendor. It was like she was floating on a dream.

Hailey gasped and turned to look at Ares.

There he sat with an engagement ring caught between his fingers. "Hailey, will you marry me?"

"Without any hesitation, I will."

She held out her hand and let him slip the ring into place.

A long-ago promise was fulfilled.

Though, she was already living her happily ever after.


THE END

# READERS

**Readers,**

I hope you enjoyed getting to know Hailey, Ares, and Judge. If you had fun reading Warrior's Instinct, I'd appreciate it if you'd help others enjoy it too.

**Recommend it**: Just a few words to your friends, your book groups, and your social networks would be wonderful.

**Review it**: Please tell your fellow readers what you liked about my book by reviewing Warrior's Instinct.

**Discuss it!** – I have a SPOILERS group on Facebook.

If you're following the **Cerberus Tactical K9 Team Bravo series** or you're reading the Iniquus World in chronological order, the next book is: ***RESCUE INSTINCT***

If you want to learn more about Remi and T-Rex read: ***DANGER ZONE***

If you want to find out more about Reaper and the surveillance at his home that was the warning Ares needed to keep his protectees safe, read: ***FEAR THE REAPER***

If you are new to Iniquus and want to start at the very beginning, here is an excerpt from book one in the Iniquus chronology, ***WEAKEST LYNX.***

*Are you ready? Turn the page and let's go!*

# WEAKEST LYNX

## Chapter One

THE BLACK BMW POWERED STRAIGHT TOWARD ME. HEART POUNDING, I stomped my brake pedal flush to the floorboard. My chest slammed into the seat belt, snapping my head forward. There wasn't time to blast the horn, but the scream from my tires was deafening. I gasped in a breath as the BMW idiot threw me a nonchalant wave—his right hand off the wheel—with his left hand pressed to his ear, still chatting on his cell phone. Diplomatic license plates. *Figures.*

Yeah, I didn't really need an extra shot of adrenaline—like a caffeine IV running straight to my artery—I was already amped.

"Focus, Lexi," I whispered under my breath, pressing down on the gas."Follow the plan. Give the letter to Dave. Let him figure this out." I sent a quick glance down to my purse where a corner of the cream-colored envelope jutted out, then veered my Camry back into the noonday DC gridlock, weaving past the graffitied storefronts. I recognized that the near-miss with the BMW guy probably wasn't his fault. I couldn't remember the last ten minutes of drive time.

I watched my review mirror as a bike messenger laced between the moving cars on his mission to get the parcel in his bag to the right guy at the right time. Once he handed over his package, he'd be done—lucky him. Even though I was handing my letter off to Dave, the truth was that wouldn't be my endpoint. I wasn't clear about what an endpoint would even look like. Safe. It might look like I was safe, that I had my feet back under me. But that thought seemed like it was far out on the horizon, and right now, I was just looking for something to grab on to, to keep me afloat.

When I finally parked in front of Dave Murphy's mid-century brick row house, I sat for a minute, trying to regain my composure. I'd pushed this whole mess to the back burner for as long as I could but after last night's nightmare... Well, better to get a detective's opinion. Dave had handled enough crackpots over his time with the DCPD that he'd have a better grasp of the threat level. Right now, even with all my training, I was scared out of my mind.

I glanced down at my hands. The tremor in them sent the afternoon sunlight dancing off my brand-new engagement and wedding rings. I felt like an imposter wearing them—like a little girl dressed up in her mother's clothes. *I'm too young to be dealing with all this crap,* I thought as I shoved my keys into my purse. I pulled my hair into a quick ponytail and stepped out into the February cold. Casting anxious glances up and down the street, I jogged up the stairs to bang on Dave's front door.

The screen squeaked open almost immediately as if he'd been standing there waiting for my knock. "Hey, Baby Girl," he said, stepping out of the way to let me in. Dave had been calling me Baby Girl since I was born because my parents couldn't decide on my name, and that was how I was listed on my hospital ankle tag.

"Glad I found you at home." I walked in and plopped down on the blue gingham couch. It had been here since I could remember. The fabric was threadbare and juice stained by his five-year-old twins. On a cop's salary, fine furnishings ranked low in priority. Right now—edgy and confused—I appreciated the comfort of familiarity.

Dave shifted into detective mode—hands on hips, eyes scanning me. "Long time, no see."

"Where are Cathy and the kids?" I asked.

"They've got dentist appointments. Did you come to tell us your news?" He lifted his chin to indicate my left hand and settled at the other end of the couch, swiveling until we were face to face.

"Uhm, no." I twisted my rings, suddenly feeling drained and bereft. What wouldn't I give to have my husband Angel here? The corners of my mouth tugged down. I willed myself to stay focused on the reason for the visit. My immediate safety had to take priority over my grief.

Dave raised a questioning brow, waiting for me to continue.

"Angel and I got married Wednesday. I'm Lexi Sobado now." My voice hitched, and tears pressed against my lids. I lowered my lashes, so Dave wouldn't see. But his eyes had locked onto mine, and he never missed much.

"Married? At your age? No introduction? No wedding invitation? Why isn't he here with you now?" Dave angled his head to the side and crossed his arms over his middle-aged paunch. "I'd like to meet the guy," he all but snarled.

Dave probably thought I'd come here because my husband screwed things up already. I pulled the pillow from behind my back and hugged it to me like a shield. "I'm sorry. I should have let you and Cathy know what was going on—I was caught up, and I just..." I stopped to clear my throat. "Angel and I got married at the courthouse, and no one came with us. Not even Abuela Rosa."

"Angel Sobado. He's kin to Rosa, then?"

I gave the slightest tip of a nod. "Angel is her great-nephew. I couldn't bring him with me today because he deployed with the Rangers to the Middle East Thursday. That's why everything happened so fast. He was leaving." The last word stuck in my throat and choked me.

Dave leaned forward to rest his elbows on his knees. Lacing his fingers, he tapped his thumbs together. "Huh. That's a helluva short honeymoon. Married Wednesday. Gone Thursday." Dave's tone had dropped an octave and gained a fringe of fatherly concern.

His compassion gave me permission to break down. But those Angel-emotions were mine. Private. Right now, I needed to hold myself in check long enough to get through my mission of handing off the letter. I shifted my feet back and forth over the rug as I glared at my purse.

"Might even explain the expression on your face," Dave said, narrowing his eyes. He slouched against the arm of the over-stuffed couch.

Stalling wasn't going to make this any easier. I reached a hesitant hand into my bag, pulled out a plastic Zip-loc holding the envelope, and held it up for Dave. "The expression is because of this," I said.

Dave took the bag. After a brief glance, he hefted himself to his feet. Over at his desk, he pulled on a pair of Nitrile gloves, then carefully removed the letter.

Dearest India Alexis,

> *O my Luve's like the melodie*
> *That's sweetly play'd in tune!*
> *As fair thou art, my bonnie lass,*
> *So deep in love, am I:*
> *And I will love thee still, my dear,*
> *Till a' your bones are white and dry:*

*Till a' your veins gang dry, my dear,*
*And your skin melt with the sun;*
*I will luve thee until your heart is still my dear*
*When the sands of your life shall no more run.*
*And fare thee weel, my only Luve,*
*And fare thee weel a while!*
*And I will come again, my Luve, so I can watch you die.*

Dave read the words aloud then stared at me hard; his brows pulled in tight enough that the skin on his forehead accordioned. "What the—"

"Someone shoved the poem under the door to my room, and it's scaring the bejeezus out of me." I gripped the pillow tighter.

Dave peered over the top of his reading glasses. "Last night? This morning?"

"Wednesday morning." I braced when I said it, knowing it would tick Dave off that I didn't bring this to him immediately. Ever since my dad died, his buddies had stepped in and tried to take over the fathering job, even though I'd be turning twenty in a few days.

True to my expectations, Dave was red-faced and bellowing. "*Wednesday?* You waited two whole days to tell me you've gotten a friggin death threat?"

Yup, this was exactly the response Dad would have given me.

Dave jumped up, pacing across the room. Obviously, he didn't think this was someone's idea of a joke. Fear tightened my chest at his confirmation. I had hoped he'd say, "No worries—someone is having fun pranking you," and then I could go on about my life without the major case of heebie-jeebies that tingled my skin and made me want to run and hide.

"It was our wedding day." I worked to modulate my voice to sound soft and reasonable. "I only had a few short hours before

Angel had to take off. So yeah, I decided to focus on us instead of this." I motioned toward the paper in his hand.

Dave took in a deep breath, making his nostrils flare. "Okay." I could almost see his brain shifting gears. "When you first picked up the letter, did you get any vibes?"

"You mean, ESP-wise?"

He nodded stiffly, his eyes hard on me.

Vibes. That wasn't the word I would have chosen to explain my sensations. "I didn't hear anything. It was more like an oily substance oozing over me." I tucked my nose into the soft cloth of the pillow and breathed in the scent of cinnamon fabric freshener. "I vomited." My voice dropped to a whisper. "It felt like evil and craziness, and I can still smell that stench." A shiver raced down my spine.

Dave's lips sealed tightly; he was probably trying to hold back a litany of expletives. Finally, he asked, "That's all?"

"Yes."

"Did any of your neighbors notice anyone unusual lurking around? Did you check with management and run through the security tapes?"

"Dave, didn't you hear? My apartment building burned to the ground three weeks ago. I assumed you knew. It was on the news."

Dave's eyebrows shot straight up.

"I've been living in a motel the Red Cross rented out for all the families displaced by the fire. But to answer your question, no, nobody saw anything, and there were no cameras trained on my motel corridor." I curled my lips in to keep them from trembling. I was used to holding my emotions in check. I trained myself to present a sweet exterior, a costume of sorts, but right now, I was filled to overflowing, and my mask kept slipping out of place.

"Shit." Dave ran a hand over his face. "I had no idea. I'm

letting your parents down. Apartment burned, married, husband gone, and now a death threat." His eyes narrowed on me. "Do you think that about covers all of your surprises for me today?"

I paused for a beat. "Yeah, Dave, I think that's it for today." Okay, even if he was like family, the way Dave was talking pissed me off. I was frightened. I wanted a hug and his reassurance. What I was getting was... Dave's brand of love. He wouldn't be this red-faced and agitated if he wasn't worried about me. Tears prickled behind my eyelids, blurring my vision.

"Hey, now. Stop. We'll get to the bottom of this. Did you already let Spyder McGraw know what's going on?"

I wiped my nose with the back of my wrist. "Spyder's still off-grid. I have no idea when he'll get home."

"Were you assigned a different partner while he's gone?"

"No, sir. I only ever worked for Spyder—he sort of wanted to keep me a secret." I still couldn't believe Mom had sat Dave down and told him all about my apprenticeship with Spyder McGraw. Under Spyder's tutelage, I was following my dream of becoming an Intelligence Officer, learning to out-think and out-maneuver the bad guys trying to hurt American interests. And like anyone heading toward a life in the intelligence community, my skills needed to go under the radar. Now that my mom had died, only four people—Spyder, the Millers, and Dave—knew that side of my life. I would prefer Dave didn't know.

"Still, did you consider bringing this to Spyder's commander? Iniquus would probably give him a heads up. Get a message to him."

"Iniquus is my last resort. Sure, Spyder told me to talk to them if I ever found myself in trouble." I sucked in a deep breath of air. "Bottom line? He never wanted them to know I worked for him, well, for them. Safety in anonymity and all that." My fingers kneaded the stuffing in the pillow. "Besides, I guess I was hoping this would all just go away."

Dave's eyes were hard on me. "You know better. Once some psycho's caught you on his radar, you're stuck there until someone wins."

"Okay, so I make sure it's me who wins."

"Exactly right." He considered me for a minute before he asked, "You've kept up with your martial arts training?"

"I have a sparring partner who's pretty good. We rent time at a Do Jang twice a week."

Dave lowered his head to read over the poem again. He put the letter and envelope back in the Zip-loc and placed it on his mantle. Pulling off his gloves with a snap, he looked down at them. "I hate these things. They give me a rash. Look, I'm going to take this down to the station and open a file. If you get anything else, I want you to bring it to me right away. Understood?"

"Yes, sir."

"This is the only poem, letter, communication of any kind you've gotten?"

I nodded. For the first time since I walked into Dave's house, I became aware of sounds other than our conversation and the thrumming blood behind my eardrums. A football game played on TV. I glanced over as the announcer yelled some gibberish about a first down, then moved my gaze back to Dave. "You must have taken graveyard shift last night," I said.

He picked up a remote, zapped off the TV, and sent me a raised eyebrow.

"It doesn't take a psychic. You look like an unmade bed."

Dave ran a hand over his dark hair, thick on the sides, sparse on top. He hadn't used a comb today or bothered to shave. He was hanging-out-at-home comfy in jeans and beat-to-hell tennis shoes. It looked like the only thing I was interrupting was the game re-run.

"Double homicide. Turned into a long night up to my ankles in sewage."

"Yum." I tried on a smile, but it was plastic and contrived.

Dave narrowed his eyes. "We need to move you. Pronto. It's priority one. You need to be someplace secure where I can keep better tabs on you."

"I've been looking since the fire, but I haven't found anything."

"Would you consider buying?" he asked.

"Yes, actually—I'm looking for a low-cost fixer-upper I can work on to help me get through this year without Angel." I followed Dave into the hallway. "Diversion, and all that."

"How about here, in my neighborhood? I could keep a better eye on you—and you won't be showing up at my door with a suitcase full of surprises." He grabbed his coat from the closet and shrugged it on. "I'm taking you over to meet my neighbor. She has the other half of her duplex on the market." He looked over his shoulder at me. "You shouldn't be running around without a jacket." He handed me an oversized wool parka that smelled like raking leaves. He kicked a Tonka truck out of the way, and we moved out the front door.

On the front porch, I slid into the shadows and took in the length of the road—no cars, no barking dogs, everything quiet.

Dave glanced back."Coast is clear."

I tucked the coat hood up over my ponytail. Screened by Dave's broad back, I started across the street. Down the road, a car motor revved. I reached under my shirt and pulled out my gun.

### *Enjoying the read?*

Continue reading Weakest Lynx today.

# THE WORLD of INIQUUS

## Chronological Order

Ubicumque, Quoties. Quidquid

Weakest Lynx (Lynx Series)

Missing Lynx (Lynx Series)

Chain Lynx (Lynx Series)

Cuff Lynx (Lynx Series)

WASP (Uncommon Enemies)

In Too DEEP (Strike Force)

Relic (Uncommon Enemies)

Mine (Kate Hamilton Mystery)

Jack Be Quick (Strike Force)

Deadlock (Uncommon Enemies)

Instigator (Strike Force)

Yours (Kate Hamilton Mystery)

Gulf Lynx (Lynx Series)

Open Secret (FBI Joint Task Force)

Thorn (Uncommon Enemies)
Ours (Kate Hamilton Mysteries)
Cold Red (FBI Joint Task Force)
Even Odds (FBI Joint Task Force)
**Survival Instinct** - (Cerberus Tactical K9 Team Alpha)
**Protective Instinct** - (Cerberus Tactical K9 Team Alpha)
**Defender's Instinct** - (Cerberus Tactical K9 Team Alpha)
Danger Signs - (Delta Force Echo)
Hyper Lynx - (Lynx Series)
Danger Zone - (Delta Force Echo)
Danger Close - (Delta Force Echo)
Fear the REAPER – (Strike Force)
**Warrior's Instinct** - (Cerberus Tactical K9 Team Bravo)
**Rescue Instinct** - (Cerberus Tactical K9 Team Bravo)
**Heroes Instinct** - (Cerberus Tactical K9 Team Bravo)

Coming soon, more great stories from the ex-special forces security team members who live, work, and love in a tightly knit family.

FOR MORE INFORMATION VISIT
WWW.FIONAQUINNBOOKS.COM

# ACKNOWLEDGMENTS

My great appreciation ~

To my publicist, Margaret Daly who is my rock.

To my cover artist, Melody Simmons

To my editor, Kathleen Payne

To my Beta Force, who are always honest and kind at the same time, especially Elisa Hordon, Michele Carlon, and Kim Schup.

To my Street Force, who support me and my writing with such lovely enthusiasm.

Thank you to the real-world military and intelligence communities which serve to protect us.

To all the wonderful professionals whom I called on to get the details right, including Jonathan Kitchens and his expertise in getting K9 Houston to the top of the truck. Please note: This is a work of *fiction*, and while I always try my best to get all the details correct, there are times when it serves the story to go slightly to the left or right of perfection. Please understand that any mistakes or discrepancies are my authorial decision making alone and sit squarely on my shoulders.

Thank you to my family.

I send my love to my husband. Every day, I am content knowing that my life is better because of you. Thank you.

And of course, thank YOU for reading my stories. I'm smiling joyfully as I type this.

I so appreciate *you*!

# ABOUT THE AUTHOR

Fiona Quinn is a six time USA Today bestselling author, a Kindle Scout winner, and an Amazon Top 100 author - Amazon All-Star.

Quinn writes suspense in her Iniquus World of books, including Lynx, Strike Force, Uncommon Enemies, Kate Hamilton Mysteries, FBI Joint Task Force, Cerberus Tactical K9 Series Alpha and Bravo, and Delta Force Echo series.

She writes urban fantasy as Fiona Angelica Quinn for her Elemental Witches Series

And, just for fun, she writes the Badge Bunny Booze Mystery Collection with her dear friend, Tina Glasneck, as Quinn Glasneck

Quinn is rooted in the Old Dominion, where she lives with her husband. There, she pops chocolates, devours books, and taps continuously on her laptop.

**Visit www.FionaQuinnBooks.com**